SHACKLETON'S STOWAWAY

SHACKLETON'S STOWAWAY

by Victoria McKernan

Alfred A. Knopf
New York

THIS IS A BORZOI BOOK PUBLISHED BY ALFRED A. KNOPF

Published in the United States of America by Alfred A. Knopf, an imprint of Random House Children's Books, a division of Random House, Inc., New York, and simultaneously in Canada by Random House of Canada Limited, Toronto.
Distributed by Random House, Inc., New York.
KNOPF, BORZOI BOOKS, and the colophon are registered trademarks of Random House, Inc.

www.randomhouse.com/teens

Library of Congress Cataloging-in-Publication Data
McKernan, Victoria.
Shackleton's stowaway / Victoria McKernan. — 1st ed.
p. cm.
SUMMARY: A fictionalized account of the adventures of eighteen-year-old Perce Blackborow, who stowed away for the 1914 Shackleton Antarctic expedition and, after their ship Endurance was crushed by ice, endured many hardships, including the loss of the toes of his left foot to frostbite, during the nearly two-year return journey across sea and ice.
ISBN 0-375-82691-2 (trade) — ISBN 0-375-92691-7 (lib. bdg.)
1. Blackborow, W. Perce, 1894–1949—Juvenile fiction. 2. Antarctica—Discovery and exploration—Juvenile fiction. [1. Blackborow, W. Perce, 1894–1949—Fiction. 2. Antarctica—Discovery and exploration—Fiction. 3. Shackleton, Ernest Henry, Sir, 1874–1922—Fiction. 4. Imperial Trans-Antarctic Expedition (1914–1917)—Fiction. 5. Endurance (Ship)—Fiction. 6. Survival—Fiction. 7. Stowaways—Fiction. 8. Adventure and adventurers—Fiction.]
I. Title.
PZ7.M4786767Sh 2005
[Fic]—dc22
2004010313

Printed in the United States of America
February 2005
10 9 8 7 6 5 4 3 2
First Edition

For Sylvia and Oliver, who will stow away somewhere, sometime, and for Sue and Tom, who will let them

~V.M.

ACKNOWLEDGMENTS

I would like to thank the family of Perce Blackborow for sharing their memories: his daughter Joan Randle; his son James Williams, and his wife, Rose; and his youngest brother, Reginald, and his wife, Grace. For sharing not only memories but their lovely home, warm hospitality, and the history of Wales, special thanks to Perce's grandson John Blackborow and his wife, Jacquie.

Thanks to Elizabeth A. Rajala, Billy Bakewell's daughter, who provided me with generous conversation, handwritten pages of her own recollections, and her father's memoirs.

Special thanks to Robert Stephenson of Antarctic-Circle.org, who shared his vast knowledge, steered and connected me to innumerable sources, answered countless questions, and placed his fantastic personal library at my disposal.

I am grateful to my agent, Kathy Anderson, for making it all seem so easy and to my editor, Joan Slattery, for making the thorny thrust of great editing always feel like a bouquet of posies.

CONTENTS

June 15, 1916

I am warm. How amazing to feel this way. Not just not cold *but actually* warm. *The little stove is glowing. Whenever someone throws in another penguin skin, I can hear it crackle and hiss. It isn't a proper stove, of* course, *but it is so warm now, I can open my sleeping bag. It isn't a proper sleeping bag anymore either, just a soggy piece of reindeer skin, so worn out that I have poked my finger through it a couple of times. It's no worse than any other, though, and better than some. The really bad thing is that they shed. The air is always full of little reindeer hairs. We pick them out of our food and brush them out of our eyes. We breathe them in and sneeze them out. But it isn't the worst thing. Not by far.*

It's hard to say what exactly is the worst thing when you are stranded on a narrow scrap of rocky beach on a tiny island in the coldest place on earth. We have been here two months now. We may never leave.

Some people would say it isn't fair that a fellow has survived two shipwrecks before the age of twenty. The way I see it, it would have been a whole lot more unfair if I didn't! For right now, I am still alive. That's pretty good, considering.

I haven't written so much in this journal lately, but I want to tell something more now while I have a chance. Only it's hard to concentrate. It's just so nice to be warm for once. It's hard to describe the cold of Antarctica. It gets so cold here, you can't smile or your teeth will crack. If you take your mittens off for one minute, your fingers freeze. Even wrapped up, you can't keep away the frostbite. Noses, ears, and feet, they get it worst.

The fire is smoky, but we're used to that. And I suppose it stinks too—burning penguin skins can't smell good. But there are so many worse smells here. If someone from the outside world walked in just now, they would probably start gagging. For one thing, there are twenty-two men crowded in here and no one has taken a bath or washed clothes for over a year. Unless you count getting dunked in the sea or splashed by waves.

Besides that, the ground beneath our hut has started to melt. It isn't actually a hut at all, just our two wooden lifeboats turned upside down on top of some rocks. We have piled up more rocks all the way around and hung what was left of old tents to keep out the wind. We call it the snuggery. When all of us are packed inside, it's very snug indeed. But the ground is mostly ten thousand years of frozen penguin guano. Guano *is a science word for what comes out of a penguin. We sailors have some other words. Call it what you like, it still stinks. The ground oozes with it. When the others walk around, you can hear it squish. So no, we can't be smelling too good. But I don't care. I am warm. It must be fifty degrees in here now! The doc wants it even warmer so the chloroform will vaporize. Chloroform is a kind of anesthesia. Doc Macklin is about to cut off my toes. Bad enough frostbite kills the flesh. That's what happened to my feet. Nothing to do now but amputate.*

The doc wants a lot of light for the operation, so they

have lit every lamp. These aren't proper lamps, of course, just lumps of seal fat in old sardine cans. (They also stink.) Usually we just light one or two, but now there are a dozen, and it's nice and bright. That's another thing I miss—light. It's the middle of the winter here in Antarctica, and the sun only comes up for about six hours. But there are usually storms or thick clouds, so we don't see much of even that. I can't remember the feel of sun on my face. I have not been out of this hut in two months.

Our lives are now measured in terms of what they are not. When our not-quite sleeping bags are not-so wet we are happy, or at least not-so miserable. We live in not-exactly a hut with not-really a stove and we are not-quite starving. And not-yet dead.

Eighty degrees now, says Doc. The water is boiling on the stove. He drops the instruments in the pot to sterilize. The clink of metal gives me a sick feeling. I try to think positive, and I would never say it to the others, but honestly, I don't know if I can go on much more. It would be different if we knew rescue was coming, but we don't know. The boss, Mr. Shackleton, went off two months ago to try and get help. He took five men in the third lifeboat. It's a small boat, hardly bigger than the ones that make our hut. They have to cross eight hundred miles of the roughest ocean in the world and find one small island. The ordinary wind here is like a hurricane, and the waves can be higher than a castle wall. They need to see the sun to navigate, and the sky is cloudy almost all the time. The chance of landing on that island is about the same as throwing a pebble from shore and hitting a leaf floating in the middle of a great lake.

Doc says of course he'll make it. Any day now, Shackleton will be sailing up in a good strong ship, and what a feast we'll have. Bread and jam and cakes. We think about food all the time, especially sweets. No one is actually starving, but all we eat is penguin. Penguin for breakfast, penguin for dinner. Penguin boiled, penguin stewed, penguin fried in penguin fat. I think I would let them chop off both feet for a piece of bread and butter!

I feel bad for Doc. It's kind of worse having to do it, cut off someone's toes. To Mom and Dad, Harry, Teddy, Jack, Charlie, and William, if I don't see you again, know I love you and had a grand adventure down here. I'm glad I did it.

chapter one

Two years earlier—1914

As far as shipwrecks go, the first one was not so bad. "Piece of cake," Billy Bakewell declared as he swung his duffel bag up onto his shoulder. "Why, I got shipwrecked once in the South Pacific—now there was trouble! Island crawling with cannibals. Poisonous snakes in every tree. And this after we floated for six days on bits of wood just to get there!"

"And the hurricane—" Perce Blackborow added with a quiet smile as he cinched his own bag tight. "And the sharks swimming all around."

"How'd you know there was a hurricane?"

"Any story you're telling must have at least a hurricane or two."

Billy threw a playful swing at him, and Perce ducked. The ferry eased up to the dock. The gate opened, and the crowd began to squeeze up the narrow gangplank. It was only two days ago that their own ship, the *Golden Gate,* had wrecked in the river Plate near Montevideo. It was not such a big deal as shipwrecks went, except to the owner, of course, and the captain, who had failed to keep her off the rocks. The anchor had dragged at night during a storm. For the sailors on board, the wreck was a bit of a bump and tumble, no more. They were close to shore, and it was little trouble to get everyone off and most of the cargo too. But it was soon clear that the *Golden Gate* would not be sailing anywhere soon. Billy and Perce had to find another ship. They heard there was more opportunity in Buenos Aires and decided to take the ferry over.

6

"True, though, you've never been shipwrecked before," Perce said as the two flowed slowly off with the crowd.

"Naw," Billy admitted. "But close. Many times. More times than I can count."

"That's very impressive," Perce said. "Considering this was only the second ship you've been on in your life!"

Billy laughed. In many ways the two could not have been more different, yet they had become good friends at sea. William Bakewell was a bold and carefree American who seemed like he could get along anywhere and do just about anything. He was twenty-six and had indeed sailed on only two ships. But one of those had taken him around Cape Horn, about the roughest passage a ship could make. Before that he had worked as a lumberjack, driven cattle in Montana, and worked on the railroads. He was a small man, just five and a half feet tall, and lean as beef jerky. Although he was fond of the tall tale (he had not been to the South Seas and certainly never seen a cannibal), he didn't really have to exaggerate his life very much. He had left home at the age of twelve, with nothing but adventure ever since.

Perce Blackborow, on the other hand, knew little of the world. He was from a small neighborhood in the city of Newport, in Wales. He was only eighteen. He had gone to sea full-time at fourteen, but he had worked only on merchant ships around England before this. The *Golden Gate* had been his first ocean crossing. Perce was only two inches taller than Billy but had a stockier build, with broad shoulders and strong arms built from rowing and lifting cargo. His face was tanned and toughened by the outdoors. His brown hair was cut short and not very well. Barbering wasn't exactly high on a sailor's list of skills. He had pale blue eyes, as blue as a glacier, according to Billy. Perce had never seen a glacier, so he didn't know about that.

The two friends wove their way through the crowd, trying not to bump people with their sea bags. Perce had never seen so many different people. Short, brown-skinned people with glossy black hair carried huge bundles tied up in cloth. Indians, he guessed, bringing goods to market. The cobblestones clattered with passing carriages and carts, wheelbarrows, bicycles, and burros. There were merchants and sailors, tradesmen with their tools, peddlers with carts of fruit, children with shoeshine boxes or trays of sweets to sell. They all went about their business and ignored the two. Sailors were common enough in a port city.

"Come on," Billy said. "There's bound to be an inn nearby, and we can start asking about ships."

An experienced sailor shouldn't have trouble finding a new ship in a port like Buenos Aires. Except that after the wreck of the *Golden Gate,* there were nearly a hundred of them trying. Billy started down the dock. He acted as if every day he was dropped suddenly into an exotic new country on the other side of the world where he couldn't speak the language and had no way home. Perce didn't feel quite so nonchalant. There were too many people and too much noise. The colors seemed too bright. And the smells! No more fresh sea breeze. The air was hot, thick, and dusty. Tar and fish mixed with tobacco and sweat. Through it all floated the perfume of manure from the donkeys and horses and dogs. Then a delicious aroma of roasting meat drifted through the sour air. Billy and Perce followed the smell and found a man squatting beside a little iron pot of hot coals. On top of the pot was a grate, and on the grate were strips of beef on sticks. They had skipped breakfast in order to catch the ferry, and Perce was very hungry.

"Come on, Baker boy." He grabbed Billy's arm. "My belly's howling."

They only had a few local coins and weren't sure what they were worth. The man at the grill said something in Spanish and held up two fingers. Perce looked at the coins in his palm.

"Give him a big one," Billy suggested. "He can give us change."

"What if he cheats us?"

"Go on—it smells so good, I don't care if he does. Besides, if you act like you know what you're doing, people usually think you do."

That simple it was. Perce handed over a coin, and the man gave them back some other coins, then handed each a stick of grilled meat. It glistened with fat and sparkled with little red flecks. The man pointed to a bottle. It was filled with red sauce. Ketchup! Perce did like ketchup. It wasn't as thick as Heinz ketchup back home, but this was Argentina after all. He poured the red sauce all over his meat. He took a big bite. Then his mouth exploded. His tongue was on fire, and his eyes flooded with tears. Water poured out of his nose and his eyes. It was like someone had run barbed wire up his nose and his tongue had been stung by a thousand bees.

The meat vendor smiled and nodded. "Ah, *bueno*!" he said. "*Muy picante,* eh?"

Billy took a bite of his meat. He had skipped the red sauce.

"Not bad. Not bad at all," he said. "Tastes kind of like the spiced monkey you get in Borneo." (He hadn't been to Borneo either.) Perce coughed and took deep breaths, trying to cool his mouth. The man at the grill pointed to a little building down the street.

"Cantina," he said, laughing. "*Cerveza!*"

A cantina turned out to be a tavern, and *cerveza* was beer. So now they knew four words in Spanish—*tavern, beer,* and *very spicy*. It was eleven o'clock in the morning, but the cantina was busy. Sailors with only a short time in port didn't waste any time going after fun, and for most of them, fun was getting drunk. Perce had been drunk once and didn't like it. He had felt stupid during and terrible afterward. Mostly he didn't like it because he was afraid he might miss something.

"That's because you're just a pup," Billy ribbed him. "Puppies always find everything exciting. Wait until you get stuck at some rotten dull job in some rotten dull place working for some rotten bad boss. Then see how friendly the whiskey can be!"

Perce had begun working on the docks of Newport when he was twelve years old. He had seen his father trembling with exhaustion at the end of a fourteen-hour day. He knew about hard, dull work. That was especially why he wanted more out of life.

There were a couple of men at a table nearby who had obviously made close friends with a bottle of whiskey. One was snoring with his face on the table; the other was talking to a woman who was trying to sweep the floor, but he was so drunk, he slurred his words.

Just then the door swung open and a frowning man peered into the dark interior. He looked sea-roughened, but not like a common sailor. Someone with rank. A bosun at least, maybe an officer. When he saw the two drunkards, he strode up to their table.

"You buggers! I've better things to do than search all over the docks for you."

"Ah, Mr. Greenstreet!" The talkative one smiled stupidly. "Come and join us for a pint!"

"You were gone all night. You missed your watch."

The sleeping man picked up his head and squinted at the daylight.

"You're both sacked," Greenstreet went on. "You can come pick up your kit until three. After that I'll have it put out on the dock."

"Oh, come on, sir, you wouldn't short a man his wee bit of fun." The talkative man was almost whining. "We've been two months at sea!" The other man just glared silently.

"See Mr. Cheetham to get paid off."

"Paid off, eh?" The second man pulled himself slowly up from the table. He was over six feet tall and looked like he could pull up whole trees with one thick arm. He let out a string of curses. Perce hoped the woman sweeping the floor didn't understand English. The big man threw a punch. It was fast but sloppy. Greenstreet ducked most of it. Chairs scraped and glasses clinked all over the cantina as men cleared back out of the way.

11

"Should we help him out?" Perce asked tentatively. Perce didn't want his friend to think he was shy of fighting.

"Well, let's give the man his chance."

"But it's two on one, and they're twice his size."

"Watch. He might know what he's doing."

Billy was right. This man Greenstreet knew how to let a man blow off a bit and not get crazy and not get anyone hurt. It turned out to be hardly a fight at all. A little shoving, a lot of swearing. Then two Spanish men came out from behind the bar. One had a stick, the other a sock with lead pellets in the toe. The two drunk sailors backed off. Everything went back to normal.

"Don't bother the others when you come for your things." Greenstreet gave them a disgusted look and left.

"Come on." Perce grabbed his duffel bag.

"Where you going? I haven't finished my beer."

"Didn't you hear the man? There's two places just opened on a ship!"

"Well, for a raw pup you've got some wits after all," Billy said as he gulped the last swallow. Perce and Billy grabbed their kit and hurried outside. The man walked fast and was half a block away before they caught up to him.

"Sir—Mr., uh, Greenstreet—sir," Billy called out. The man turned.

"I'm William Bakewell. This is Perce Blackborow. We lost our ship in Montevideo. She ran aground," he added in case the man might think they had been fired themselves. "You'll be needing some new hands."

Greenstreet gave them a quick look-over. "Experience?" Bakewell explained that he had experience with both sail and steam. No navigation to speak of, but he could keep a course. He mentioned his two last ships, craftily avoiding the fact that they were his *only* two ships.

"And you?" Greenstreet turned to Perce. Next to Billy, he had little to offer. There were a hundred men within shouting distance with more skill and experience.

"Ordinary seaman, sir," he said quietly. "Very willing."

chapter two

"Ernest Shackleton!" Perce said excitedly. "What I'd give just to meet him!" When Greenstreet had told them exactly what they were applying for, Perce could hardly believe it. The Imperial Trans-Antarctic Expedition, under the command of Sir Ernest Shackleton. Billy hadn't heard much about Shackleton, although he was a legend in England.

"So he's the guy that *didn't* make it to the South Pole?"

"Well, yes, but—"

"And the Brit that *did* make it—what's his name?"

"Robert Scott," Perce reminded him.

"Yeah, Scott, he died on the way back, right?"

"Yes, but—"

"And that Norwegian guy—Amundsen. He actually got there and came back alive. So he won the race."

"There's more to it than that," Perce said with exasperation. Americans were so bloody stuck on winning and losing. "Do you know how far it is to the South Pole and back?"

"Farther than anybody in their right mind would ever want to go!" Billy laughed.

"It's almost two thousand miles!" Perce said. "And when Shackleton went, back in 1909, he didn't even knew what to expect. No one had seen much beyond the coastline. That'd be like you setting off to walk across the United States, only you didn't even know if there were mountains or deserts or what to cross. Shackleton pioneered the way!"

Perce was surprised at how little Billy knew. In England,

polar explorers were regarded as heroes. Magazines printed long stories about them, and people packed lecture halls to listen to them speak. Perce remembered his father reading the newspaper stories aloud to the family. How Shackleton led his men across endless miles of the Ross Ice Shelf, hauling heavy sleds with all their equipment. Sometimes the ice would crack beneath them, opening a huge crevasse hundreds of feet deep. They found an enormous glacier, a mountain of ice blocking the way. Shackleton and his men clawed their way up. For weeks they trudged across a high plateau where the air was so thin, they could barely breathe. It was freezing cold. Blizzard winds knocked them down. They walked for 660 miles. They were almost there, only ninety-seven miles from the South Pole, when Shackleton turned around.

He knew they didn't have enough food. They were already desperately hungry and exhausted. They suffered from frostbite. They were only covering six or eight miles a day. He knew they could reach the South Pole, but he didn't think he could get them all back alive. He could be the most famous explorer in the world, but instead he turned around.

Perce was eleven years old then, far too old to cry, but as he heard about the desperate struggle at the bottom of the world, he couldn't help it. "Two years after that, Scott made another try for the pole," Perce explained. "He followed Shackleton's route. It still wasn't easy, of course, but at least he knew what to expect. Scott did reach the South Pole but found out Amundsen had already been there by a different route. Then Scott and his men all died on the way back."

"How?"

"No one really knows. They were found dead in their tent months later. Starved, probably."

"And now Shackleton wants to go back and cross the whole continent." Billy shook his head. "Is he *nuts*?"

"Think what an adventure this would be!"

"Are *you* nuts?"

The *Endurance* was the most beautiful ship the two had ever seen. She was a barkentine, 140 feet long. Not terribly big compared to the modern ships that filled the harbor, but strong. She had clean lines and a sturdy hull built of oak and fir. While she had a coal-burning engine, she was also fully rigged to sail. Perce and Billy weren't the only ones enchanted by this ship or the journey she was about to make.

Word had spread fast. When they arrived at four as instructed, there were at least fifty other men on the dock, waiting to be interviewed for the two open positions. Some men eyed each other suspiciously, some talked and joked, but all were trying to measure their competition. Billy leaned over and whispered to Perce.

"By the way, in case anyone should ask, I'm Canadian."

"Why?" Perce asked, puzzled.

"They're all Brits!" Billy nodded toward the ship. "Not likely to take a Yank along. But Canada is still tied up with England. Got their queen on their money and everything. Besides, I cut enough lumber up there, I ought to be an honorary citizen at least!" Billy grinned. He recognized a couple of sailors from the *Golden Gate* and went to talk to them. Perce stood off by himself and looked at the ship.

What was it like to go someplace that no one had ever been before? To set foot on land that no human had ever walked on? There was no place left like that except Antarctica and the moon. And no one was ever going to set foot on the moon after all. Perce hoped he would at least get a chance to see Shackleton. What was it like to be a great man? Would you know it if you were? And how many had the challenge? And what if a man was challenged and failed? Perce gave a little shiver of dread. What if, by some miracle, he was taken on for this voyage and things got tough and he turned out to be weak? What if he was a coward? A hundred things could go wrong on a trip like this. What if he wasn't strong enough, smart enough, brave enough?

Perce watched the men on the deck of the *Endurance*. What about them convinced Shackleton that they should go on such an expedition? Five thousand had applied; why had these twenty-five been chosen? Only one man was idle. He stood on the bow, leaning casually against the railing, smoking his pipe and looking down at the crowd of men below. He was a small man, slightly built, with a mustache and neatly trimmed beard. He had a relaxed posture about him, as if nothing ever bothered him. He might have been a small-town schoolteacher or shopkeeper, until you saw his eyes. He had a keen steady gaze, an alert watchful look that missed nothing.

The man saw Perce and nodded. He might even have smiled, Perce couldn't really be sure. He thought he saw the pipe bob just a little. A few minutes later, the man left his place, came along the railing, and stood at the top of the gangway.

17

"Gentlemen." The voice was surprisingly strong coming from such a small man. "My name is Frank Wild. I am second in command of this expedition. Thank you all for your interest in joining our ship."

Frank Wild—Perce was even more awestruck. This man was a polar legend in his own right. He had been on Scott's first *Discovery* expedition and by Shackleton's side on the heartbreaking Furthest South.

"We don't want to waste anyone's time," Wild went on. "You understand of course that we require experienced sailors, so Mr. Greenstreet, our first officer, has already narrowed down the list of your names based upon ratings and experience. I will interview the following men aboard the ship." Wild took out a piece of paper and began to read off the names of men who would be interviewed. William Bakewell was the first name on the list. Perce was tense as he listened to name after name. Exclamations erupted throughout the crowd as each name was called. Perce felt dizzy and realized he was holding his breath. Name after name floated through the hot tropical air. Twenty in all. Perce Blackborow's was not among them.

"It was only because I've had experience with sail." Billy tried desperately to cheer his friend up. "Most of those blokes have only worked on coal ships. Shackleton wants to sail as much as he can to spare the coal. And they decided to hire on only one man, not two after all. If they'd taken two, you know you'd be on. Except you're also too young," he added. "I am sorry."

"I never liked the cold anyway," Perce said gloomily.

They sat on the dock, their feet hanging over the water, their backs to the *Endurance.* Perce didn't really want to look at her anymore. It was bad enough to be turned down, but for Billy to go! Scrawny old Billy, who had only worked on two ships and didn't even know who Shackleton was an hour ago! Perce had a wicked idea to go tell Shackleton exactly what Billy had said about him being nuts.

"I'll ask around for a ship for you," Billy said.

"Thanks. I'll find something." But it wouldn't be Antarctica. It wouldn't be with Shackleton. "With the war starting, I can get easy passage back to England and join the navy. I'll sink a few German ships and be a hero or something." Two fat pelicans paddled around below them, looking for treats.

"Come on." Billy slapped his back. "Let's go find you lodging, then I'm gonna buy you a ripping big feast with all the ketchup you can handle." Since he was now crew, Billy would have a berth aboard the ship. Perce would have to find a bed somewhere else.

"All right." Perce tried to sound enthusiastic. They got up and were startled to find Frank Wild standing there. He had approached so quietly that neither had heard anything. It seemed a long time before he spoke, but that was just because of the way he was, like he made his own kind of time.

"Your mate spoke well of you," Wild said. "Said you were a good worker. And I understand you're from Wales. Any experience with dogs?"

Dogs? Perce thought quickly. Wales was full of sheep—

and sheepdogs. Shackleton must be taking dogs to Antarctica to pull the sleds. *If you act like you know what you're doing, people usually think you do. . . .*

"Yes, sir!" Perce answered with confidence. He had never owned a dog, but the neighbors did, and he had sometimes played with it. "I'm good with the dogs, sir." It wasn't exactly a sled dog: it was a funny-looking little thing, hardly bigger than a cat, with black wiry fur and legs comically short for its long body.

"They're pretty rough," Wild said. "Working dogs."

Perce nodded and made a slight murmur of agreement as if he knew all about working dogs. Little Blackie's hardest work each day was shifting position from doorstep to doorstep to keep himself comfortable as the sun moved down the lane.

"So we could use an extra hand on board here for a week or so. Just until we sail," Wild went on. "Give a hand with the dogs and help the cook in the galley."

"Yes, sir!" Perce tried to keep his voice steady. "I could do that, sir."

"It's only a week or two." Wild's piercing eyes studied him. "Only while we're in port."

"Yes, sir. I understand."

"You can bring your kit on board, then. Bakewell here will show you the fo'c'sle bunks."

chapter three

The dogs were not impressed with the beautiful ship *Endurance*. They did not know or care who Shackleton was. They had been on a long boat journey already, and they didn't want to go on another. They were bred for cold, and now they were hot. They were bred to run, and now they were cooped up. They were surly and restless. What they wanted to do was fight. With each other or with the men who were handling them; it didn't matter. There were sixty-nine big dogs, and sixty-eight of them were in a bad mood. When they weren't snarling at the men or snapping at each other, they lunged after the pelicans that waddled around the dock. Perce yanked on the chain of his dog and urged him toward the gangplank.

"Come on, pup," he said sweetly, as if he were coaxing his baby brother. The dog looked at him with a cold, scary gaze. One eye was brown, the other pale blue. His lip pulled back, and he snarled.

"Hey," Perce said sharply. "None of that." The harsh tone seemed to work better. All the dogs were half wild, but this one was the meanest he had handled so far. "Sit!" Perce commanded. The spooky-eyed dog's lip twitched again, showing teeth. Another dog was balking at the gangplank, causing everyone else to bunch up behind.

"Down!" Perce pulled up on the chain with both hands and used his knee to push the dog's hindquarters down. Surprisingly, it worked. Nearby, a sailor by the name of Walter How had a more gentle mutt, a great shaggy brown beast with white paws. While they waited, the brown dog dropped to the dock and rolled over to have his belly scratched. Perce's dog, seeing this, growled.

"No!" Perce jerked the chain. His dog obeyed, but barely. The brown dog whined and waved his white paws in the air. Just as the men ahead of him started to move again, Perce heard a shout. Out of the corner of his eye he saw a giant mass of fur galloping toward him. A dog was loose. *Dog, hell,* Perce thought with real fear. *That thing's a wolf!* Walter's dog yelped and jumped to his feet, cowering behind Walter with his tail between his legs. Perce's dog lunged, nearly pulling his arms out of the sockets, but Perce managed to hold him back. The wolf-dog leaped on top of Walter's dog and clamped his teeth on the back of his neck. The whole dock erupted in howls and barks, clanking chains and curses, as every dog tried to get in the fight.

Walter kicked at the beast, but it was like kicking a tornado. No one could let go of his own dog to help. Perce looked around for somewhere to tie his charge, but the nearest bollard was on the other side of the dock.

Then the wolf lunged and clamped his fangs on Walter's boot. The man fell, and the wolf started shaking his foot like a chew toy. In desperation, Perce swung his own dog around by the leash and threw him into the water. Then he grabbed the tail of the wolf and yanked it away from Walter. The wolf turned and snapped at Perce. Perce fell backward and the wolf leapt toward him. Perce kicked, hitting the beast square in the chest. Perce jumped to his feet. The wolf was stunned for the moment, so Perce ducked his head and ran square into him with his hardest tackle. Perce was a good rugby player, and the rough game now served him well. He knocked the animal backward, clear off the dock, then tumbled in after him.

With these two splashes, it was all over. A couple of men fished out the dogs. Billy tossed Perce a rope and helped him climb back on the dock. The men started talking and joking.

"Bloody fools—" Greenstreet strode down the dock, spreading the men and dogs farther apart. "Keep some distance here—these are wild dogs, not ladies at a tea party!"

Walter How's dog was whimpering. He had some blood on his neck, and one ear was torn.

"He all right?" Perce asked. His wet clothes made a puddle around his feet. He felt self-conscious with people looking at him.

"Fur's thick, thank God. He ain't bad hurt."

"Your foot all right?"

"Sore, but the boot took the teeth. Thanks, mate, I owe you."

Perce nodded. He went to retrieve his wet dog. The brown and blue eyes looked at him with a new mixture of respect and loathing. Frank Wild walked up, and all the men stopped their rude talk.

"All sound? All right, then. Let's get these dogs aboard." He caught Perce's eye and gave him a nod, then he walked away.

"Jeez—he could've said well done or thanks or something," Billy said.

"Wasn't nothing." Perce shrugged. The crazy-eyed dog lifted his leg and peed on Perce's wet trousers.

chapter four

The two weeks in port were wonderful and terrible. Perce worked hard. Although it was a nasty job, he actually preferred cleaning out the dog kennels to working in the galley. He liked being out in the fresh air. The cook, Charlie Green, was a good fellow, but a little serious. Charlie had cooked on merchant ships for several years but had never been in charge before. He was taking his responsibility very seriously. The potatoes had to be cut a certain way, the carrots sliced just so.

He was a small man with bushy eyebrows and a luxurious handlebar mustache. His voice was squeaky, which sometimes got on Perce's nerves. Although he was thin, his hands and arms were incredibly strong. He could hold a forty-pound bag of flour at arm's length. Charlie had also been hired on at Buenos Aires after the original cook was fired for drunkenness. This meant he and Perce both had to get familiar with the galley and learn where everything was. The galley was very small, only about six foot by ten, so cooking three meals a day for twenty-eight men was a challenge. The pots and pans were huge.

"I could bathe two of my brothers at once in that big pot!" Perce told Billy. "And all the laundry as well."

For breakfast, they fried four pounds of bacon and scrambled sixty eggs. Charlie baked twelve loaves of bread every day. Perce found kneading all that dough was harder work than rowing against a tide. It was also hot and stuffy down there, so Perce was glad when Charlie didn't need him.

Even with the stink of dog, it was better on deck. Mostly, on deck he could listen. All the sailors liked to tell Perce their stories, and he liked to hear them. He was never much for talking anyway and sure didn't have tales like theirs.

During meals, Perce acted as steward, serving the officers and scientists in the wardroom, so he got to hear their stories as well. Some had been to Antarctica before, with Shackleton or Scott.

"This'll be the third time for old Tom Crean," Wild told Perce one night. "He'll never tell you himself, but there's plenty men would be dead without his being along. On Scott's last expedition, he and another bloke dragged a mate on a sled for sixty-five miles. Finally the other man got too weak to pull, so Crean went on alone, walking another thirty-five miles to get help."

Perce listened with horror as Wild told him the details. Crean had only two chocolate bars and a biscuit to eat. A blizzard was rushing in behind him. He walked for eighteen hours without stopping. When he got to the hut, he collapsed. But only a few days later, as soon as the blizzard stopped, he led the rescue party back out to find his friends. A few months later, Crean went out in the party to search for the missing Scott and found the leader's dead body frozen stiff in his tent.

Tom Crean was second officer on the *Endurance*. Unlike most officers, Crean had come up through the ranks and understood the sailor's life on the "lower deck." He had grown up very poor on a potato farm and joined the British navy at the age of fifteen, in a borrowed suit with empty pockets. Crean's nickname was the "Irish Giant," for he was five feet ten, the tallest man on the ship. He was also one of the strongest and, at thirty-seven, one of the oldest. His face looked like a rocky cliff that had been carved by waves. Though he was gruff, all the sailors both liked and respected Crean, and Perce was sorry that he would never get to know him.

There wasn't much time to get to know anybody, since it took so much work to get the ship ready. The expedition would be away for two years and had to bring every single thing they could possibly need, from extra sails to extra buttons. They had ten tons of flour and two of powdered milk. Perce had never heard of powdered milk. The first time he mixed it up, he didn't stir it enough, and there was crunchy grit in the bottom of the cups, which caused much loud complaining and not a little spitting.

There were cases and cases of tinned meat, tinned butter, and tinned fruit. There were six thousand cans of sardines and twice that of soup. The sacks of oatmeal alone could have filled Perce's bedroom back home, top to bottom, wall to wall. Thirty thousand pounds of vegetables—potatoes, cabbage, carrots, brussels sprouts, cauliflower, rhubarb, and parsnips—had been chopped and dried and pressed into cubes. One three-inch cube would feed ten men.

"German company called Knorr makes 'em. So now there's a war on, we don't have to pay the blighters!" Charlie laughed.

There was scientific equipment as well: huge nets for dredging up sea life, crates full of collection jars. There were sleds and fur sleeping bags, candles, matches, extra mitts, socks, oilskins, harnesses for the dogs. Once they got to Antarctica, a party of men would stay ashore for the winter, so there was also wood to build a hut, linoleum for the floor, cots and blankets, lamps, coat hooks, and all the little things one could want for a cozy home in the long polar night. Everything had to be stowed so it wouldn't shift or spoil and where it could be found when it was needed. That was not easy on a small ship like the *Endurance*. Every inch of space was crammed with something. There was also the problem of coal. The hold was packed, and hundreds of extra sacks were wedged into every available space on deck, stuck behind dog kennels, and packed against the gunwales.

Shackleton arrived a few days after Perce started working, but Perce hardly ever saw him. Every day some important person wanted the famous explorer to come to dinner. Since money to pay for the expedition was always needed and since these people controlled the money, Shackleton had to go. He spoke briefly to Perce when he first arrived. He shook his hand and welcomed him aboard, thanked him for his hard work, and wished him well. Perce had never met anyone like him before. Shackleton was not a tall man, but he was square and solid, built like a bull. His blue-gray eyes were sharp and penetrating. One minute they were twinkling and merry as a boy's at a fair, the next as solemn and fiery as Moses's in a Bible picture. Shackleton had a kind of force about him, an energy that hit you right away and stayed with you even after he left.

"He makes you feel like you've been friends all your life," Perce said to Billy.

"Yeah, and like he's about to ask for all your pocket change and leave you feeling glad to give it!" Billy laughed.

Finally, on October 24, 1914, Frank Wild assembled the crew and told them they would sail in two days.

"Do any final shopping and post your letters. Half the crew will have shore leave tonight, the other tomorrow night. Any man fighting ashore or coming back drunk will be fired."

The men drew lots for their night off. Billy drew the first night but switched so he could spend the final night ashore with Perce. They started walking along the dock toward the bright lights and music of Buenos Aires.

"Hey! Hey, Bakie—Blackie!" Tim McCarthy, one of the sailors, ran up after them. "Where you two headed?"

"Don't know."

"Well, come on with me, then. I know a place where the steaks are two inches thick and the barmaids are cousins to the angels. *Distant* cousins," he added with a meaningful wink. Tim McCarthy was a carefree Irishman who seemed completely nonchalant about the impending journey. "Can't go off to the ice without one last warm kiss. What about you, young laddie—" He shoved Perce on the shoulder. "You kissed many girls yet?"

"Dozens," Perce assured him. "Back home, I have to make 'em stand in line. Sometimes all around the block."

"Aye, and charged them a penny apiece, I suppose."

"Only the mean ones."

They all laughed. Tim was twenty-six and came from a family of fishermen from County Cork. He had been at sea since he was three years old. "We usually start at two," he explained. "But I was a lazy little sod." Tim's older brother had sailed to Antarctica with Captain Scott on his last expedition.

"The sailors didn't like Scott so much, God rest his soul," Tim said. "He was all rules and regulations. Made them wash the decks every day, even when it froze to ice right away. The word is that Shackleton is the one to be with!"

The night was cool, and the whole city seemed to be out enjoying it. The little restaurant Tim took them to was crowded. The steaks were indeed thick and juicy. They shared a little jug of red wine and toasted to the voyage. Perce had never tasted red wine and found it sour.

Tim and Billy talked excitedly about the expedition. Perce listened to their banter with growing sadness. His stomach was all in knots, and for one horrible minute he felt tears welling up in his eyes. He ducked his head, he didn't want to ruin their last night with his own disappointment. But Billy had noticed and suddenly offered a solution.

"Stow away," Billy said simply.

Perce stared at him in disbelief.

"Really. We can sneak you back on late tonight and hide you somewhere."

"Why, sure—in a locker!" Tim suggested, his eyes bright with the idea. "Everyone will be busy in the morning, getting out of the harbor. You just have to hide for a couple of days."

"Shackleton won't turn the ship around just to put you off," Billy added.

"The worst that can happen is he'll put you off on South Georgia Island," Tim said. "We're stopping at the whaling station there to wait for the ice to open." He took another big bite of his steak. "Then you'll get work on a whaling ship. That's nasty work, but you're no worse off. But you'll have two weeks to prove yourself first."

"You can't be drunk because we've only had a glass apiece, so you must be mad," Perce said. Even so, his heart was beating with new hope.

"Oh, come on, you're a damn good worker, and we need the extra hand anyway," Tim insisted. "Shackleton's thinking he's going to have scientists working those sails! In the Drake Passage! Why, half of 'em were seasick all the way over from England with the sea flat as a duck pond."

"Come on, Perce," Billy urged. "Tim's right. Shackleton can't throw you overboard. The navy doesn't even flog people anymore."

"Walter How is on watch tonight," Tim said. "He'll let you aboard. He owes you for saving his tail in the dogfight."

"I didn't . . ."

"Oh, shut up and say you will!" Billy's eyes were sparkling with the excitement of a wicked child with a brilliant scheme.

"Come on, lad—" Tim lifted his glass. "What have you got to lose?"

chapter five

On October 26, 1914, at ten-thirty in the morning, the *Endurance* sailed from Buenos Aires. The dock was lined with people waving and cheering. The men cast off the lines, and the ship slowly pulled away. Everyone stood on deck to watch the city fade away. All but one. Perce Blackborow crouched silently in a dark cramped corner of Billy Bakewell's locker. With every bob of the ship, Billy's oilskin jacket banged against Perce's face. Billy had not washed his socks lately either, Perce noticed. But he didn't care. He was going. He was really going.

Two hours later, beyond the protective waters of the harbor, every motion of the ship felt a hundred times bigger. Perce broke out in a cold sweat. His head was spinning, and his stomach churned. So this was seasickness. He had never felt it before. He had thought that those who suffered from it were probably just sissies. Now he took back every bad thought he had ever had for them. Hours and hours went by. His legs were cramped. His elbows and shoulders hurt from banging against the walls. Just when he thought he might die, the door opened and a stream of fresh air flooded in.

"How you doing?" Billy whispered. "Here. Some water and a biscuit."

"I need . . . I . . ." Perce couldn't get the words out because a hot stream of vomit erupted behind them. Billy quickly grabbed a bucket.

"Here. Watch your aim."

It was a long awful day followed by a long awful night.

The locker was dark and airless. Every now and then Billy or Tim cracked the door open and handed in a biscuit or a cup of water. Sometime during the night one of them even took away the bucket to empty it. By then Perce was beyond throwing up.

All the next day the ship rolled and tossed. Perce bumped and banged up new bruises. Finally, by evening, the ship was far enough from land. Billy pulled Perce out of the locker. His legs were so cramped, he could barely stand. He hobbled a few steps down the narrow passage. Suddenly they heard footsteps. The watch was just ending, and several men were coming below.

"Go! Get away!" Perce whispered. He didn't want his friends to get in trouble for helping him.

"Quick! In here." Billy opened another sailor's locker and shoved Perce in. Perce crouched down in the new locker while Billy disappeared in the other direction.

When the sailor opened his locker a few minutes later, he was surprised to find an extra pair of boots. He was even more surprised to discover these boots had feet inside them and these feet were attached to Perce Blackborow. The sailor shut the door. A few minutes later, Frank Wild yanked the door open, grabbed Perce roughly by the front of his shirt, and hauled him out. Perce was now shaking so hard, Wild practically carried him to Shackleton's cabin.

Shackleton was sitting at his desk. He was terribly still, his hands spread motionless on the small desk. His blue-gray eyes glinted with fury. Perce tried to stand, but his cramped legs kept buckling.

"Oh, sit him down, Wild," Shackleton barked. Wild dragged over a chair and dropped Perce into it.

"What the bloody hell do you think you're doing!" Shackleton roared. "Stowing away! You think this is a jolly lark? You think this is a pleasure cruise? We're all going to play shuffleboard on the deck? Eh?"

"N-no, sir," Perce stammered weakly.

"If I'd wanted more crew, I would have picked someone. You think I can't pick a crew? You think you know better? You think I need a boy not six months at open sea? To sail the roughest ocean in the world to the worst place on the entire planet? You think you can clean behind your own ears?"

"Y-y-yes, sir. I mean, no, sir." Perce was hoping there wasn't anything left in him to throw up. Perce glanced at Wild, but the man just stood there behind Shackleton, with his usual calm gaze that betrayed nothing.

"I mean to work hard, sir," Perce blurted. "I do."

"Oh. You mean to work hard. Do you have any idea what we're getting into?" Now Shackleton came from behind his desk and stood in front of Perce. His face was red. His voice roared. "We are going to the most desolate place in the world. It is always cold and always dangerous. Do you have any idea what it is to walk through a blizzard when you can barely stand? Have you ever spent an hour trying to wiggle your foot into your boot that has become a solid block of ice?"

Perce didn't think there was an answer, so he said nothing.

"Stowaway!" Shackleton said, his voice dropping a little. "Who helped you?"

"No one, sir. It was my idea. I wanted to go so bad.

Please, sir. I—I won't let you down." He was clutching the arms of the chair so hard, his fingers were white.

"Well, you'd better not because I can't get rid of you now." Shackleton's eyes narrowed, and his voice dropped to a terrible whisper. "But do you know that on these expeditions we often get very *hungry*—" He leaned even closer until his face was just inches from Perce's. "And if there is a *stowaway* available, he is the first to be *eaten*?"

Perce almost fell backward out of his chair. Frank Wild turned his face away. Perce saw his shoulders shaking, just a little bit. Slowly Perce Blackborow realized what had just happened. Wild was laughing, and Shackleton was going to give him a chance.

chapter six

Life aboard a ship has a rhythm all its own. The clock is important, but time to a sailor is tracked more by the movement of the sun, the moon, and the stars. The ocean swells begin to feel like your own pulse. The creaks and groans of the ship become familiar as your own heartbeat. A sailor can feel the smallest change in the wind the way a mother can sense when her baby is waking up. Perce felt at home on the sea. He especially liked being on dawn watch. This time, from four to eight in the morning, was the quietest time. He loved to watch the night slip into morning as the sky changed through a hundred shades of blue.

By now, however, as the *Endurance* had sailed farther and farther south, that lovely shift from night to morning had vanished. It was early December, but down here, where the seasons were flip-flopped, it was summer, and the sun only set for a couple of hours. By midsummer, it would never set at all. Even now, though, the sky never got dark. Perce could only see the brightest stars in those dusky hours.

Still, he liked this watch. If the weather was fair and the ship was on a steady course, there was time to just sit and think and watch the ocean. There was nothing in the world like this feeling. It was sort of lonely, but not in a bad way. He felt partly sad, partly happy, longing for something, but wanting nothing. He knew he was one tiny person in one small ship in the middle of an enormous ocean, but it was the right place to be.

Especially right for me, Perce thought. The *Endurance* was three days out from South Georgia Island now, and he was still aboard. He felt a shiver of happiness and disbelief as he remembered that day. They had spent a month on the island, anchored near the whaling station, waiting for the ice to open up. Every day Perce had expected to be handed his papers and put ashore. But each day passed with no summons to doom. Then just five days ago, Greenstreet stopped Perce after breakfast and asked him to report to Shackleton's cabin. Greenstreet had dropped no hint as to his fate. Perce tried to prepare himself for the worst. And it would be worst, for now he had friends and a taste of adventure and the stink of dead whales in his nostrils. He definitely wanted none of that.

Perce took a deep breath and knocked on the wooden door. Shackleton was sitting at his little desk, a stack of letters folded neatly beside him, an account book open on the bench.

"We're leaving tomorrow, Perce," he said sternly. With barely a glance, he tossed some papers on the bench toward Perce. Perce was so nervous, he just looked at them, afraid to pick them up.

"Well, go on," Shackleton said. With a sinking heart, Perce picked them up, expecting his discharge papers. His hands shook as he unfolded them.

"You can read, can't you?"

"Aye, sir."

"So you know what those are."

Perce nodded. Now his heart was beating so hard, he couldn't talk. It was the ship's articles, the legal document that all the sailors had to sign to be aboard.

"And you're sure you want to go on?"

"I—I do. Yes, sir," he stammered.

"Why?" Shackleton fixed a steady gaze on him. Perce tried to think of a good answer. There was science and the glory of England and all that, but he couldn't lie to Shackleton.

"I can't really say, sir. It's just the adventure of it. And the chance of it. And a test, I suppose."

"A lot of men have failed that test."

"Aye—" Perce stopped. He was about to say he wouldn't fail, but that would be stupid. He had no idea how he would do. He pictured Tom Crean bravely trudging alone through the snow to save his mate. "Aye, but I want to have a try," he said simply.

"You're a good lad, Perce, a good sailor. You have a whole life ahead of you—why don't you go home and live it?"

"Thank you, sir." Now it was all he could do to keep from shouting. "But I think I'd rather live this one here first."

Shackleton sighed and gazed at the map of Antarctica pinned to the wall. Perce couldn't tell what he was thinking.

"Then sign the articles," Shackleton said. "And write your family. Tell them what god-awful mischief you've got yourself into."

Perce grinned with relief. "Yes, sir! Thank you, sir!"

"You'll continue helping Charlie in the galley and serving as steward. Sort out your sailor's duties with Mr. Greenstreet. You've been learning the ropes well enough, but it will do you good to learn the books as well." Shackleton handed him a great fat copy of *The Manual of Seamanship*. "You must try to keep up your other studies too. Borrow whatever you want from the library. Everyone is welcome to the books, and a good story helps to pass the time."

"Thank you, sir."

He forced himself to walk calmly out of the cabin. He restrained himself until he was halfway down the passageway, then broke into a run, nearly crashing into Frank Wild as he came out of the wardroom.

"Steady there—ship sinking?"

"No, sir. Sorry, Mr. Wild. And thank you! If you had a say in keeping me, sir. Thank you!"

Wild just nodded and went into Shackleton's cabin.

"You couldn't talk him out of it, Boss?" he said as he took out his pipe.

"Damn fool boy. Stowing away to bloody Antarctica." Shackleton grinned and leaned back in his chair. "How the hell could I talk him out of it? Just the damn fool sort of thing I might have done myself."

December 5, 1914
Grytviken Whaling Station,
South Georgia Island

Dearest Mother and Father,

I am writing to tell you what god-awful mischief I have gotten myself into. Please excuse the swear, but that is what Sir Ernest Shackleton told me to tell you. Yes, that *Shackleton! I have a place aboard his ship* Endurance, *and tomorrow we leave for Antarctica. It is a long story how I came to be here, and someday I will tell it when I get back. Do not worry about me, because I will be fine. I will only be on the ship, of course, not going to the South Pole, though I hope to walk on an iceberg. I don't know how long before I can write you again. After we land Shackleton and his men in Antarctica, we might take the ship back here to South Georgia for the winter. But if Shackleton can find a good harbor down there, we will stay. That is safe too, so don't worry. So there is no way to tell you yet. It might be six months or a year before another letter. Give my love to Harry, Teddy, Jack, Charlie, and William. Say I will bring them a penguin for a pet. Do not worry for me, because I am with Shackleton.*

Your loving son, Perce

Perce could only imagine the surprise when his parents received that letter a month or two from now. What are they doing right now? he wondered. His mother would have already made her Christmas fruitcake. His father would be worrying about paying for the winter's coal. At least they would have Perce's wages from the *Golden Gate* to help with that. Maybe there would be a little extra for new boots. He pictured his five younger brothers in the annual "try-ons," when they got out the winter coats and boots to see who fit into what. Even the most careful mending couldn't always make a jacket last through all six boys.

Perce walked up to the bow of the ship and looked all around. They had seen a few icebergs already, but now that they were farther south, they had to be extra alert. The news from the whale-ship captains was not good. They said there was much more ice in the Weddell Sea than anyone could ever remember. Shackleton was worried. The Antarctic summer was short, and his plans were big.

First they had to sail almost two thousand miles across the Weddell Sea, then find a good place to set up the winter camp. Since there were no good charts of the coastline, this would not be easy. Once they found a place, Shackleton would take twelve men ashore for the winter. They would build a hut and spend the winter months getting ready for the crossing. The scientists would do their research, and the dog drivers would train their teams.

Right now, Perce knew, another ship, called *Aurora,* was sailing from New Zealand to the opposite side of Antarctica. The *Aurora* would come through the Ross Sea and land another party onshore. Shackleton, Scott, Amundsen, and most of the earlier explorers had started from the Ross Sea. The men from the *Aurora* would go out in dog sleds along Shackleton's old route and lay depots of food and fuel for him.

Next spring, Shackleton would choose a team of six out of the group who had spent the winter onshore. They would make the overland journey. The *Endurance* would return to pick up the remaining men, then sail back to Buenos Aires.

It all sounded very neat and organized when the men were talking about it, but Perce knew how difficult it really would be. No one had ever gone inland from this side before. Shackleton would have to find a completely new route to the South Pole, then continue across to the Ross Sea. The entire distance was about fifteen hundred miles. He could only carry enough supplies to get a few hundred miles beyond the South Pole. Then he would have to rely on the depots. There were no radios strong enough to cover such a great distance so the two parties couldn't communicate. Shackleton would not know if the supplies had been left until he got past the South Pole. If there were no depots, he and his men would die. At least Frank Wild's brother was aboard the *Aurora*. Everyone knew he would lay the depots or die trying. If everything worked well, Shackleton and his men would arrive at the Ross Sea in early fall and the *Aurora* would pick them up.

Perce's thoughts were interrupted by a cold drip on the side of his face. A squashy plop landed on his shoulder. It was a big oily glob of whale blubber. There was a ton of it hanging from the rigging. They had bought it from the whalers on South Georgia for dog food. When the sun warmed it up, it dripped all over the deck. Perce brushed the glob off his jacket. Some of the dogs smelled the fat and started to howl. Perce went over to Sampson's kennel and let him lick the grease off his hand. Sampson was the biggest dog they had, but also the most gentle. Most of the dogs had settled down by now, but some might still bite his whole hand off for a taste of whale blubber.

The bell sounded the end of the watch, but Perce lingered on deck. There was something different about this morning. He wasn't sure yet what it was, just a feeling in the air. The sea felt different too. There was a subtle change in the rhythm of the swells.

Tom Crean, officer of the next watch, came on deck and nodded to Perce.

"You didn't hear the bell?" He spoke with a thick Irish accent.

"I did. It's a fine morning, though."

"Aye."

Mrs. Chippy, the ship's cat, strode over to Perce and rubbed against his ankles. Despite its name, the big striped tabby was actually a male. The carpenter, who on a ship was often called "Chippy," had named him before anyone took the trouble to check. Mrs. Chippy didn't seem to mind. He swaggered around the ship like he was king of the world.

"Come to watch with us, Mrs. Chippy?" Perce scratched the cat behind the ears. "Or is it just a little dog fun you're after?" Mrs. Chippy's favorite game was to run across the kennel roofs to tease the dogs. He seemed to know exactly how long the chains were and always stayed just an inch out of reach.

"Wants his breakfast prompt, he does," Crean laughed. Perce usually fed Mrs. Chippy scraps when he cleared the table after breakfast. Crean leaned against the rail beside Perce and turned his binoculars out to sea. Crean was not one to fill up the morning with idle chat, though with his Irish wit he could, and often did, outdo any man aboard with tales and song.

"Do you feel the change?" Crean nodded his chin toward the horizon.

"Something's different," Perce agreed. The temperature hadn't really changed, but the air felt cold in a different way.

"Ice," Crean said simply. "We're coming to the pack."

The pack ice was the final barrier. The big icebergs could be dangerous, but they were fairly easy to avoid. In the pack, plates of ice crowded together like water lilies on a pond. There was no way around, only through. The whalers had not been able to get through just a couple of weeks ago.

"Would you fancy hanging off a boom in these seas?" Crean's rough face cracked into a broad smile. "That's how they used to do it down here a hundred years ago. The ships were slow, and some sailed in the winter when it was dark day and night. You couldn't see the ice. So they'd hang a lad out over the side on a boom. He had to listen for the sound of water hitting the iceberg. Feel for a bit of icy air blowing against his face. That'd be your job!" Crean laughed. "Though you'd have been a first-class idiot to have stowed away back then!"

Perce was glad to live in the modern age.

chapter seven

Perce was scrubbing out the porridge pot an hour later when the cry came.

"Ice ho! Pack off the port bow!" The shout sent everyone running. Perce dropped the pot and joined the crowd of men squeezing up the narrow passages to the deck. Shackleton was on the bridge, looking through his binoculars. Perce ran to the rail.

"Wow!" Giant white plates of ice floated across the entire horizon. There was not more than two feet of open water between any of them.

"It's half a mile long, maybe more." Tom Crean pointed. "But not so wide. There's clear water on the other side."

"How can you tell?" Perce asked. "All I can see is ice."

"Look at the clouds." Crean handed him the binoculars. "Watch the reflection off the bottom of the clouds. It's different over the ice from over open water. You see a touch of blue with open water." Perce tried to see the difference, but the light was so strange, it was hard to know what he was seeing. Billy appeared beside him, yawning. He had done the midnight-to-four watch and was sleeping when the shout came.

"Dang," he said. "It's like a jigsaw puzzle! How are we gonna get through that?"

"Very carefully," Crean said somberly. He went off to talk to Shackleton. Billy rubbed the side of his face that was still creased from his pillow and shivered. He was wearing only a jacket over his undershirt.

"You should have brought your mother along, Billy,"

Perce chided. "Someone to tell you to put your sweater on when you're going out in the cold."

"Yeah. But better to have my grandpa along with his mule whip to knock the living daylights out of that one." Billy cocked his head in the direction of the ship's bosun, John Vincent.

"What trouble now?"

"He tore his own sweater on a nailhead and offered himself mine till his gets itself mended."

It wasn't long into the voyage that John Vincent had showed himself a bully. At first it was small things. He took the best of the food at meals. He made everyone move bunks several times until he found the one he liked best. He was the bosun, so he did have some authority over the other sailors, but this usually meant assigning chores, not stealing another man's clothes. Perce looked closer at the red mark on Billy's face and realized it was not from any pillow.

"What—"

"Yeah—" his friend interrupted. "You'd think he'd know how to hit a man without leaving a mark." Vincent claimed to have been a professional boxer. He certainly looked like one. His shoulders were broad, his neck thick, his arms heavy with muscle. Before signing on with Shackleton, he had worked on fishing trawlers in the North Sea. That was some of the roughest work you could find, and it attracted the roughest men. The six sailors and Charlie the cook all shared the small cabin called the fo'c'sle at the bow of the ship. While it was fairly roomy as far as fo'c'sles went, it was still close quarters, and this would be a long enough voyage without a bully on board.

"He'll settle down when we get busier," Billy said. He didn't sound very convincing. "His hide's as thick as a mule, so he can't hardly be feeling the cold anyway."

"Well, take my sweater for your watch," Perce offered. "I have that extra wool shirt too, if you roll the sleeves up."

"Thanks." The two friends fell silent. There wasn't much they could do about Vincent except watch each other's back. He hadn't done anything really bad, and they would look like whiners going to Wild or Shackleton over a "borrowed" sweater. Billy pulled his jacket tight around his neck.

All day, they sailed along the edge of the pack ice, looking for a way through. Frank Worsley, the captain of the ship, had never seen pack ice before. He was from New Zealand and had sailed mostly in the South Pacific. Shackleton and Wild spent the whole day on the bridge, guiding him. The men were kept busy working the sails. Perce had "learned the ropes" from Billy and Tim and now worked almost as well as anyone. There were dozens of lines and cables, halyards and winches, and a sailor had to know exactly which one to grab when the order rang out. A mistake or delay could bring disaster. On the *Endurance* they were lucky, for they didn't have to rely only on the sails like earlier explorers: they had the coal engines. Perce could not imagine how Captain Cook sailed down here over a hundred years ago entirely at the mercy of wind power. How could you steer through pack ice when it might take fifteen minutes or more to turn your ship about?

"Look there! We got company!" Tim was up in the rigging and pointed down at the ice.

"Penguins!" Billy laughed. "Look at them! All dressed up fancy in their fine tuxedos to greet us."

"Those are emperor penguins," Crean explained. "Biggest ones down here. I knew three fellows who sledged through a month of the worst Antarctic winter to collect some of their eggs."

"Why?" Perce asked.

"I never was too sure about that. But it probably wasn't much crazier than any other reason we come mucking around down here."

There were ten emperors in this welcoming committee. They stood together solemnly like a bunch of bishops. They looked up at the ship as it passed only inches from their floe, heads tilted up in silent puzzlement.

"They must think we're from another planet," Perce said. "From Mars or someplace."

A little while later, they saw a large flock of Adélie penguins. These birds were much smaller and more playful than the emperors. They chattered and squawked and waved their little flipper wings in excitement. They leapt out of the water and slid across the ice on their bellies like kids on toboggans. Sometimes a whole group of them waddled over to the edge of their ice floe and just stood there, looking at the water as if daring someone to be the first to jump in. Finally one would jump, or maybe get pushed, and all the rest would follow.

Perce would like to have stayed and watched the playful birds all afternoon, but he had pots to scrub in the galley. He yawned. It was almost two o'clock, and he was on watch again at six for the second half of the dogwatch. While most watches were four hours long, the dogwatch was broken into two shifts, four to six and six to eight in the evening. This gave all the men a chance to eat supper and shifted the rest of the schedule around a notch so that no one was always on the same watch. Perce squatted down and scraped the last scraps into Mrs. Chippy's bowl. The big cat meowed happily, and Perce scratched his head. When he stood up again and turned to leave the galley, John Vincent was blocking his way.

"What a good little Peggy you are," the man sneered. "Done all your cooking and washing up; now it's time for mending." He thrust his torn sweater at Perce. "I'm on again at eight—I'll need it by then."

"Then you'd better get to work, hadn't you?" Perce said, making no move to take the sweater.

"You'll sew it with broken fingers if you mouth off like that again!" the man snarled.

"Why, I was just offering some advice," Perce responded calmly, though his heart was beating hard. "You'll want time to do a nice job, seeing as how we all like to keep up appearances down here."

John Vincent grabbed Perce by the front of his shirt and shoved him back into the galley. He pushed the sweater into his face. Perce knocked Vincent's arm away. This only made him angrier.

"Did you just hit me?"

"If I did, you wouldn't have to ask." Perce's voice was still calm, but there was force behind it.

"If this sweater isn't mended before I—"

"Hey, Blackborow!" A strong voice interrupted from the companionway. "Blackborow? Are you down there, lad?"

"Aye, sir." John Vincent glared at Perce and squeezed one

hand into a threatening fist, then stepped back as Frank Hurley appeared. Hurley was the expedition's official photographer. He was a big, strapping Australian with thick, curly brown hair and steady, challenging blue eyes.

"Ah, good." Hurley looked from one man to the other. If he felt the tension in the air, he didn't say anything.

"Blackborow—lad, what you doing now? Not on watch, are you?"

"No, sir."

"No potatoes to peel?"

"Not for a while."

"How do you do with heights, lad? Afraid of heights?" Hurley was buckling on a belt of canvas webbing. Beside him were two crates of camera gear.

"No, sir." Perce looked doubtfully at the equipment and the belt. "Not so far anyway, sir."

Hurley laughed. "Fancy a climb up the mast, then?" Hurley had already earned a reputation as a daring, some said reckless, man. He would go anywhere, do anything to get a good photograph. On South Georgia, he had lugged his heavy equipment up mountains and glaciers. He also had a brash self-confidence that annoyed some of the men. They thought he was stuck-up. Some called him "The Prince."

It was true that Hurley could seem a bit full of himself, but it wasn't all hot air. Hurley had traveled all over and really knew how to do a lot of things. He had been to Antarctica before too, with an Australian expedition.

"Come on, then, while the sky's clear. Grab that box, would'ya?"

Perce picked up a crate and followed Hurley up on deck. Hurley clipped a line from his belt to the large box camera. He slung the strap over one shoulder and across his chest.

"I want to take the cine camera too," Hurley explained. "Got to take advantage of a good clear day like this for moving pictures, so I can't carry the plates as well." Hurley tossed Perce another safety belt like his own. Perce buckled it on and picked up the case of glass plates.

"Clip the box to your belt so you can't drop it. Don't fall overboard, or it'll drag you to the bottom." Hurley grinned. "You can clip the safety line on the rigging as you climb if you want to. Boss likes that," he said, as if he would never consider actually doing such a thing himself. "Once on top, we'll just scoot out the yardarm. You'll hand me a plate when I'm ready. Handle them only by the edges—can't have greasy fingerprints all over the glass." Hurley turned his back on Perce and, without any further instruction, began to climb up the rigging.

Perce knew almost nothing about photography. He had seen advertisements in magazines for modern cameras. Some were as small as a packet of cookies, but they were still too expensive for anyone he knew. Most people who wanted a photograph went to a studio, where they sat in front of a painted backdrop and came back a week later for the picture.

Hurley climbed the shrouds as easily as a monkey, despite the heavy camera. Perce followed more slowly. He hadn't done much top work yet. The ropes were frozen with spray from the waves. He knew half the men would now be watching them instead of the penguins, and he didn't want to slip and make a fool of himself. The heavy box banged against his back. When Hurley reached the main yard, he turned and waited for Perce. The strong wind made his eyes water, but he didn't look like the cold bothered him at all. He wore only a sweater and jacket, no gloves.

"Nice view, eh?"

Perce hadn't exactly noticed the view yet. He was just trying to hang on for dear life. Down on the deck, it hardly seemed the ship was moving. Up here, the mast waved back and forth like some crazy carnival ride. Hurley climbed out along the yardarm as if he were strolling down the sidewalk. Perce carefully eased down and sat where he could hold on to the mast. He shifted the box of plates around so he could get to it more easily and waited. And waited.

Hurley looked around in every direction. The wind blew colder. Perce was bareheaded and had only the thin gloves that were in his jacket pocket. At least he wasn't getting beat up by Vincent in the galley, he thought cheerfully. And what nice fresh air there was. You couldn't get much fresher than this! Back home, the coal smoke poured out of chimneys and left fine black grit all over everything. The stink of sulfur sometimes made your eyes water and your lungs burn. Perce shivered and tried to think of the nice fresh air, not how bloody cold it was.

"Look there!" Hurley shouted. Perce turned to look. A great spout of water shot into the air only a hundred feet from the ship.

"A whale!" It was bigger than any whale Perce had ever seen. "It's as long as the ship!" he cried excitedly.

"Blue whale." Hurley shaded his eyes and watched it. "Beauty! Hand me the cine camera."

Hurley wound the camera and shot some footage of the whale, then handed the movie camera back to Perce and went on watching the ice. He didn't even pick up his box camera for a good ten minutes. What was he waiting for? The scenery wasn't really changing much. There was water and ice and ice and water. Finally Hurley took up the camera.

"Hand me a plate," he directed. Perce opened the box and carefully drew out one of the glass plates. When Hurley worked with the equipment, every movement was precise and sure. But it was different from just a workman with his tools, Perce thought. It was more like his mum changing a baby's nappy or pulling a splinter out of someone's hand. There was a tenderness about it.

Hurley slipped the plate into the camera, then pulled the black cloth over the back of his head. Perce waited for the snap of the camera lens. He waited some more. He watched the shape of Hurley's head beneath the black cloth. The man barely moved. The wind howled through the rigging. Perce could feel the vibrations in his legs. What was Hurley waiting for? Despite the cold and the frantic swaying of the mast, Perce began to feel sleepy. A click snapped him back to his senses. Perce opened his eyes and saw Hurley tossing off the black cloth.

"Right, then."

Perce shifted the heavy box full of plates. "That's all? Just one?"

"All you need when the one is right." Hurley grinned and sprang to his feet. Perce unwound his stiff legs.

"Begging your pardon, sir—"

"Oh, blast it, lad—you don't have to 'sir' me. I'm not an officer."

"Sorry, sir. I mean, all right. But could I ask, how do you know when the one is right?"

Hurley grabbed Perce by the back of his jacket and helped him up. He steadied him as they both held on to the mast.

"Look out there." He pointed off the beam of the ship. "What do you see?"

"Ice, sir."

"And this way?" Hurley turned Perce so he was looking toward the front of the ship, the direction Hurley had taken the photograph.

"More ice. And the foremast."

"Ah, but you don't just see ice, do you? You see shapes of ice and shapes of water. You see light and dark. And you don't just see the foremast. You see the mast and the yardarm and the rigging. Altogether you see squares and lines, foreground, background. Now watch awhile."

Hurley leaned easily against the mast, barely holding on. "See when the shapes come together in a way that pleases your eye."

Perce clung to a halyard and shivered.

"See there." Hurley held up his hands again to frame the scene. "How the yardarm crosses straight up against that channel of water?"

"Is . . . is that the most pleasing?" Perce asked.

"Could be," Hurley laughed. "That's up to you. There

are some rules—you don't want a mishmash of lines every which way. But it's bloody cold up here to be discussing them now, don't you think? I wouldn't mind a cup of tea."

"Yes, sir."

"Right, then." Hurley slung his camera over his shoulder and helped Perce with the box of plates. "Thanks, mate." He swung his feet over and began to climb down the frozen rope ladder. Perce took one last look at the horizon. The ship was turning slowly to port. As her bow shifted, Perce saw a line of square ice floes laid out point to point like stepping-stones in a garden. The sun caught them at a certain angle and made them seem like they were floating above the surface of the water and pointing the way to the end of the world. It was very dramatic. Very beautiful. There were so many different ways to look at the world.

chapter eight

Crack! Perce woke with a start as he flew through the air. He fell back on the bunk a good two feet from where he had been sleeping. He felt sharp claws scramble up his legs as a terrified Mrs. Chippy clawed his way to Perce's head. Perce tucked the cat under one arm and pulled his pillow over his ears. The timbers of the ship creaked.

"Worsley's at the helm again," Billy groaned from the bunk below. "Get your helmets on, boys." After a week in the pack, each helmsman had developed his own technique for steering the ship through the ice. Frank Wild took a smooth steady course, finding openings that no one else would have seen. Mr. Greenstreet liked to chug along slowly, nudging the bergs gently aside with the bow. Captain Worsley thought it great fun to back the ship up in an open lane of water then build up speed and ram the floes as hard as he could, smashing them apart. The collisions made the whole ship shudder, but it was worst in the fo'c'sle.

"A rat in a maze. That's what we are. A rat in a maze." John Vincent threw his blanket back in anger. "Eight bloody days and we've got nowhere."

"And no one told you there was going to be ice in Antarctica?" Billy said.

"Shut up!" John Vincent kicked the side of his bunk so hard, the whole cabin rattled again. Mrs. Chippy fluffed up his fur and hissed. "And if that damn cat keeps thumping around in here all night, I swear I'm going to throw it overboard." He grabbed his jacket and stomped out.

"Sure, and let the mice come and chew your ugly face off," Perce muttered after him.

"Now *that* I'd pay to see." Billy turned over and stretched. "Did you hear the bell?"

"No, but if Worsley's taken the helm, the watch must have changed."

Perce flung back his own blanket. He couldn't tell what time it was. It was midsummer now and light all the time. "I'm wide awake now anyway. I'll go check," he said to Billy. Mrs. Chippy gave him a brief indignant look, then curled up in the warm place he left behind. Up on deck there was none of the bustle of a crew change. Some of the dogs were barking and pacing in their kennels. They had been disturbed by the crashing as well. Worsley was still at the helm. He was grinning like a schoolboy who had just captured the flag. First Officer Greenstreet was back by the stern, leaning over the railing. He straightened up as Perce approached, then looked at his watch.

"Up early, aren't you? Watch doesn't change for another ten minutes."

"Had a bit of a toss below."

"That sod. Going to split the ship in two one of these days. We had clear water for a good three hours, doing seven, eight knots. Then more of this." Greenstreet nodded at the pack ice. "I think he was happy to see it. Smooth sailing bores Mr. Worsley."

Perce heard hammering from below and leaned over to see McNeish, the carpenter. He had built a small wooden platform off the stern and was now pounding the last nails to fasten a railing in place.

"What's that for?" Perce asked.

"Fancy you should ask. We're just needing a volunteer to try it out."

"Aw, not that one, sir!" McNeish growled in his thick Scottish accent as he climbed back up on deck. "'e makes a good piecrust, 'at one does. Don't want ta lose him overboard."

"Then watch he doesn't fall, Mr. McNeish." Greenstreet smiled. "Watch he doesn't." Greenstreet turned to Perce. "What was it you said to me when you was begging for a job back in Buenos Aires? Oh, yes, *very willing* it was. *Very willing.*"

Uh-oh, Perce thought. So far *very willing* had got him up the mast and down in the bilge. It got him peeling thousands of potatoes and hauling up wet, stinky drift nets for Clark the biologist. Greenstreet pointed down where chunks of ice were churning in the wake of the ship.

"The rudder is getting dinged by all the ice. We thought we might put a man out there with a pole to push the floes away and help keep it clear."

The little platform bucked and bobbed with every swell.

"You'll need seaboots," Greenstreet said. "Some in the port locker there." Perce got a pair of the rubber boots. He tugged his wool hat snugly over his head and pulled up the hood of his oilskin jacket. The bell sounded the change of the watch. He would have liked a cup of tea and a bit of breakfast, but he was on duty now. He swung one leg over the side.

"Wait a minute—use yer 'ead, boy." McNeish scowled. He tossed Perce the end of a rope. "Tie yourself up, lad. I meant it about the piecrust."

"Thanks," Perce said as he tied the line around his waist. McNeish handed Perce a long iron pole. Perce looped the tether strap around his wrist and tried the pole out on a small chunk of ice. There was a satisfying thwack, and the ice bobbed away. Right, then, this would be easy enough. Perce straightened up and looked around. The pack ice stretched as far as he could see. In clear water the ship could be making two hundred miles a day. In the pack, she was doing barely thirty.

Ten minutes later, this new job didn't seem quite so easy. The platform grew slippery with freezing spray. Every now and then a big wave washed over and sucked at his ankles. He bent his knees and tried to balance, but he still slid and skipped around like a jerky marionette.

"How are you doing there, Blackie?" Tom Crean appeared at the railing. "Having fun yet?"

"Yes, sir. Great fun. Get to practice my dancing steps too!" He jabbed away another chunk of ice. "Are you needing any practice yourself, sir? I'd be glad to give you a go."

Crean laughed. "We'll change you off on the half hour."

How long had he been out here already? Cold air blew down from the sky and up from the sea, finding its way through the smallest opening in his clothing. The pole began to grow heavy. Perce's legs were starting to feel jiggly. A single large plate of ice drifted toward the propeller. Perce poked it. It floated lazily out of the way and bumped into another floe. Suddenly both chunks rose up out of the water. A great enormous head appeared between them. The shiny black snout of a killer whale poked through. One cold dark eye fixed itself on Perce. Pods of orcas, or killer whales, were common down here, but he had never seen one so close. Perce could smell the foul, fishy breath as the great snout edged closer to the platform. Each tooth was as big as a man's fist. He saw the fin of a second whale break the surface about ten feet away, then another behind that.

The sea was calm and smooth as glass. He saw the black-and-white pattern of the first killer whale as it dove down and circled slowly beneath the stern. Perce leaned over the railing to get a better look. It was scary, but also fascinating. He watched the giant beast make another lazy circle. Suddenly, with one flick of its powerful tail, the whale rocketed up, knocking the bottom of the platform. Perce went flying.

Time stood still as he stared down into the gaping mouth of the killer whale. The tongue looked plump and pink as a ham. The platform slammed back down on the water and Perce's feet slipped out from under him. He crashed down and slid across the platform. His feet plunged into the sea, and cold water rushed into the boots. It seemed to slosh up all the way to his heart. He grabbed frantically at the flimsy railing. He couldn't even cry out; terror seized his throat. At the same time, he had strange, slow thoughts. *What a stupid way to die! Will I simply slide down that spongy throat? Or will I be crunched hard between those teeth first?* In the same half second all this went through his mind, he felt a hard yank around his waist. The safety line caught him as his knees slid over the edge. He scrambled backward to get his footing. The enormous head fell back with a splash, and Perce felt the rope yank him up. For a few seconds, he was a puppet on a string, dangling mere inches from the cold, stinking maw of the killer whale. Then the solid timbers of the ship smacked against his back. He turned and clawed up the side. Big hands grabbed his arms and pulled him roughly over. Tom Crean fell backward with Perce on top of him.

"Jesus, lad!" Crean gasped. "Where were you when the good Lord was handing out brains!" Perce rolled off and jumped to his feet. His legs were shaking so, he could hardly stand.

"What—why—" Perce swallowed. "Why did it do that?"

"Do what?" Crean said gruffly as he got up. "Try and eat you for breakfast? He was hunting! What the bloody hell did you think he was doing? Come to pay you a friendly visit? That's how they hunt the seals! Smash those great ugly heads up through the ice just like that. Knock the seal off into the water and *chuuuck* . . ." Crean made a gruesome smacking noise.

Perce leaned against the stern rail. He crossed his arms tightly. He didn't want Tom Crean to see he was shaking. "Thanks. I—I'll be more careful," he stammered.

"Accchh—get yourself below and warm up. They got no business putting you out there, knowing nothing about nothing. Accchhh. Here—" Crean began to untie the knot in Perce's safety line. Perce held his breath so Crean wouldn't feel his stampeding heart.

"You've seen them hunting like that? Knocking up the ice?" He tried to keep his voice steady, like he was just asking a casual question.

"Aye. And worse." Perce thought he saw stony Tom

Crean shudder. "Almost made a Jonah out of me," he said. "Years ago on Scott's first expedition. We were crossing some bloody rotten ice. Full of cracks it was. Had no business there, not one of us knew what we were doing back then. But Captain Scott tells us to go on across. So we go. And we're leading ponies besides." The knot had tightened with the jerk, and Crean had to work at it. "Aye—we were waltzing with the devil that day. Ice breaking up all around us. Ponies over there on a wee bit of ice, us over here on another, and the killers all around. Those cold eyes. One pony finally went in, and we couldn't pull him out. Didn't want to see him eaten alive. Had to kill him there in the water."

"You shot the pony?"

"Didn't have a gun. Put an ice ax through his skull." Perce shuddered as he pictured it. The knot finally came free. Crean retied the safety line to the deck rail so it was shorter. "There you go. Next man out might only get his leg bit off," he said.

"If the rope doesn't break."

"Or the beast don't leap twenty feet clear up out of the sea."

"Aye. There's always something." Perce and Crean both laughed.

chapter nine

A few days later, as Christmas approached, the *Endurance* was still making slow progress through the pack ice. Charlie was busy making mince pies and nut bread, so Perce was busy chopping nuts and rolling out piecrusts. The Christmas pudding came from a tin but still had to be steamed for hours. The galley was warm and damp with the condensation. The wardroom was decorated with paper lace streamers. Someone had brought a box of Christmas crackers, and he set each place with one of the brightly colored favors.

"Oh, will you look at all this!" Tim whistled in appreciation as he came in with a load of coal for the stove. "Hey, Billy, come see how the high society does things now." Billy stuck his head inside the wardroom. He had just come off watch. His eyebrows were white with frost, and little icicles clung to the hair around his face.

"Luuv-ly, just luuv-ly," he said in an exaggerated imitation of Tim's Irish accent. "What're these things?" Billy picked up one of the Christmas crackers. Drops of water fell from his frosty face and splashed on the tablecloth.

"Hey, don't be melting all over my nice table!" Perce snapped his dish towel at him. Billy ducked.

"You don't have crackers in *Canada*?" Tim stressed the word; he knew Billy's deep dark secret, and laughed at the expression on his face. "Hardly matters anymore, does it? But I'll keep your secret."

He wiped the coal dust off his hands and took the bright paper toy from Billy. "Snap the ends apart and it makes a noise. There's a little toy inside and a paper crown. Some have confetti too. Me mum hates that kind."

"There's some for us too," Perce said, nodding toward a box on the bench. They would have their own Christmas celebration in the fo'c'sle. It was how things were on ships. Common sailors didn't mix with the officers and scientists. Shackleton wasn't very strict about this and in fact treated everyone so alike that some of the officers grumbled. He had them scrubbing floors and working the lines alongside the sailors. He encouraged the sailors to take an interest in the science experiments. But for social activities, dinners, and parties, everyone stayed with their own kind.

"You gonna do up the fo'c'sle next, Blackie?" Tim said. "We could use a little fancy froufrou up there."

"Orde Lees did all this, not me," Perce said as he tacked another decoration in place. "Must have spent the whole night snipping paper."

"Well, at least he finally took himself a job around here." Tim snorted as he stoked the stove. Thomas Orde Lees, an upper-class captain from the Royal Marines, had earned a reputation for ducking out of hard work.

"I'm sure he'll show you how to cut paper lace if you ask him nicely," Perce teased. Every child knew how to cut paper lace, but Orde Lees would certainly make a big deal out of it.

The sailors nicknamed him the "Old Lady," for he was forever fussing and fretting about little things. He collected odd bits of scrap like a magpie and spent hours carefully mending his favorite old green slippers. Orde Lees had been taken on as a motor expert (Shackleton had brought along three experimental ice tractors), but so far he hadn't shown himself to be very mechanical. Whenever anything needed fixing, it was usually Hurley who did it.

Perce knew Orde Lees better than the other sailors did but still didn't know what to make of him. He was snobby, but then most of his class were. But when Charlie hurt his knee and Orde Lees was appointed cook for a few days, he didn't try to boss Perce around. In fact, he admitted he didn't have a clue about cooking and let Perce run the galley. The other officers and scientists found him at least a little peculiar, but even they would enjoy the decorated wardroom.

"Well, you can frill the fo'c'sle up as much as you like." Tim picked up the empty coal hod. "I've got watch, so I won't be down there anyway."

"Only an hour watch," Billy said. "Aren't we doing just hours tonight so everyone can have Christmas?"

"Sure, but who's my relief?" Tim sniffed. "If you see Master Vincent jumping up from the table to take my place, you sound the trumpets, eh?" There was nothing Billy and Perce could say to that or do about it.

"Will you keep me a plate warm?" Tim's easy smile returned. When there was nothing you could do, might as well be happy doing nothing.

"Aye, of course."

"And some pudding?"

"I'll hide you some."

"Good lad. Custard too! And put it where Mrs. Chippy won't get to it. No paw prints in my pudding!"

"Aye, will you have a silk cloth and silver spoon as well?"

× × ×

The dinner was a feast, with many courses. (And many plates to be washed afterward, Perce thought dismally.) It was funny to watch a bunch of grown men snapping the crackers open like children and searching through the confetti for the tiny prizes and tissue paper crowns inside. Captain Worsley got a pirate ring. Tom Crean and Frank Hurley both got little dolls. Shackleton got a whistle.

Finally Charlie brought out the Christmas pudding. According to tradition, he had doused it with brandy and set it on fire. Little blue flames danced smoothly over the black surface. The men cheered. Perce followed with bowls of custard and bottles of brandy. The men drank toasts to family and friends back home, to "wives and sweethearts," and to the king. It was all very loud and merry. Then someone offered a toast to all the British soldiers fighting in the war. The men grew quiet. Out here it was easy to forget there was a war going on in Europe. It had started only a few days before the *Endurance* left England. They didn't know what was going on. Who was winning? How many countries were fighting by now? How many men had died? They would have no news for at least a year.

"To our boys." Shackleton raised his glass.

"Our boys. Hear, hear," the men murmured.

Perce went back to the galley and stacked the plates. There was no need to scrape them clean. With such fancy food, the men had eaten every morsel. There would be no Christmas tidbits for the dogs. He did manage a scrap of herring and a spoonful of custard for Mrs. Chippy, who was waiting expectantly by his bowl. Low rays of bright sunshine streamed in through the window as Perce quickly washed the plates. When he was finished, he went up on deck.

The cold air felt good after the hot, steamy galley. The pack ice was loose today, and the ship was making slow, slushy progress. Perce leaned on the railing and watched cloud shadows shifting over the ice. He knew his mates were having a good lively party in the fo'c'sle, but he wasn't ready to join them just yet.

Perce thought about the war. He had forgotten all about it until the toast. Now he felt embarrassed by that. But out here it seemed so remote. War was in history books. War was Napoleon. He didn't know anyone who had been in a war. A couple of the old men on the docks back home had been soldiers in India or Africa, but it wasn't the same. All of Europe was fighting now. There was talk it might spread to the whole world. Japan, even, and the United States. Was that possible? That every country in the world was fighting? What for? If he hadn't come here, he would be in that war himself right now. Some of his friends from home must have joined up. Some might already be dead.

Perce heard footsteps on the deck and turned to see Shackleton. He was wearing his coat and hat, so Perce knew he had come on deck to stay awhile. He leaned on the railing beside Perce and took out his pipe. His face was flushed from the warmth of the wardroom, the food, and the drink. He looked like someone who enjoyed a party but was also glad when it was over.

"You worked hard tonight, Perce. Thank you."

"Glad to, Boss."

Shackleton looked him up and down.

"You all right, lad?"

Perce blushed. He didn't want Shackleton to see every little thing he worried about show up on his face.

"Yes, sir. Of course. It's a fine Christmas."

"You missing your family?"

"Some. But I'm glad I'm here.

"You look like you're a thousand miles from here." Shackleton laughed gently.

"I was just thinking."

"Ah. And what were you thinking?"

"About the war. How strange it seems out here. Having a war at all, I mean. I was wondering if—well, it's so grand out here. And there's so much to do—science and all that, but even just putting it all together." He faltered. "Figuring out how to get here and make it all work—exploring, I mean. I was thinking, sir. What if there were just more places to explore?"

"I'm not sure I follow."

"I've only read about war in history, in school. Richard the Lionheart, Alfred the Great. It all sounds very exciting in a way. Men have a chance to be someone. To test themselves, I guess it is. But isn't that what exploring is for too? When you tried for the pole, sir—wasn't that like a battle?"

"Oh, yes." Shackleton's face, unlike his own, was hard to read. Perce hoped he hadn't said the wrong thing.

"But in a real battle," Perce went on, "everything gets wrecked and people die. It doesn't make much sense really, having a war."

"Most people don't think exploring makes much sense either," Shackleton laughed.

"Everyone loves exploring. It's a grand thing."

"They like the idea of it. They like the stories in the newspaper and the lantern slide shows, but to most of them, it's just entertainment."

"But if you do this, sir—I mean, when you do this, crossing all of Antarctica—people will know it's important."

"Ah." Shackleton warmed his hands on his pipe and stared out at the ice. His face was hard now, but his voice was quiet. "But it isn't, though. Not really."

"Why do you do it, then, sir?"

"Why?" Shackleton turned back and smiled at Perce. "I don't suppose I'm good for much anything else."

chapter ten

After Christmas, there was a long good time. There were gales and patches of thick pack ice, but more often, there were sunny skies and open water. Whenever the pack ice was too thick to sail through, Shackleton ordered the *Endurance* anchored to an iceberg to wait. He didn't want to waste the coal. Although the men were eager to make distance, they also enjoyed these breaks. If there was a good solid floe, they had a chance to get off the ship and play soccer or hockey on the ice. The first time Perce walked out on the ice, he felt very nervous. Wild assured them the ice was twenty feet thick and not about to crack, but it was still very strange to walk on an island of ice floating over an ocean thousands of feet deep. The memory of the killer whales was still fresh for Perce, and he never ventured anywhere near the edge where they might get him.

Orde Lees, in his most eccentric style, had brought along a bicycle and took it out one day to ride on the ice. It was not a huge success, except as a comedy show. Later that night, some of the other men awarded him a stack of prize certificates. There was one for the longest Antarctic bicycle ride and another for the shortest. There was a prize for the highest point reached and for the lowest, for the fastest ride and the farthest south latitude reached. He was also voted the most fashionably dressed bicycle rider in Antarctica and elected president of the South Pole Gentlemen's Bicycle Association. Orde Lees took the mocking with good humor.

One day when they were anchored to an iceberg,

Captain Worsley spied a big Weddell seal about a mile away. Since the ice was good and solid, Shackleton said they could go hunting. He had brought dried food along for the dogs but needed to save this for the long overland journey. The dogs were not exactly fond of the dried food either. It was made of shredded meat mixed with fat and cereal and pressed into bricks. These bricks, called pemmican, were so hard, it took an ax to break them up. They were eager for fresh meat. Frank Wild got the rifle, and Hurley lowered a sledge down to the ice. Crean brought up a pile of harnesses.

"This looks way too big for a dog," Billy said, picking one up.

"Oh, you're the bright one, aren't you!" Crean laughed. "You're not really thinking I'm going to take a pack of wild dogs out after fresh meat, do you? We'd have a bloody riot. Now turn around; I'll show you how to put it on." Until the dogs were better trained, the men would pull the "butcher's wagon" themselves.

The harness was of simple design. There was a broad band of canvas that went around the hips, held up by two narrower straps like suspenders that crossed over the chest. At each end of the hip band, there was a metal grommet hole. The pulling ropes, called traces, were looped through these holes so that they could shift and allow a man to move freely while pulling.

They hooked up the traces and started off. It was a bright sunny day, and the empty sled was easy to pull. Frank Wild led the way, stopping every now and then to look back at the ship, where Worsley waved directions from the crow's nest.

After about fifteen minutes, they could see the seal for themselves. It was a handsome fellow with mottled black-and-white fur. The seal lifted its head and gave them a lazy look, then yawned, scratched itself with one flipper, and closed its eyes.

"Mr. Wild, are we just going to walk right up to it and ask it to dinner?" Billy said.

"Pretty much," Wild laughed. "They aren't afraid of us. They don't have any natural predators on land. Orcas are the only danger for them. We could walk right up and whack it on the head if we wanted to. Still, I like the bullet. Makes it quick."

When they were only about twenty feet away, Wild lifted the rifle, squeezed the trigger, and sent one shot right through the seal's brain.

"Right, then." Wild shouldered the gun. "Since we don't have so far to go, we'll take it back whole. More for the dogs that way, and Clark wants to poke around in the guts."

"Just so he keeps them off the dinner table," Perce muttered. Clark, the biologist, had annoyed more than a few with his habit of dissecting penguins on the wardroom table. Perce and Tim grabbed the dead seal's tail; Billy took one flipper and Vincent the other.

"One, two, three, heave!" Tail and flippers came up, but the six hundred pounds of blubber in the middle didn't budge. It was like trying to lift a half-ton bag of jelly. Crean and Wild watched, amused. Billy went around to the seal's head, but there was nowhere to get a grip except by sticking his hand inside the mouth. They tried heaving again, then pushing and rolling, but their efforts just got more comical. Finally Wild showed them how to line up on one side and roll the seal toward themselves while Crean tipped the sled up on its side and shoved it under the blubbery mass. Another push and the huge seal was on.

After a half mile of pulling the loaded sled, they were all sweating. It was a warm, sunny day, almost twenty degrees above zero, with a bright sun and no wind. Soon the men had stripped down to shirtsleeves.

"I'm aching in places I didn't even know I had muscles!" Billy grunted.

"Y'er saying you have a headache, then?" Tim teased. Billy snatched up a handful of snow and threw it at him.

"Shackleton pulled like this every day for months at a time," Perce pointed out.

"Well, Shackleton can drag the bloody moon around for all I care," Vincent grumbled. "I signed on as a sailor, not a damn cart horse. This isn't sailor's work."

"Aye! A sailor's far too delicate! Just look, my poor little hands are all rough and red!" Tim said in a high girly voice. The men laughed, and that made Vincent even angrier. After a minute or two, when they had the sled moving along well, he suddenly shoved Tim with his shoulder so hard, Tim fell and almost got run over.

"Hey, watch out," Crean said, pulling on the brake. "She can get away from you."

"Sorry, must have slipped," Tim said, glaring at Vincent.

"No need to get all bunched up," Wild said evenly. Perce was pretty sure he had seen what really happened.

When they got back to the ship, they tied a rope around the seal's tail and hoisted it up alongside.

"Pay attention, lads," Wild directed. "Butchering is a job for everybody." He put a pot under the seal's head to catch the blood, then slit the throat. The blood was dark red and smelled awful. The dogs up on deck went crazy. Next he slit open the seal's belly. A great pile of steaming, slimy guts fell out on the ice. Tim turned away, and Perce heard him trying not to retch. Wild showed them all how to slice the blubber off in chunks. Then Crean took the knife and sliced off a piece of the dark liver. "This'll be good for our Sally!" he said happily. One of the bitches was pregnant, and Crean was fussing over her like an old grandmother. After the seal was all cut up, Perce hurried to wash so he could help Charlie prepare supper. He was tired but felt good. This was real Antarctic business now! Sledging and killing seals and the ice all around and the ship running well and everything just right with the world.

chapter eleven

Days passed quickly as the *Endurance* made slow but steady progress. The sun never set, and the strange light played tricks on the eyes. The air was so clear and the distances so vast that it was hard to know how close or far away something was. The light bounced between ice, sea, and clouds, conjuring mirages. Sometimes the icebergs seemed to be hanging upside down in the sky. Sometimes they looked like magical buildings in a fairy city, full of jeweled towers and domes.

The mood aboard ship was light. Some of the men thought up elaborate practical jokes. Once they got Charlie to boil up some spaghetti and put the strands in one of Clark's collection jars. They told the biologist they had found it in the stomach of a penguin and watched as he spent all afternoon trying to identify the strange worm. Clark would never admit they had been pulling his leg.

Even Shackleton seemed more relaxed as they got closer and closer. Tim and Billy started up a band in the fo'c'sle. They made drums out of tarps stretched across pails. They pulled strings across cigar boxes for a banjo and fiddle. Mrs. Chippy meowed with pain, ran away, and cowered in the stern. Fortunately, Leonard Hussey, the meteorologist, played a real banjo, and they often had singsongs at night. Once a week on Sundays, if the ship was moored or at least wasn't rocking too badly, they brought out the gramophone and listened to records. That was a real treat.

Along with the ordinary chores of running a ship, the

men were busy with science experiments. Hussey kept careful track of the weather, measuring the wind and the water temperature. Clark dredged up great piles of mud from the ocean floor. Reginald James, the physicist, did lots of things with numbers that no one understood. James Wordie, the geologist, had to make do with examining the odd stone from a penguin stomach. He was about the most eager to get to land and mess around with real rocks.

One evening in early January, Perce took a bowl of dinner scraps to Sally's kennel. Mrs. Chippy scowled at him and sniffed in disgust. He didn't like to see any choice bits going to the dogs.

"But didn't I give you some sardines just last night?" Perce laughed at the cat's haughty scorn. "And Sally's in a family way. Due any day now and needs a little something, don't you know?" Perce went up on deck and squatted by Sally's kennel. The big dog was whining and scratching at her blanket. She came to the front of the box when Perce approached, but she wouldn't take the treats he offered. She panted and lay down, then got up again and walked nervous circles in her kennel. Perce dropped the scrap bucket and ran back down the companionway. He found Tom Crean playing cards in the wardroom.

"Mr. Crean, I think you'd best come, sir. I think Miss Sally is about to have her pups."

"Miss Sally!" Hurley laughed as Crean jumped up from the table. "Why, Crean, I thought you got her married off to Sampson all right and proper. Shouldn't she be Missus?"

"I'll have her married off to you if you don't watch out!"

Crean jumped over Hurley's outstretched legs and grabbed his jacket.

"Wager, anyone?" Worsley piped up. "Number of pups? What time born? How many dogs—how many bitches?"

"I'll wager a shilling on five," Hurley offered his bet. "Three girls and two boys."

"I'll take two to one on six—an' half and half . . . ," Worsley jumped in.

"A chocolate bar on six—all born by the end of the watch!" The bets began to fly as Perce followed Crean out to the deck.

"Oh, will you look at that!" Crean's rough face cracked into a smile. A steaming wet little puppy wiggled on the straw. "Sweet Mary—now look at the dear little thing!" The Irish Giant was cooing like a schoolgirl. He opened the kennel and nudged the newborn pup closer to Sally's nose. She seemed unsure what to do for a minute, then began to lick the pup.

"Atta girl, there's a good mum," Crean encouraged.

"It's so tiny," Perce marveled. "And listen to it. Sounds more like a little kitten."

Crean got a rag and helped Sally clean her puppy off. The newborn puppy was lost in his enormous hands. "It's a boy!" he said proudly. The puppy was breathing well and wiggling vigorously. "A fine little boy." He steered the newborn toward a teat and grinned when the pup began to suckle. Sally looked up, puzzled at this new situation. Crean stroked her head and murmured soft words until she relaxed.

They had four pups by midnight. Crean named them Roger, Toby, Nelson, and Nellie. Nobody had predicted just right, but Tim came closest. He bet there would be four puppies by midnight, though he thought there would be two girls and two boys. He won six chocolate bars and shared them with the whole fo'c'sle that night. Shackleton brought out a bottle of rum, and they all drank a toast to Sally's new pups. Tom Crean stayed up with the new mother until morning, dozing fitfully with only a blanket around his shoulders, his big body crouched protectively against the kennel.

Good fortune came with the puppies. The ice thinned, and the *Endurance* made progress. On January 9, the men saw open water. They were through the pack! The next day, they sighted land. Shackleton named it the Caird Coast, after Sir James Caird, the Scottish businessman who had put up most of the money for the expedition. It was still far from where they needed to go, but it was reassuring to see any land by now.

Day after day, they sailed through clear water. The puppies grew fatter, opened their eyes, and began to yip at the world. The sky was blue and the ocean even bluer, the mood optimistic.

"Isn't it strange," Billy said one day as he and Perce stood watch together, "how, when things are going well, you can hardly remember when they were bad? Doesn't it seem now like there was never a pack of ice holding us back? Like every day was just like this—nothing but fair winds and endless clear blue seas?"

It was true about the forgetting, but not about the endless clear blue seas. On January 16, with only two hundred miles to go, Tim shouted down from his lookout at the top of the mast.

"Ice ho! Pack ice dead ahead!" The news went down to

Shackleton's cabin, and he came on deck. His face looked serious, but he simply took the binoculars and looked out at the new obstacle. Then he scanned the sky, where thick thunderclouds were piling up.

"Well, nothing we haven't seen before," he said calmly. "And a bit of weather on the way too. Shall we furl sail, Mr. Worsley?"

"Furl topsail!" Worsley commanded from the deck below. The men on deck began to haul on the sheets, and Perce leaned over the yard, gathering the stiff, frozen canvas as it was hauled up. Sometimes the ice was so thick on the canvas, they had to kick it off before they could furl the sail. The wind whipped through his hair and made his eyes tear. Perce could actually feel the pressure of the advancing storm. He looked over and saw Tim, balanced easily on the footropes even as the gusts whipped his clothes. Tim grinned and howled. As much as they all hated actually being in a storm, the approach of one was thrilling. Like watching a herd of wild horses stampeding toward you. You knew you were about to get smashed, but what a magnificent sight! Perce lashed his part of the sail into place, climbed back down, and ran to the foremast to repeat the process with the next sail.

Shackleton wiped the icy spray off his face and rubbed his frozen hands together. "Well, at least with a day or so of this, the pack ice should all blow away!" he said optimistically.

But for the next two awful days, Sally's puppies were the only creatures who really stayed optimistic. While the blowing snow scoured the decks, they snuggled deep into their mother's thick fur. While Perce and Charlie were smashed and bashed around the galley, trying to heat up some stew, the puppies slurped their mother's warm milk, rolled over, and went to sleep again. When the ship was tossed dangerously close to the iceberg and the men on deck fell back in terror, the puppies played and wrestled in their cozy bed of straw.

Finally, early on the morning of January 18, the gale began to fade. Worsley cautiously steered out from behind the protection of the iceberg. They were all dismayed at what they saw. The storm had not blown the pack ice away but had brought in even more. As far as they could see, in every direction, there was only ice. They were so close now, only eighty miles from the bay, one good day's sail in clear seas. But eighty miles was as good as eight hundred if you couldn't cross it.

Everyone's nerves were on edge. Shackleton never left the deck. He paced like a caged lion. Perce watched him, feeling like his own heart might break. With winter approaching, the success of the entire expedition was coming down to a matter of days. In the fo'c'sle at night, some of the sailors were grumbling.

"Even if, by some magic, the ice opens up and we get through tomorrow, it will still take at least a week at best to unload all the supplies," Vincent said. "And nothing's been happing at the best now, has it? We should be on our way back to South Georgia right now!"

"A retreat now might be even more dangerous," Tim pointed out. "The ice could trap us on the way back and freeze us in the middle of the Weddell Sea. We still have time to find a safe harbor down here." Frozen for the winter in a protected bay near land would be uncomfortable but safe. Frozen in the middle of the sea, where the ice moved and shifted with crushing force, could be catastrophic.

"He won't risk our lives," Perce insisted. "He turned back before he reached the pole, didn't he?"

"Aye, but that was a clear decision," Walter How said. "They had twenty days of marching and five days of food. Here, he doesn't know what's the safest thing to do."

"Can't know," Perce said, a little defensively. "None of us can know. It all turns on the ice." He could only guess at the agony Shackleton was going through.

The ship puttered slowly along for days, nudging her way through the ice. This was different from the pack ice they had encountered before. It was thicker, slushy, and sticky. It made a strange sucking sound as it washed against the wooden hull.

"It's like a bowl of bad dumplings," Tim said.

"I've had a few of those in my life, I'll tell you," Billy said.

"Oh, you have, have you? And how bad were they?"

Perce gave an exaggerated groan. He knew what was coming.

"Why, my granny's dumplings were so heavy, my gramps had to brace up the table," Billy said.

"Oh, light enough for a table, were they?" Tim took up the challenge. "Ours we had to eat sitting on the floor. In case you dropped one, you see, you wouldn't break your foot."

"And tough!" Billy went on. "Why, there was a cook at one of the logging camps, used to make dumplings so tough, we'd put 'em outside in a dish for the bears."

"So they were tender enough for a bear to bite through?" Tim said. "What a treat!"

"Ah, well, yes, but they were so sticky, it would glue their fangs together."

"My gran's would bounce, you see—like a rubber ball,"

Tim countered. "One hit the floor one day, bounced clear out the window. Knocked a bird out of a tree. Bounced down the road and killed a cart horse. Bounced all the way to the dock, onto a ship, and went right through four decks and put a hole in the bottom."

"It sank the ship, did it?" Billy played along.

"No, not entirely. The ship went down, but it landed on the dumpling and bounced right back up again. Shot up out of the water, it did. You can see it today, upside down in the town square where it landed."

Perce laughed. Clearly there was no way to beat an Irishman at this game. "What about you, Perce," Billy asked, "did your mother make a good dumping?"

"They weren't too bad," Perce said seriously. "Nice and light they were, in fact. The only bad part was how the angels in heaven used to come down wanting some. They'd be flying all around the house. Neighbors would start complaining, y'see, flocks of angels clogging up the lane. And all that heavenly singing. It gets to be a bit much. Hallelujah this and hallelujah that. We used to have to go out with the flyswatter and chase them away so we could eat in peace."

The three friends laughed. There was not much else they could do. The slushy ice got thicker. By Saturday morning, the ship was stuck.

chapter twelve

Days passed. Weeks passed. The *Endurance* remained trapped. The men tried to keep busy. They took walks on the ice, read books, and played cards, but the confinement was starting to get on everyone's nerves. Sometimes Perce climbed up in the rigging and sat on the yardarm just to be by himself. From there he could see for miles. Miles and miles of ice.

Then one night in late January, he was startled awake by a great boom like a cannon shot. The ship trembled. Everyone ran on deck, and Tim climbed the rigging for a better look.

"Crack dead ahead!" he cried triumphantly. As if by magic, a channel of water had opened only fifty yards in front of the ship.

"Can we break through?" Perce asked Crean.

"We'd be mad not to try. Nothing much else to do today, is there?"

"Right, then!" Shackleton's blue eyes sparkled with excitement. "Shall we give it a try?"

There was a festive feeling in the air as the sailors sprang to work. Perce and Billy climbed the rigging and unfurled the sails. The frozen canvas snapped alive and sent a shower of ice to the decks. Down in the engine room, men began to shovel coal furiously. Full power, all sails set. Captain Worsley expertly steered the *Endurance* back and forth to knock her hull free of ice. When she floated free, he pushed her forward. Full power, full speed. Perce felt the timbers shudder with the impact. Nothing happened. Worsley tried again. Full power, full speed—a few bits of ice crunched off. Worsley reversed the engines, but there just wasn't enough room to get up any speed.

"It's like a mouse pushing against a pyramid," Billy said.

"There's still a great chunk of ice built up on the keel here," Crean said as he leaned over to examine the hull. "Might help to knock it off." He looked up at Perce and Billy. "Can you two bring up the stern platform? Swing it around the side here."

"Yes, sir." Perce was glad to have something to do.

"Tim—fix us up some lines. Where's the bosun? We can use his muscle."

Crean explained his plan to Shackleton, who agreed it might help. McNeish helped Billy and Perce release the stern platform and secure it to the side near the bow. Crean, Perce, and Vincent each tied a rope around his waist. Tim tied the other ends around the ship's rail, and Billy, Greenstreet, and McNeish each stood by, ready to pull them up if the ice suddenly broke out from under them.

"Choose your weapons, boys!" Crean picked up an iron pike. It was eleven feet long and an inch thick, with a flattened wedge at one end. Perce, being a good three inches shorter than Crean, chose an eight-foot pole that he had often used for chipping ice off the rudder. Vincent armed himself with a pickax. They climbed down to the platform and began to whack at the ice. It was awkward work, but it felt good to be doing something. They chipped and pried and stabbed. Little shards of ice went flying. Occasionally, a small chunk broke off, but mostly nothing happened.

"It's just freezing on thicker as soon as we knock it off," Vincent grumbled.

"Then let's knock the whole block of it—off—once and for—all!" Crean's words were broken up by heavy breaths as he chopped at the ice with all his might. He was sweating, but he never stopped. He worked with a demon energy. Perce thrust his pike harder, trying to match Crean stroke for stroke. Crean grinned at him. "It's a challenge you want, do you? You know you're half my size, Blackie."

"Aye," Perce laughed. "But I'm also half your age."

Perce's arms ached, but he wasn't about to slack off in a race. The men on deck began to cheer them on. Even Vincent began to swing faster. The iron pikes rang. Ice chips flew. The platform jerked around under their feet. Sweat ran down into Perce's eyes. Crean's face was red. Still, the ice would not come free. They began to slow down. The cheering faded, punctuated only now and then with a feeble shout of, "Come on, lads!" Finally Crean stopped. He rested the tip of his long iron pike on the platform, leaning the other end against his shoulder. He wiped the sweat from his forehead.

"All right, lads." His breath came in fast white bursts. "She's not ours today. It was a good try."

Vincent needed no urging. He handed up his pickax and quickly climbed back on board. Perce's whole body trembled with fatigue and frustration. This was just too cruel. With a last thrust, he stabbed at the stubborn ice.

"Come on, Blackie." Crean smiled and took the pike from his shaking hand. "It could still all break up tomorrow. Go on up now."

Perce grabbed the rope and started to climb. Suddenly there was a crack, and the huge ice chunk broke off. The bow of the ship, freed from the weight, swung wildly. Crean stumbled as the platform pitched up under his feet. Perce reached for him, but the wild motion of the platform jerked them apart. It all seemed to happen so slowly. The water churned. The platform heaved. The chunk of ice hit the water, then shot up into the air. Perce felt cold spray on his face, saw the milky slab of ice against the blue sky. It seemed to hang there for minutes, but it was hardly a second. Then the whole ton of ice crashed down directly on top of Crean, crushing him against the side of the ship. Perce felt a swoosh of cold air, heard the sickening crunch, saw Tom Crean's boots sticking out from beneath the slab of ice. At the same time, in the same slow motion, Perce felt himself being pulled up. He heard men shouting. The ship rolled again, and the ice tumbled away. Billy grabbed hold of his arm.

"You all right?" Tim asked. Perce nodded. Tim's hands were red and bleeding. He had been holding Crean's safety line and now had bad rope burns on his palms. Perce saw the other men haul Crean up over the side. He was limp as a rag doll. Someone was shouting for the doctor. They laid Crean out on the deck. Perce saw the big hands lying terribly still. He felt the deck shake as the doctor and Shackleton came running. It seemed like hours, but finally Perce heard a gasp and cough, followed by a loud, angry groan.

"Get offa me!" Crean coughed and tried to sit up. "Get your bloody hands offa me! Owww—Jaysus!"

"Tom? Tom, are you all right?" The men parted as Shackleton ran up. "Just lie still." Shackleton knelt by Crean and put a hand on his chest. "Don't move." Crean's forehead was bleeding, and one cheek was scraped raw.

"I'm not moving—bloody hell!" he groaned. The blow had knocked the wind and the curses right out of him. Doc Macklin, the ship's surgeon, dashed up and dropped to his knees beside Crean. He unbuttoned Crean's jacket and reached up under his sweater. He pressed his hands down the ribs, felt his arms and legs for broken bones and asked, "Can you feel this? And this? How about this?" to which Crean growled affirmatives.

"I'd know if I was broken," he said roughly, getting some of his wind back. The color was coming back to his face. He drew a deep breath, though it appeared to hurt. Macklin helped him sit up.

"No damage a nip of Irish won't cure," Crean said. The men laughed in relief. Shackleton took out his handkerchief and wiped the blood from Crean's face.

"It's me needing the whiskey, Tom," he said with a shaky laugh. "What do you mean, giving me such a scare?"

"Come on." Macklin stood up. "Let's go look you over properly." Shackleton and Macklin helped Crean to his feet. He was dazed but apparently unbroken. He favored one leg and winced when Macklin touched his ribs.

"Dang—would you take a look at this!" Billy picked up the iron pike that Crean had been using to chip at the ice. Everyone turned to look. The impact of the ice had wrapped the iron pike clear around Crean's chest. The inch-thick metal was bent like a cheap tin spoon.

"We knew you was a tough bugger, Crean!" Tim laughed. They called him "Iron Man" for a while after that or sometimes "The Anvil."

chapter thirteen

On the seventeenth of February, the sun slipped below the horizon for the first time. Complete darkness was still a couple of months away, but it was a cruel reminder that winter was coming. The *Endurance* remained stuck. Sometimes leads of water would open nearby, teasing them with the lure of freedom. Then they would attack with poles and picks, saws and shovels, trying to chop through to open water. Officer, scientist, sailor, and Shackleton himself chopped and sawed and whacked away. Even Charlie, who was busy enough making three meals a day for them all, came out and worked. He was a small man who could hardly manage the long iron pike. When he broke off a chunk of ice, everyone cheered. But always the lead would close again before they could reach it.

Once they worked twenty-four hours around the clock and cut a channel over a hundred yards long. Perce worked until his shoulder muscles ached and his legs went wobbly. Chips of ice flew up and stung his face. The relentless glare of the ice burned his eyes, but hope grew with every yard. Then, suddenly, the ice got thicker. The men stood around, leaning on their pikes, white clouds of breath puffing in the cold air, watching the measuring line go down and down. Six feet, eight feet, ten, twelve—eighteen feet thick.

Finally Shackleton decided to accept their fate. No amount of work was going to free the *Endurance*.

"Well, men," he announced. "Perhaps it's about time we tuck in for the winter."

It was February 24, 1915. They had a grand supper that

night. Not fancy as Christmas, but more extravagant than usual. Charlie made a cake with tinned peaches, and the men enjoyed a ration of grog. After supper, Shackleton stood up.

"Gentlemen, I could not have asked more from you. It has been an honor to sail with you. And it will be an honor to be stuck with you." He raised his glass, and the men responded with stomps and cheers.

"You have worked hard. More importantly, you have shown generous spirit and good humor. I'm going to depend on those qualities during the upcoming winter. We've come a long way, and fate hasn't turned out exactly as we had hoped, but we are not conquered. Not by a long shot. We are, however—for the near future, at least—stuck." He laughed as if he were merely telling them their picnic had been rained out. "As of tomorrow, we will operate as a winter station. Sea watches and ship's routines will be suspended. We'll rotate one man on night watch, unless weather requires more."

Perce sat calmly, though waves of nervousness were rippling up through his stomach. He glanced at Billy, but his face didn't betray any worry. They had both read the story of the *Belgica* from Shackleton's library. That was the first ship that had ever spent a winter in the long black night of Antarctica, just seventeen years ago. Half the men went crazy; three never recovered. One man had died; all suffered from scurvy. Crean, Wild, and a few of the others had wintered before and knew what to expect, but the rest of them? Things could get tough. Even back home in Wales, winters were tough, with long, dark days and dull winter food, too many people in the house, and all the games played to death.

"Even though we're frozen in," Shackleton went on

cheerfully, "we will be moving." He pointed to the map of the Weddell Sea that hung on the wall. "The ice here drifts in a clockwise pattern, so we'll be drifting effortlessly north all winter. Effortless or not, I expect there will be lots of duties to keep us all busy, so I look forward to the sort of optimism and enthusiasm you've all shown so far."

Those who knew Shackleton knew this was a command as much as a suggestion. Of all the qualities the Boss required in his men, optimism was the most important. He knew the damage that one negative man could have on all the others.

"So enough talk. Mr. Hussey, why don't you bring out your banjo and we'll have a bit of a singsong?"

chapter fourteen

The next morning, the men began to prepare for winter. The cabins on the upper deck would soon be too cold, so Shackleton asked McNeish to build new ones belowdecks. The men had to shift lots of provisions around. All day, they tossed sacks and carried crates while McNeish sawed and hammered and gave directions. Perce watched him slap walls up as easily as a child building with blocks. McNeish almost never measured. He could simply look at a piece of wood and know down to the quarter inch if it was right. Hurley was also a good builder, but while he needed a T square to fit a door frame, McNeish simply eyeballed it and it always came out true.

Orde Lees offered to make an inventory of all their supplies. It was the perfect task for the fastidious man. He ran around with his notebook, peering into the farthest corners of the holds and writing neat columns of numbers and weights. The men of course poked fun at him.

"Hey—I think there are 41,625 potatoes left, not 41,626. . . ."

"Oh, but 19,004 of them are small, so you might count them two for one—"

Orde Lees went on counting sardines. "You'll be grateful soon enough that someone is keeping track of your food," he said testily.

The sailors stripped the decks of unnecessary gear and stowed away extra ropes and sails. They shifted all the sacks of coal from the deck into the hold. The ship had burned through more than half her supply, so there was plenty of room below.

"At least we know where we stand now," Perce said. "We're not waiting around wondering all the time." He caught a bag of coal from Vincent and swung it on into Tim's arms. "There's some peace in knowing where you stand."

"You're an idiot, Blackie," Vincent spat. "We could be back on South Georgia like we were meant to be. Should have turned back weeks ago. Now we're frozen in the middle of God-bloody-rotten Antarctica!" He swung a sack of coal at Perce so hard, it knocked him down.

"How do you like where you stand now, boy?" he sneered. Perce leapt to his feet, his hands in fists.

"Perce, don't—" Tim pulled him back. Perce saw Frank Wild glance in their direction.

"Anytime, Vincent," Perce said quietly. "On the ice." He picked up the sack of coal, his blue eyes burning. "Anytime." He tossed the sack on to Tim, and they went back to work.

"Perce, what the hell did you think you were doing?" Billy pulled him aside later. "Calling him out like that?"

"I'm sick of his bullying. Do you want to go all winter with him shoving us around?"

"No, but I don't want to listen to you moan all night after the thrashing he's going to give you."

"I can take him."

"Sure, you can. Then you can pluck out the ship and fly us all home. Come on, Perce, fighting isn't going to solve anything."

"Who's telling me this? You've fought in every saloon in Canada."

"Some of them twice," Billy agreed, laughing. "But that was just for fun."

Perce finished coiling up a line and tied it off. Billy threw it into the locker, and they started on the next one. Perce knew Billy was right. He had let his temper get the better of him. But he couldn't take back the challenge. It was a stupid place he had gotten himself into. Growing up around the docks had made Perce no stranger to bullies or fighting, but he knew he was no match for Vincent. The worst part of it, though, wasn't the thought of getting beat, but of how Shackleton would think of him. The Boss needed them all to get along and pull together. Perce was about to mess that up in a grand way, and he hated himself for it.

He thought about his dilemma the rest of that day. Vincent was a bully and needed taking down. But fighting would upset Shackleton and be bad for everyone's morale. He could take back his challenge and avoid the whole thing. Then what? Live out the rest of the winter with Vincent puffed up even more and all the others thinking Perce was chicken?

He scrubbed the pots, his anger getting them shinier than they had been in a long time. Perce looked out the galley window and saw Shackleton walking out on the ice. He looked so small out there, alone on the endless frozen ocean. The responsibility of all their lives rested on his shoulders. Perce felt ashamed. His own quarrel was so stupid. He wouldn't make it worse for the Boss. He would make amends with Vincent and take back his challenge and just let the others think whatever the hell they wanted. Perce finished the pots, hung them to dry, wiped down the table, and swept the galley floor. Feeling much calmer now, he went off to find Vincent before he lost his nerve. He wasn't on deck or in the wardroom. Perce poked his head in the fo'c'sle and found all the other sailors talking excitedly. They stopped as soon as Perce appeared.

"What's happened?" Perce asked. "Where's Vincent?"

"Been demoted!" Tim said, eyes still wide with the surprise. "Probably sulking in the lifeboat, licking his wounded pride."

"Boss called him on the carpet after tea, and he came out with his tail between his legs," Tim said.

"Come on," Billy said, handing Perce a mug. "We had a bit of rum put by—have a toast!" Perce put the mug down on the narrow table. He was relieved to be out of his mess, but it didn't really feel like something to celebrate.

chapter fifteen

The next day, Shackleton turned his cabin into a store to issue winter clothing. To the sailors' surprise, he offered them first choice. Each man received a thick sweater and two lighter ones, a woolen helmet, a windproof Jaeger shell, five pair of woolen socks, wool mittens, felt mittens, and fur mitts.

"You'll need to wear all three if you're out in winter," Wild told them. "And you'll need this." Wild handed Perce a long piece of the flat cord they used for lamp wicks. "The fur mitts are warm but bulky. You'll find you can't do much in them," Wild explained. "Keep them tied around your neck with this so you can pull them off and not lose them. Lose your mitts and you lose your fingers."

He also gave them strange boots called finneskos. These were large, soft boots made of reindeer skin that were stuffed with special Norwegian grass called sennegrass for insulation.

"Would you look at this," Perce marveled as he looked at all the clothing laid out on his bunk. "I've never had this many new clothes at the same time in all my life! Three sweaters. And all brand-new!" He tucked two of them away in the back of his locker. If he was careful with them, he might be able to bring them home for his brothers after the trip.

Soon the men fell into a winter routine. Breakfast was at nine, then chores. Everyone took turns helping Charlie in the galley now. They shared most of the other duties too. They all scrubbed floors (though Orde Lees clearly thought such work was beneath him), and they all went out to cut ice. Wild showed them how to look for the clear blue ice that had all the salt squeezed out of it. They chopped it into chunks and brought it back on the sleds. Then they chopped it into smaller pieces and kept these in a basket by the galley door. A melting pot was always kept going on the back of the stove, and whenever a man drew out some water, he was supposed to put in some more ice. The ice in the basket got dirty, and the dirt collected in the bottom of the pot, so if the level went down too low, the water could be pretty sludgy. Keeping clean in general was a big challenge. No one did much laundry when all the water for anything had to be quarried, chopped, hauled aboard, and melted. About every two weeks, when a man was on night watch, he took a bath and washed his clothes.

"Me mum would be shocked," Tim laughed one night as he hung his socks to dry by the stove. "Wearing the same underwear for two weeks at a time."

"You washing every two weeks now?" Billy replied. "Why, aren't you the swell one!"

"Washing? Who said anything about washing? I just switch my dirties for cleans out of your locker. You haven't noticed?"

Perce laughed. Things couldn't ever get too dismal with Billy and Tim around.

The old wardroom on the upper deck was too cold now, so they cleared out a space in the hold and brought the long table and benches down there. They nicknamed it "the Ritz" after a fancy hotel in London. Shackleton had brought along a roll of linoleum for the floor of the hut, but now they decided to put it down in the Ritz. Shackleton was on his hands and knees with the rest of them, cutting and fitting it.

Soon the *Endurance* had been converted into a cozy winter home. Even the sailors who had complained about getting stuck began to accept their fate and settle in. Life felt as normal as it could with twenty-eight men crowded together on a ship stuck in the ice at the bottom of the world. Outside of football injuries and the occasional dog bite, no one ever got sick. There was no one around to give them a cold or flu. The only real threat in the polar regions was scurvy. Shackleton had seen what scurvy could do. He had suffered it himself on his first trip south with Robert Scott. Once a week, Doc Macklin examined everyone for the early signs of the disease. He checked their gums and felt their joints, asked about aches and pains. No one knew exactly what caused scurvy, but they knew eating fresh fruits and vegetables could prevent it. But those foods were impossible to get in the polar regions. Eskimos in the Arctic didn't get scurvy, however, and Shackleton was convinced that eating fresh meat also prevented it.

Shackleton had tried to get the men to eat fresh seal and penguin, but many of them would not. McNeish, like many sailors, was superstitious about penguins and all seabirds. He said that birds held the souls of dead sailors. John Vincent and some of the others were just suspicious. In their experience, the officers were always trying to keep the best food for themselves. If they offered the sailors seal and penguin, then there must be something wrong with it!

But now that they were stuck for the winter, eating fresh meat was essential. Besides keeping scurvy away, it would also help preserve the limited supply of canned meat. The next time the men were out playing football on the ice, Shackleton asked Charlie to fry up a great pot of onions in butter. Poor Charlie was crying buckets of tears as he chopped and chopped. He opened the galley door for fresh air and shivered as he chopped some more. The wind carried the smell of frying onions out over the playing field.

"Now this if you please, Charlie." Shackleton handed him five pounds of bacon that he had brought up himself from the larder. Charlie began to fry the bacon. The men began to glance over at the ship. They could smell something good. "Now how about some fresh seal steaks to go with that onion and bacon, Charlie?" Charlie realized what the Boss was doing and grinned.

"I'll make a nice gravy too, sir!" he offered. "And some yeast rolls!"

When the men came back, they were hungry from the exercise. The good smells almost knocked them over: bacon, onions, fresh bread baking, and the rich aroma of sizzling meat. Mrs. Chippy was crouched in the corner of the galley, staring at Charlie like he was God, praying, if cats could pray, that some tidbit would fall. A rumor went around that someone had found some frozen beefsteaks in the larder.

"But there wasn't any steak on my inventory list." Orde Lees frowned. "And believe me I would know about steak if there was any steak and I'm sure there wasn't. I have a list of everything on this ship. And there's no beefsteak on my list."

"Your list, hmmm," Shackleton interrupted. "Yes, I've been meaning to have a look at your list."

"Oh, you should, sir," Orde Lees said. "You should! I've worked hard on it! It's very comprehensive."

"I'm sure it is. Why don't we go have a look right now?" Shackleton threw an arm around Orde Lees's shoulders and pretty much shoved him out of the Ritz before he could go on anymore about there being no steak. Dinner was served, and by the time half the men realized what they were eating, they had already licked the plates clean. After that, fresh seal and penguin were regular features, and the dreaded scurvy was never a threat.

All they had to do now was wait out the winter. Wait for the ice to thaw and then sail to South America. No one said much about Shackleton's shattered dream. Sometimes they talked as if it might still happen, but everyone knew it wouldn't. It had been difficult to raise the money in the first place. Now, with this initial failure and with the war, it would be impossible. Still, they trained the dogs as if they would one day be running for the South Pole. The sea was frozen solid for miles in every direction, giving them lots of room to run. Crean built a small sled and miniature harnesses for Sally's pups. The first time he tried it out, they simply played and tumbled all over themselves. The traces were hopelessly tangled in minutes.

April came, and Perce tore another page off the calendar. The days were growing shorter. The men tried to stay busy. They played soccer, mended clothes, read books, played cards, told stories. They rubbed eyes off potatoes. They hunted for seal. More puppies were born. Clark dragged up nets full of slime. Hussey filled columns and columns in his meteorology notebook. It was, he declared (as if no one had noticed!), an unusually cold year. Hurley converted the refrigerator into a darkroom. He needed the thick, insulated walls to keep the film warm.

He developed his movie film and showed it to the men one night. They stretched a sheet out for a screen. Some of the men had seen newsreels before, but it was new for Perce. He tried not to let on, but it was so amazing, he could hardly keep from jumping out of his chair. There was film of them playing football on the ice! There was Charlie Green, skinning a penguin! It was very strange to see people on the screen who were sitting beside him right now.

"Just wait," Hurley told Perce. "I bet it won't be long until you can see newsreels only a day or two after something happens. Someday you won't even have to go to the cinema—pictures will come over wires like the telephone."

"So we'll all go down to the corner and crowd in the phone box to watch a moving picture?" Perce laughed. "I wouldn't mind actually, if there were girls."

"No, everyone is going to have a telephone in their own house." They all laughed at that one.

"Just you wait," Hurley went on. "Pictures could even come over the wireless, right into your home. All you need is some kind of receiver and a screen, you could put it all in a box like a cupboard."

"That's daft!" Greenstreet said. "Who would want to watch a picture show on a box in your own parlor? Where's the fun in that?"

"And someday I'll bet there'll be movie cameras so small that everyone will have one," Hurley went on excitedly. "You could take your film to a shop and get it back in a week. Or maybe even develop it yourself in the kitchen sink. And the pictures will have sound too!"

Soon the whole Ritz was roaring with a lively debate about the future. You could make a telephone call anywhere in the world! There would be telephones without wires! And with pictures! Airplanes would fly across the oceans! Shackleton wanted a special kind of camera that could photograph a whole book and shrink it down to the size of a pack of cards. "Then when you wanted to read, you would have some kind of enlarging machine and read it on a screen. Think how many books we could take along then!"

"Why not just send books over your picture wireless?" Wild said. "Then you could read the pages on the screen in your cupboard too!"

Perce laughed. Sending books through the air! That was something Jules Verne would invent for one of his wild stories.

Doc Macklin had high hopes for the future too. There would be no polio, no tuberculosis, influenza—nothing. "We'll have vaccines or cures for everything. There won't be any infections," he said hopefully. Macklin held up his own hand, bandaged from an infected dog bite. "I'll have a pill to cure this."

"How could a pill you swallow inside cure infection on your outside?" Tim asked.

"It would kill the bacteria that causes the infection. Problem is, it would have to kill only the bacteria, not the rest of you."

When Perce finally went to bed, his head was so full of the future that he couldn't get to sleep.

"What do you think about all that?" he whispered to Billy. "What if people really could fly across the oceans? With passengers and cargo and everything?"

"Be a lot of sailors out of a job."

"It would be an awful lot easier to get down here, though."

"Just our luck, the plane would get stuck."

"I like the wireless with pictures, though. Have you ever heard a wireless?" Perce asked.

"No. But I do think that might catch on. Imagine if we could hear some news down here," Billy sighed. It had been five months since they had any contact with the outside world.

chapter sixteen

On May 1, the sun set for a long winter night that would last until July. For a few weeks, it was still light in the middle of the day, but those hours dwindled fast. Before long, it was dark all the time. Around noon, there was a faint twilight glow on the horizon, but it was barely enough to do outside chores. It was too dark and cold to play football. The seals and penguins had disappeared, so there was no hunting. They had laid in meat enough for three months, so there was little worry about food, but everyone missed the activity.

The men built "dogloos" out on the ice beside the ship, out of ice blocks and frozen sealskins piled over with ice and snow. For bedding, they stuffed sacks with straw. Each dog was staked by its own dogloo, its chain frozen securely into the ice. The dogs seemed happy with the new accommodations. The ship was less crowded and much less noisy. Still, it felt claustrophobic.

There were only so many games of checkers and cards one could play, and some of the men were getting "cabin fever." The scientists had expected this long, dark confinement, but the sailors had not.

John Vincent grew more surly. He didn't like to read and was always bored. Billy, on the other hand, was finishing a book every other day. The other sailors called him "the librarian." But they also asked him to recommend good books. There were so many to choose from. Perce didn't know where to start. He once borrowed a book called *Anna Karenina* just because it reminded him of a girl back home called Anna.

Perce thought about her a lot these days. She had never actually been his sweetheart in real life, but out here the faraway Anna was becoming more real than real could be. She had dark straight hair and dark brown eyes that sparkled when she laughed. She laughed a lot and wasn't afraid of anything. Perce had known her since they were small but never thought much about her except that she always wanted to play with the boys. She could run faster than most of them and row better than some. Anna was the youngest of nine, and everyone said her poor parents were just too worn out by then to do anything about her.

He had always thought of her as just one of the kids in the lane until one spring, when he was fourteen, just a week before he first went to sea. He had picked up an extra job painting boats with Anna's brother Hugh. One day, Perce was surprised to see Anna ride up on Hugh's bicycle. It was the first really warm spring day and the first time Perce had seen her without the drab bulk of winter clothes. She was thirteen or even fourteen now, he realized, and hadn't been roughhousing with the boys lately. She was dressed in old clothes, and her hair was tied back in a ponytail, but Perce didn't really notice that because there was a golden curtain hanging behind her, pushing away everything else in the world. How could a girl be the same girl you've seen all your life but completely different? The way she looked at him too, like she knew all the secrets in the world.

"Where's Hugh?" Perce asked. His voice came out strangled, and he blushed. He ducked his face and fixed his attention on the complicated job of opening the can of paint.

"Buggered his shoulder playing rugby yesterday," Anna

said. "Doc had to come and pop it back in. You could hear it crackle like breaking a chicken's neck!" She laughed, and a thousand songbirds died from envy. "So I'm here for him. Said a warm, dry day we shouldn't waste, and the rest were off fishing." Her hair was shiny in the sun, her lips like she had just eaten raspberries. Her wrists, where she had rolled up the sleeves of her brother's shirt, were covered in a delicate downy fuzz.

They painted all day. She was good at it. She had a way of holding the brush so it barely touched the wood, leaving a perfect, smooth stroke of crimson paint. Sometimes now it was all he could think about, the row of red hulls glistening in the hot sun, the shine on Anna's hair, the graceful little hands, the feel of her skin as their hands or wrists would bump in the work, once her whole leg.

"Aw, well, that Tolstoy can be rough going." Billy jostled Perce back to reality. "Try Kipling," he suggested. "He's got some bang-up adventure stories. Also H. G. Wells. You'll have to stand in line for it, but *The Time Machine* is super. Greenstreet is reading it now, and Hurley claimed it next."

Perce had never read a novel before joining the *Endurance*. He had read stories in magazines, but there weren't many novels around. And between work and rugby and looking after his brothers, there just wasn't much time. Now he discovered how wonderful it was. Books took you someplace else. He could lie on his bunk with a novel and be sailing in the South Pacific instead of frozen stuck in Antarctica. When he finally got his hands on *The Time Machine,* he read it straight through without stopping. He even tried reading Shakespeare but found it even rougher going than Tolstoy.

"Oh, Shakespeare," Billy laughed. "He's a pretty good writer, that fella. But he's got some strange words. And sometimes just too many of them!"

Shackleton loved books and liked to talk about them, even with the fo'c'sle hands. He also encouraged the men to keep journals and gave them all notebooks. Some wrote every day. Orde Lees wrote pages and pages and pages about every little thing. Perce didn't know what to write about.

"Tell how things are," Hurley suggested. "Like a letter to a friend." But Perce was never good at writing letters.

"Do it like in the encyclopedia," Billy said. "Or like a school report or newspaper story."

That was an even worse idea. Perce had never liked school reports, and most news stories were boring.

"Do you keep a journal?" he asked Crean when they were working in the harness room one day.

"A journal? What would I put in a journal?"

"I don't know. Things that happen?"

"Not much happens." Crean ran his fingers over a harness strap, feeling for worn spots. "Then when something does happen, it's either a great good thing—like Sally's pups—so I'll remember it just fine, or it's a bad patch, and why in heaven's name would I want to remember that at all?"

There was some truth to that, Perce thought. "What if it's a bad patch but you can't help remembering anyway?"

Crean laughed. "That's why God made whiskey and the Irish make songs."

Perce gave up the idea of a journal. The blank notebook sat on his shelf by his bunk for a couple of weeks. Then one night he couldn't sleep. A blizzard had been raging for three days. It was dark and cold, and everyone was cooped up and cross. Even Mrs. Chippy hissed at him when Perce tried to move him off the table. It seemed the winter would never end. Perce felt alone and crowded and scared and mad all at the same time. He didn't know what to do with himself. Cry or scream or get an ax and chop a hole in the boat and sink and be done with it. He saw the notebook and grabbed a pencil and just let everything tumble out the way he felt it.

Sometimes I hate this ship! I am the stupidest person alive for stowing away! I want to run off across the ice and keep going and not look back. Sometimes I hate everyone here, even Billy. Well, not him so much. Just seeing him all the time. The same faces and the same smelly socks and the same old jokes. I want to see girls in Sunday ribbons—yellow, blue, pink, green. I long for color. I want to eat color. I hate everyone. Well, not the dogs. I love the dogs. And Mrs. Chippy. But everyone else—yes! I hate them all!

Sometimes the dark feels evil. Like a live thing out there, wanting to get you. Or a monster. It is always out there and nothing we can do about it. Everything is just dark, dark, dark. I know the earth is still turning. I know the sun will come back one day. But sometimes I can't believe it. I can't remember sunlight.

× × ×

It felt good to write all that. It was like opening a window in a stuffy room and letting fresh air in. And with the fresh air came better memories. Perce took up the pencil and wrote some more.

But then I'm on night watch and the Boss comes and sits with me and talks. Just ordinary talk. Like he isn't the Boss and I'm not nobody. He remembers I have five brothers and asks questions about them. He has eight sisters. He asks why I first went to sea and what else do I want to do in my life. I don't know that. Don't know much beyond this for now. But just because he asks, I think there might be something. So then I don't hate everyone anymore. I don't want to run off across the ice. I believe the sun will come out again and the ice will melt and Endurance *will sail free again. So maybe things are really all right.*

chapter seventeen

June came. They had been stuck for three and a half months. Shackleton worked hard to keep up spirits. They had birthday parties nearly every week. On Frank Wild's birthday, Charlie brought out a big round cake all covered in coconut. He called it a snowball cake. When Wild cut into it, however, the cake exploded, throwing gobs of frosting all over. Charlie had frosted a balloon for a trick. So for Crean's birthday, everyone was suspicious. It looked like a regular cake, but Crean stood back and poked it very delicately with the knife. When nothing exploded, he tried to cut it. Hard as he tried, the knife wouldn't go through. This time Charlie had frosted a brick. When there were no birthdays among the crew, Shackleton declared it was the birthday of the king of Tonga or the sultan of Mesopotamia. Sometimes he sent Billy searching through the encyclopedias for obscure occasions to celebrate. They celebrated the invention of the tin can and the transcontinental railroad.

Shackleton insisted that all the men gather together in the Ritz for a little while every night. He knew how easy it was for some men to feel isolated and depressed and he didn't want them hiding away alone in their bunks. On Sunday nights, they listened to records on the gramophone. At least that was one benefit of being stuck in the ice: they never had to worry about the needle skipping and ruining the record. On clear nights, they often went outside to watch the southern lights. Beautiful curtains of light and color danced across the sky. Gold and green and pink shimmered so bright sometimes, it was like fireworks.

× × ×

On July 26, the sun finally peeked above the ice again. In August, the seals and penguins began to return, and by September, they started to feel the first hints of spring. From the crow's nest, they could see cracks appearing in the ice. October came with brilliant sunshine and mild weather. The temperature at midday often went up to twenty degrees. Open lanes of water began to appear in the ice. One day Perce woke to a strange feeling. It took a few minutes to realize what it was. The ship was floating. After eight months, she was a real ship again.

Perce ran up on deck, where everyone else was gathering. The ice around the hull had melted enough to give them a little pool of water. All over the ship, loose gear rolled off tables and tumbled off shelves. Even the dogs knew something exciting was going on and set up a loud howl.

"Let's hoist the mainsail," Captain Worsley ordered. They knew they weren't going anywhere soon, but the sail would help keep the ship steady. Perce, Tim, and Billy scrambled aloft. After being furled for so long, the sail was frozen solid, but they knocked the ice off with gleeful kicks. From the yardarm, they could see patches of open water in the distance. Their own little pond was hardly bigger than the *Endurance*'s hull but, soon enough, the sea would be open and they would all be going home.

A few days later, Perce had a strange dream. He dreamed an orca had come up under the ship and was pushing it over. He started sliding out of his bunk but held on so the orca wouldn't get him. He could hear the eerie calls of whales all around him. Perce woke in a cold sweat. First he was relieved that it was just a dream. Then he realized it wasn't. Perce sat up and rolled right out of his bunk. He slid into the side of Tim's bunk. Everything was tilted at a crazy angle. The ship was full of strange noises: groaning, creaking, and screeching. The screeching was so loud, he could hardly hear Tim. Then there was a loud crash, and Billy came tumbling out of his bunk above.

"What the hell!"

"What's happening?" Tim shouted.

"Don't know. Let's get out of here." Perce gave Tim his hand and pulled him up out of the bunk. Clothes, books, boots, and jackets had been thrown everywhere. They had to scramble out, walking sideways like crabs. The squealing, grinding noise got louder. It was like being in the jaws of a giant machine. They struggled to open the fo'c'sle door. In the Ritz, chess pieces, books, lamps, and empty sardine tins had been thrown in a pile on one side. Mrs. Chippy sat contentedly licking at the spilled sardine oil. Lopsided didn't matter much to a cat. The benches and tables had slid down the sloping floor. Curtains hung out from the walls. Other men were stumbling through, fighting their way to the deck. The bell began to clang.

Once on deck, Perce stopped and stared. The flat, endless ice plain they had lived in for months was torn apart. But rather than opening up the sea for their escape, it was trapping them more than ever.

Great jagged slabs of ice were piled up all around the

ship, lifting her hull half out of the water, tipping the *Endurance* until she was almost on her side. Deck planks were snapping, and metal halyards screeched like fingernails on a chalkboard. Shackleton stood on the bridge, calmly giving orders in the chaos. Wild directed the men as they came on deck.

"Billy," Wild shouted. "Help McNeish with the lifeboats." The *Endurance* was heeled so far over, the lifeboats on the port side were in danger of being crushed against the ice.

"Blackie, Tim," Wild commanded. "Help get the dogs on board." Dogloo city was a wreck. The dogs howled with fright. Some of the chains had come free, and the loose dogs ran everywhere. Others were trapped and buried in their dogloos. Huge slabs of ice stuck straight up like tombstones in a giant's graveyard. Perce grabbed an ax in one hand and a pike in the other. It was hard even getting to the dogs through the maze of broken ice. Perce began to chop the chains free. Crean was digging Sampson out of his collapsed dogloo.

"What's happening?" Perce had to shout to be heard over the noise of crunching ice.

"Pressure!" Crean shouted back. "Ice starts to break up, and the current jams it all together. Then the wind catches the broken slabs like sails and pushes it up more."

It was scary to see blocks of ice that weighed ten tons piled up around them like a child's building blocks. Crean freed Sampson and led him to the safety of the ship, with the four grown pups running right behind. Hurley had his hands full with Shakespeare but grabbed another dog from Perce. They bolted in opposite directions, almost pulling him in two.

Hurley swore, yanked on the leashes, and muscled the dogs back to his side. It was a frantic race, but within ten minutes every dog was securely on board the ship. They were so terrorized, they even forgot to fight. They just cowered in corners and whined.

McNeish came running, as much as anyone could run on the sloping deck.

"She's sprung fore an' aft, Boss!" he announced. "There's two foot of water in the hold, and the pump's froze up."

"Very well," Shackleton said evenly. "Get some men on the hand pumps. Can you stem the leaks?"

"Timbers is split, sir. I might build a cofferdam, though. Might keep the water back from the engines."

"Take whatever men you need."

"You two—" Wild pointed at Perce and Tim. "Help Hurley secure the dogs, then relieve the men on the pumps. You there—Bill, Vincent, the rest of you there—get the pikes, let's try to push some of this ice back from the ship. The rest of you with McNeish."

McNeish took his men belowdecks. "I need all the planking you can find," he directed. "Packing cases, shelves—get the doors off the cabins! Go!"

Perce dragged a frightened dog along the tilted deck. His heart was beating hard, but he felt surprisingly calm. There was just no time to be afraid.

They worked all day and all night. McNeish and his crew sloshed waist deep in the freezing water as they tried to stop the leaks. The sailors, officers, and scientists worked shoulder to shoulder. They were so wet and dirty, you could hardly tell one man from another. Fifteen minutes on the hand pumps—fifteen minutes' rest, half hour chopping at the ice or helping with the dam down below. Perce pounded nails and stuffed blankets into cracks, then went back to the pumps. The labor was extreme. The water was pouring in so fast, they had to pump full out. After five minutes, his arms ached. After ten minutes, his shoulders and neck were in a spasm.

The night became a blur. Once Perce fell asleep while holding a board in place on the dam. Once he found a mug of soup in his hand and didn't know how it got there. The strangest thing was how the Boss was everywhere all the time. When a shift finished on the pumps, there he was with mugs of chocolate. When the strips of blanket floated out of the cofferdam, it was Shackleton's hand that caught them. His clothes were as wet and dirty as any of theirs, but he never rested, never seemed tired.

Finally, late the next morning, the efforts began to show success. Water still came in, but slower. Shackleton ordered an hour's rest. Charlie had somehow managed to cook with the galley at a crazy tilt and now dished out big bowls of porridge. The men ate hunched over, too tired to speak. Some fell asleep at the table, their heads beside the empty bowls. And always, the terrible screech and groaning of the pressing ice continued all around them.

Perce saw Crean come into the Ritz. His clothes and face were covered in ice. His eyes were red. Perce realized he hadn't seen him below at all. He must have been working outside all this time. Shackleton went to him, and the two men talked briefly. Then Crean caught Perce's eye and nodded toward the companionway. Perce got up, gathered an armful of empty bowls on his way, and dropped them in the galley. Then he got his coat and hat and went up on deck. He blinked at the bright light after the darkness below. The sight was shocking. The deck was all twisted and broken. Rigging had snapped, and a couple of loose lines still whipped around. Blocks of ice the size of train cars were piled against the side. The beautiful *Endurance* was a shattered wreck. For a moment, he felt more sad even than scared.

"Can you still stand up, lad?" Crean smiled.

"No one's standing up much on these decks," Perce replied. "But I'm strong yet."

"Good. Help me with a wee job, then." Crean walked over to the port side. There were crates of provisions on the deck: rolled-up tents and sacks of sleeping bags, tins of paraffin and boxes of food. "The Boss has an idea that we might like to have the lifeboats ready," Crean said. "But we don't want to make a big fuss about it. I need a hand to load all this mess in."

Perce looked down at the ice where the lifeboats had been lowered. Another hundred feet out, he saw Hurley and the other dog team leaders packing the sleds. He realized what they were doing now. They were getting ready to abandon the ship. The *Endurance* was done for. He knew it already, of course. Probably everyone knew. But knowing something in the back of your mind was one thing. Knowing something in the way of packing the lifeboats was another. The pressure ice had caused too much damage. There would be no fixing her, no sailing away, no escape. Perce felt his head go all hot and his stomach lurch. He took a gulp of cold air, but it didn't help. He grabbed the rail, leaned over the side, and threw up.

"Sorry." He wiped his mouth on his sleeve.

Crean put a heavy hand on his shoulder. "You'll do all right, Blackie," he said quietly. "We've a bad time coming, but you'll do all right."

chapter eighteen

"When you follow ships for a living," Billy said sadly, "you have a feeling they get to be human." All the sailors felt that way. Even the scientists who had never been interested in ships before had grown fond of the *Endurance*. She was a valiant little ship and had carried them far. But ten million tons of crushing ice were too much for her. They worked for three more days in a desperate attempt to save her. They worked around the clock. When they were too tired to move another step, they dropped for exhausted naps. In the wreckage of the galley, Charlie still managed to cook a few hot meals.

On the third day, while some men still pumped to keep her afloat, others began the long, sad task of emptying her out. Shackleton and Wild found a stable section of the ice floe about fifty yards away. All day long, like a line of ants, the men carried off everything they could.

Charlie cooked one last hot meal. Perce helped him hand the bowls out, bracing his back against the downhill side of the doorway and his feet up against what used to be the floor. The men ate silently, too sad, too tired to talk. Even if they wanted to talk, no one could hear over the death noises of the ship. Planks and timbers screeched as they were twisted by the ice. It was like an endless thunderstorm. Sometimes a whole row of planks would start snapping one after another, so it sounded like gunfire.

At five o'clock, Shackleton gave the order they had all been waiting for. Abandon ship. The men took their personal bags and began to climb over the shattered decks and down the broken side of their ship. They made a slide out of canvas and slid the dogs down one by one.

The men set up the tents on the ice. Shackleton had never planned for twenty-eight men to sleep in tents. They were crowded, but crowding at least provided some body heat. There were two large tents and three small, all made of canvas. Some were held up with hoops; others needed poles and ropes to stake them out. The tents did not have floors sewn in; there were separate groundsheets. These were also made of canvas and provided very little protection from the ice.

The men worked in a daze, like zombies. Perce held up a tent pole, while Tim pounded a stake in. Perce glanced back at the ship. The crushed hull stuck up out of the ice. Her mast was still erect. One lonely light still burned. Maybe Shackleton was wrong. Maybe tomorrow the ice would open and she could be saved. McNeish was a good carpenter; maybe . . .

"Hey, Perce." Tim nudged him. "It's done; you can let go."

Perce wearily let his arm drop. After the tents were erected, Wild gathered the men up to distribute sleeping bags. There were only eighteen warm reindeer fur sleeping bags; the rest were woolen.

"I think the best way to distribute these would be by lot. Are you all agreeable to that?" Shackleton asked.

"Oh right and see how that turns out," Vincent grumbled. "See how many of the lower deck wind up with fur."

"I have eighteen blue-tipped matches and ten red."

Shackleton shook a metal box. "Blue get the fur bags." He held the box up so no one could see in, and the men began to draw lots.

The lottery did seem to be rigged, but not as Vincent had suspected. One after another, the *sailors* all drew the blue matches. Charlie Green got one, and so did the coal stokers and the engineers. One after another, everybody from the "lower deck" walked away with a warm reindeer fur bag. It was purely by chance, Shackleton insisted, that he himself got a woolen bag. Purely by chance, in fact, that all the most senior officers, Crean, Wild, Worsley, Greenstreet, and the others, drew the red matches. Orde Lees drew one of the blue matches and walked off with a warm fur bag, smiling over his good luck, apparently clueless. Perce and Billy looked at each other.

"How d'ya think he did it?" Billy asked.

"There's only blue in the tin," Perce guessed. "Some had red matches already. Easy enough to hide one in a mitt."

"Damn good of them."

"Aye."

By seven o'clock, despite the conditions, most of the men were fast asleep. Perce thought he would never sleep. He was more tired than he ever thought possible, but he felt all jangled inside. He turned on his side and pulled the sleeping bag tighter over his head. The fur was nice, thick and silky, but it did little to cushion the hard ice beneath him.

He thought of his comfortable bunk on the *Endurance*. He thought of his bed back home. He had always shared a bed with one or two of his brothers. On a really cold night or in a scary storm, all five might pile in with him. He would growl at them for wiggling too much and groan when stray elbows and ankles jabbed him. But it was nice to wake up all snuggled like a litter of puppies, with a soft, curly baby head under your chin. Perce would carefully untangle all the arms and legs to creep out of bed. Sometimes he had to wiggle his toes to find out which were his own feet.

Just as he was working himself up into a grand misery of homesickness, he heard footsteps outside. He lifted up the skirt of the tent and saw Shackleton and Wild. They were walking around the tents, checking the ice, checking the dogs, keeping all well. He could hear the murmur of their quiet talk and smell the pipe tobacco. They did not look like stranded explorers on a splintering ice floe but simply two old friends out for a stroll. Perce's anxiety melted away and in seconds he was asleep.

In the morning, in those odd minutes between deep sleep and fully awakening, Perce was happy. He was still half in a dream. Everything was quiet and peaceful. He heard footsteps crunching outside and thought it was the milkman coming up the front walk. Then he opened his eyes, and all dreaming ended. Perce sat up. His brain felt foggy and dull. He thought there was something wrong with his ears, for he heard nothing but a low hum. Then he realized that it was just the quiet. The horrible screeching and groaning death noises of the *Endurance* had been with them for so long, the silence was strange. The other men in his tent began to move and shift until all eight were awake.

The tent flap opened, and Wild poked his head in. He had a crate full of mugs of hot tea. Perce sleepily took one and passed it back. Then another until everyone had a cup.

Frank Wild squatted outside, watching with a half smile on his face. "I'm certainly glad you're liking your breakfast in bed," he chided. "If any of you gentlemen would like your boots cleaned, just put them outside!"

Perce felt ashamed. Wild and Shackleton had been up all night and worked hard to fix a hot drink and no one had even said thank you. "Sorry, Mr. Wild. Thank you." The others realized their rudeness, and the tent rang out with appreciation. "But can you make it cocoa tomorrow?" Tim teased.

The day was gray and overcast but not terribly cold. Hussey's thermometer read six degrees above zero. The men came out of their tents, moving slowly with aching muscles and sore backs. No one said much. Shackleton didn't push them but waited until everyone sorted themselves out. Finally, after everyone had a hot drink and some time to get moving, Wild gathered the men for a meeting. They sat on sleds and crates. Some smoked their pipes, others just sat quietly in a daze. Shackleton walked among them, talking casually to each man in his easy way until all were assembled. Then he stood before the group. Whatever fear was in his heart, the men never glimpsed it. The Boss appeared relaxed and confident. There was no sign of his sleepless night.

"Well, boys, we made a damn good try of it. But it looks like what the ice gets, the ice keeps. Ship and stores have gone—so now we'll go home!"

Some of the men smiled. A few cheered. This simple

assurance was really so absurd that maybe, just maybe it might be true.

"You all know the general plan," Shackleton went on. "We're going to load everything we need on the dog sleds and two of the lifeboats. McNeish has built sleds for the boats so we can pull them along. Then we'll march northwest, toward Paulet or Snow Hill Island. It's a bit of a walk to be sure," Shackleton said lightly. Some of the men laughed, some sat stone-faced and grim. It was 346 miles to Paulet Island.

"There's a hut there and some stores. They were put there a few years ago specifically for the chance of shipwrecked whalers. Since I helped make the supply list, I can personally assure you that there is a generous supply of chocolate!" The reassurance fell a little flat. Vincent spat on the ice.

"We're hoping to cover five miles a day," Shackleton went on.

Perce and Billy looked at each other. Five miles a day dragging several tons of food and gear over rough ice would be no easy task. It would take three months at best. And once they got there, if they got there, they were still far from rescue. They would have to camp on the island and wait for a passing whale ship to find them.

"Ideally, though, the ice will break up before that, and we can get in the boats," Shackleton said, trying to sound optimistic. "That gives us several other possible destinations: Deception Island or Clarence or Elephant Island. Worsley and I have plotted courses to all of them, so anytime the ice opens, we'll be ready. I'd like to start in a day or two if you're all agreeable. There's quite enough sorting and packing to keep us busy until then."

They had unloaded so much so quickly that everything lay about in chaos. No one was even sure what stores they had. Food and equipment, ammunition, cans of fuel, tools, and clothing were scattered chaotically everywhere. Hurley wanted to go back to the ship to try and rescue his photographs. He had left them behind in the refrigerator for safekeeping, but then the crushing ice had trapped them underwater. Shackleton wouldn't let him return for them. It was too dangerous, and the plates would be too heavy anyway.

"We need to lighten our load as much as possible, so I'm asking each of you to leave behind all but the essentials."

Perce noticed Crean drop his head and squeeze his hands when Shackleton said this. That was odd. Of all the men on the ship, Crean probably had the least attachment to possessions.

"Keep your warm clothing, of course. Two pair of boots and mittens. Beyond that, each man may carry two pounds of personal gear." There was a murmur of protest. Two pounds was nothing.

"No article has any value when measured against our survival." Shackleton raised his voice and held up his hand for quiet. Then, with perfect showmanship, he unbuckled his gold watch and held it up for all to see. He dropped the watch in the snow.

"We get through this together or not at all," he said solemnly. He took out his gold cigarette case and a handful of gold coins and dropped them in the snow. Then he picked up the heavy Bible that had been a gift from the queen of

England. He tore out the inscribed flyleaf, a page from the book of Job, and the Twenty-third Psalm: *The Lord is my shepherd; I shall not want.* Solemnly, he folded the three pages and tucked them into his pocket. Then he dropped the Bible in the snow.

"Everything is replaceable," he said gently. "Except your lives." He paused. "Though it might do to have a bit of music along, so Hussey, could you bring your banjo?"

"Aye, Boss! How about my extra strings?"

"Well, how much do they weigh?" Shackleton replied. The men laughed. Shackleton looked over the men. His ship was gone, his dream of crossing Antarctica was shattered. This was his mission now, to get these men home.

"Shall we get on with it, then?"

The men stood up and began to mill around.

"McNeish," Shackleton called. "Could I have a word?" The carpenter went over to Shackleton's side. Crean stood up slowly. He looked at Shackleton, then down at the ice again. He folded his arms and seemed uneasy.

"Mr. Crean?" Perce asked. "Are your eyes all right?"

"My eyes?"

"They're all red."

"Snow blindness," Crean said gruffly. "If you've nothing to do, Charlie was asking for a bit of shelter for the stove. Could you gather up some boards and see to that?"

"Aye," Perce said. He walked off, puzzled by Crean's abruptness.

Crean waited, shivering a little. He had been working outside most of the past three days and did have a touch of snow blindness. His eyes burned and felt like they were full of sand. But that wasn't the only reason they were red. He watched Shackleton take McNeish aside. Crean knew what was coming.

"I hate to do it, Harry," Shackleton said in a low voice to McNeish. "But you know Mrs. Chippy can't last out here. The dogs will get him or the cold will. Or he'll run off and get lost. It's going to be hard enough without that sort of thing down the road to get everyone down. We need to make a clean break. At least this way, it will be quick. I am sorry."

McNeish said nothing but nodded.

"Who's to do it, Boss?"

"Crean. All the small pups too."

"Aye."

McNeish slowly walked back to the tents. Perce was hammering some planks into a windbreak when McNeish came up to him. Perce thought he looked a hundred years old. He was carrying Mrs. Chippy in his arms. The big cat's fur was ruffled against the cold, but otherwise he looked like his usual unflappable self.

"Would you do me a favor, lad?"

"Aye. Of course."

"Could you find us a wee treat for Mrs. Chippy? He isn't coming with us, you see. You always feed him in the morning. Would you do it now? So he gets the idea everything is normal, eh? So he won't be nervous or frightened. And he'll have a nice full belly."

Perce saw Crean come out of Shackleton's tent. He was carrying a pistol. Perce swallowed and nodded. Wild came from the other side of the camp, leading the three youngest puppies. They were only three months old, playful little puff-balls. At least Sally's pups would be spared, Perce thought with relief. They were ten months old and strong enough to pull. Perce looked at Mrs. Chippy. The big cat was purring happily, but the carpenter's hands were shaking.

"Aye. I'll find him something nice." Perce swallowed hard. His own eyes started to burn, and he didn't try to pretend otherwise. There were just some things even a man ought to go ahead and cry about. He walked over to the food boxes and found a can of sardines for Mrs. Chippy's last meal.

chapter nineteen

Perce had learned a lot on this voyage so far, but the most surprising thing was that ice is not slippery. Dragging the overloaded boats was like trying to drag an elephant through sand. The sled runners simply would not slide.

"Well, you see, you don't actually slide on ice," Orde Lees was only too happy to explain. "What you slide on is water—water on top of the ice! Ice, after all, is made of crystals, and crystals are rough, just like sand crystals. But when you move a ski or a sled runner over the ice, the friction melts a thin layer of water. That's what you slide on. See? But if it's too cold—like this—the ice doesn't melt at all. No melt, no slide." Orde Lees was an experienced skier, so they figured he must know. But since he was the only one not pulling or pushing something, it was a little hard to listen to him describe why they had to work so hard.

The whole line of hauling men stretched out about a half mile. Shackleton went ahead with three men to clear a path. The ice was so cracked and piled up, they had to chop through hummocks and shovel snow into makeshift ramps. After Shackleton came the seven dog teams. There was so much gear to carry that the dogs relayed the loads, pulling one as far as the cleared path, then returning for another while Shackleton chopped and leveled a few more yards. Finally came the men pulling the lifeboats. They also had to relay, dragging one boat a few hundred yards, then walking back for the other. They had to leave the third lifeboat behind entirely. It would take all their strength just to haul two. Orde Lees's job was to ski back and forth along the line, relaying information and directions. Someone had to do it, and he was the best skier, but it was hard for the men to watch him with such an easy job.

"It's only yourself to blame," Tim chided Billy when he grumbled. "There you were with your head in a book all winter when you could've been out on the ice, learning to ski."

"I'll remember that for the next time I'm stranded in Antarctica, thank you very much!"

They had all tried the skis a few times over the winter, but it was a difficult skill that took a lot of practice. The wooden skis were eight feet long and weighed fifteen pounds each. They needed different kinds of wax for different kinds of snow. Amundsen and his team had reached the South Pole partly because they were all good skiers. But they were Norwegians who had skied since they were born. And even Norwegians would have had trouble skiing here. The sea ice was heaved up and buckled, with hummocks and holes and pressure ridges taller than a man. Orde Lees could only manage by staying in the trail that Shackleton cleared.

The men strained against the harnesses. Twelve men pulled from the front while Vincent and Perce pushed from behind. Two others pushed from the sides, trying to keep the awkward load on track. Perce dug his feet in and threw all his weight behind the sled. It was like pushing against a wall. By day's end they had covered barely one mile.

"At least we're moving," Billy said optimistically. "Better than just sitting around on our butts looking at the wreckage."

The worst part was that they could still see the wreckage they had left behind. The *Endurance*'s twisted mast stuck out of the ice, awful as a broken bone. It was a sad and quiet camp that night. The temperature was climbing. A heavy wet snow fell that kept them trapped until the next afternoon. The rough sandy ice had been bad, but now warm temperature, fresh snow, and bright sunlight made it even worse. Now they were dragging the elephant through mashed potatoes. The men sweated and struggled, heaved and hacked and strained and pulled all day. Sometimes they sank up to their hips. After struggling all day, they had covered only another mile. At this rate, it would take them over a year to reach Snow Hill Island.

October 30, 1915

I think back, almost exactly one year, to when I first looked at our ship and felt burning with how much I wanted to go. I thought about how it could get hard and would I do all right. But I couldn't have thought how it could be so slow, and confusing and dull too. When the papers write stories about explorers, it always sounds very exciting. Even when they tell how Shackleton sledged day after day after day to get to the pole, those days don't sound like so much in the papers. Now we had one of those days, and I think we are in for a lot more. It is very long and very dull and everything hurts after, so I want to cry. But tomorrow we have to just do it again and not fail. That's really more of what exploring is, I suppose.

Some are grumbling mightily tonight. Say it's all a waste of time. Vincent making fun of me for writing here. Says I'd do better just writing up my last will and testament. Well, joke is on him, then, for I haven't anything to leave anyone in a will and testament. Didn't even fill my two-pound allotment outside of clothing, so told Billy he could have another pound of books. That's two more encyclopedias and he's happy. Hurley built a blubber stove out of an old ash chute from the ship. Very clever. We cut the blubber into chunks and put it on a metal rack. Under it is a little pan of paraffin. When this is lit, it starts to melt the blubber, then the blubber keeps itself going, slowly melting, dripping, and burning in the same pan. It makes a hot, stinky, smoky fire, but it will be our only way of cooking for some time.

Mostly we are eating what we call "hoosh." That is boiled seal meat with some broken-up hardtack biscuits to thicken it. Shackleton asked Charlie today to add some chopped-up seal blubber for all the strength we need. But the blubber is oily and fishy-tasting, and some of the men picked it out.

Everyone was gloomy that night as they made camp. The men staggered with fatigue as they set up the tents. Charlie Green wobbled as he stirred the pot. Every day since they started camping, one person from each tent took a turn at being "Peggy." The Peggy had the job of fetching the hoosh for his tentmates from the main pot, then cleaning the pot out with snow. Each man had a tin mug called a pannikin, which he used for both food and drink. It became quite normal to drink a cup of hot milk with globules of seal fat floating on top. For utensils, each had a spoon and his fingers. They didn't really wash these, just licked them clean and put them back in their pockets. They ate inside the tents, sitting cross-legged on the soggy canvas, hunched hungrily over the food.

When Billy finished eating, he leaned over to put his pannikin away, then gasped and fell over.

"Billy?" Perce leaned over his friend. "What's wrong?"

Billy was crumpled on his side, his face twisted with pain. He could hardly talk. "Cramp," he hissed, arms clutching tight around his stomach.

"Tim, come give a hand. Try to relax, Billy, we'll stretch you out."

"Here, pull his knees down. Easy, like." Tim grabbed Billy's knees, and Perce held his shoulders, but Billy was still seized up.

"Jeez—he's tight as a bug. We need to warm the muscles. Anyone's hands still warm?" Tim asked.

"Aye." Walter How put down his mug, scooted over, and reached up under Billy's clothing and rubbed his palms on the bare skin.

"I'll go for Doc," Tim offered.

"Can you take a deep breath, maybe?" Perce suggested as he crouched beside his friend. Suddenly his own leg started to cramp. When Tim crawled back inside the tent a few minutes later, he felt the muscles clutch in the back of his neck. It would have been comical if it didn't all hurt so much. Doc Macklin came with a jug of warm water. "You've all got to drink more," Macklin explained as he knelt beside Billy. "Everyone's cramping up tonight. The Boss is walking like a beggar, and Crean is groaning like an old lady." He felt Billy's knotted stomach muscles. "Though none so bad as this." He mixed hot water with four lumps of sugar and some brandy and gave it to Billy by spoonfuls until he could sit up enough to drink it down.

"I know you men are knackered after the work, but you can't just sit right down in the cold. Walk around a little. Like a horse after a race." Finally, his muscles relaxed by the warm drink, Billy fell asleep, his cramp subsided. Perce lay awake a long time, watching the frost form on the inside of the tent.

If Shackleton really was limping like a beggar the night before, it didn't show in the morning. Perce was the Peggy for his tent that day. When he went to fetch the breakfast hoosh, he saw the Boss far out on the ice with Wild, Worsley, and Hurley. They looked small and lonely against the gray sky. He knew they were surveying for the day's journey, and the very thought of it made Perce shudder. A little while later, after they had finished breakfast and Perce was rubbing out the pots with snow, Shackleton came over.

"Bit of a rough go yesterday, eh, lad?"

"A bit, sir."

"Is Billy doing better?"

"Much better. He slept fine after Doc saw to him."

"Good. Haven't much time to do your studying these days, have you?"

Perce looked down at the pots. He wasn't sure if the Boss was chastising him or not. "You've been so busy with all this hauling," Shackleton added quickly as if he immediately read Perce's mind. "But let me ask you something." Shackleton sat down on a crate beside Perce. "I know we all like the sense of getting somewhere, but this man hauling, well, doesn't seem to be working very well, does it? Not for lack of trying, mind you. I know everyone is working very hard."

"We haven't got very far," Perce agreed.

"We were out scouting this morning."

"Aye, I saw you."

"The ice is pretty bad. All broken up as far as we could see. But there appears to be a good solid floe not too far away. We were thinking about camping there awhile until the ice breaks up. What do you think? Do you think the men would mind?" Perce felt a flood of relief at the idea.

"Might be a good idea," he said.

"We'll have a meeting in a little while to talk about it. Tell the others in your tent, will you?"

"Aye." They both stood up. Shackleton staggered a step and Perce saw him wince.

"Are you all right, Boss?"

"Just a twinge here and there." He rubbed his hands over his lower back. "Ah, when we get home, I'm going to lie down in the green grass. Let the sun beam all over me for about ten days. Maybe just in my knickers. What do you say, lad? Sound good?"

"I haven't any knickers decent enough for that, sir," Perce said. Shackleton laughed.

chapter twenty

They called their new home Ocean Camp. It was a good, thick chunk of ice, almost a mile square. Best of all, it was only two miles from the remains of the *Endurance*, where so much had been left behind. That first afternoon, most of the men went back to see what they could salvage. Everyone was in a jolly mood as they set out, but when they got close to the wreck, they fell silent. The *Endurance* was little more than a twisted pile of wood, half sunk and crushed like a child's toy run over by a train. It was a horrible sight.

"Doesn't it seem a hundred years ago," Perce said. "And it's only been a week since we left her."

"Father Neptune got us, boys," Billy said with some admiration. "Poured out all his vengeance for trespassing in his domains."

McNeish, Hurley, and Crean went on board first to check for danger. The mainmast was about to fall, so they cut it down. The mizzen fell with it and made a terrible sound. The sorrow didn't last long, however, once the plunder began. The next few days became a combination pirate raid, treasure hunt, and Christmas all rolled into one. They brought back planks of wood and built floors for the tents. They pried up the entire wheelhouse and turned it into a galley for Charlie. Much to Billy's delight, many of the encyclopedias were rescued. They salvaged boards and ropes and rolls of canvas. They spent hours prying out every precious nail they could get. Hurley found a metal coal hod and more pieces of the ash chute and improved the blubber stove.

"Look at that," he said proudly. "We can melt two and a half gallons of water in thirty minutes with ten pounds of blubber for fuel. That's double what we were doing!"

Best of all, they recovered the third lifeboat. No one had liked the idea of all twenty-eight men crammed into two lifeboats. Now all they needed was for the ice to break up enough to use them. Meanwhile, they worked on a more comfortable wait.

"Do you know that big iron pot we had?" Charlie asked Perce one day. "It was in the pantry locker."

"Aye."

"Could you have a look for it? Be a great thing to 'ave! All's we got is this thin one now, and I don't think it will last. Hurley's new stove gets too hot, y'see."

The wreckage shifted day by day, so when they found the pantry locker, the door was under two feet of water and eight inches of slushy ice.

"Anyone fancy a swim?" Perce said. No one was exactly jumping for the opportunity.

"Would be mighty good to have that big pot," Billy said wistfully. "I'll bet if we sent a *big strong fellow* down with a rope around him, he could find it well enough." He looked pointedly at Tom Crean.

"I'd say we're better off sending a *skinny little fellow* down." Crean grinned. "And have the big strong fellow hold his ankles."

"Well, there's an idea!" Billy replied quickly. "Not a *good* idea, but an idea! What do you say, Perce?"

"I say it's fine of you to volunteer!"

"Oh, I would, you know, Perce, but after all, it's you who knows what the pot looks like."

"Why, it looks just like a pot, Billy. Two handles and a big pot-shaped thing in the middle."

"And since you won't be seeing much down in the dark water anyway, it doesn't matter much what it looks like, does it?" Crean added. "I imagine it's more a groping sort of job."

"Groping. Yes, that's what I'd expect. So don't you agree we'd do much better with a *tall fellow* like Tim here!" Billy clapped Tim on the back. "His arms are much longer—why, he's practically built for groping!"

They finally decided by drawing straws. Billy lost. He stripped off his clothes and waded into the freezing water.

"Oh, jeez—I don't know enough swearwords for this!" Billy gasped.

"Easier if you just plunge on in, mate," Tim encouraged.

"Oh, you think so? Oh, blast—let's get on with it." Crean grabbed hold of his ankles, and Billy took a deep breath, closed his eyes, and plunged, shrieking with the cold. He felt around in the dark murky water for the cupboard latch, then felt around in the mess of floating junk for the big iron pot. He was almost out of breath when his fingers struck the dense metal. He grabbed hold of it just as Crean yanked him out.

Billy held the pot triumphantly aloft. The other men cheered. Tim threw him a blanket, but Billy waved it off.

"I'm half froze already, might as well get some more!" He plunged in twice more and pulled out three more pots before Crean, afraid to risk turning him into an icicle, called a halt to the effort. They rubbed him with blankets until his skin was red as a lobster, but Billy didn't warm up for hours.

Pots were good, but the real quest was for food. Right now the ration was about half a pound of food per man per day. It wasn't starving, but it wasn't much. Back home, a man could easily eat a half-pound steak for dinner. They had carried off several tons of food when they first left, but there was much more in the ship's hold.

"Only we have to break through decking a foot thick and three feet underwater," McNeish explained. "With nothing much to stand on and no tools to speak of."

"It's impossible." Vincent scowled. He sat on a piece of rubble and began to roll a cigarette.

"Aye." McNeish nodded somberly. "Impossible it is. You know what that means, Blackie?" He winked at Perce.

"Impossible?" Perce knew what Shackleton would say. "Means it's going to take a little longer?"

"Machines!" Hurley was bristling with energy. "That's what we need, boys—machines!" Hurley was never happier than when he was creating some new useful thing out of old bits and pieces. The task of breaking through the deck was a good challenge. He sharpened one of the ice chisels and rigged it to a block and tackle. They could hoist it up and let it drop like a pile driver. It took half the day to get through the thick deck, but once it was pierced, they could insert a long saw and the job went quicker. A couple of hours of sawing and finally they had an opening three feet square.

Wild wouldn't allow any more diving. "It's too deep, and no one's going to last long enough to get much out anyway. Get the boat hooks and we'll see what we can drag out."

They still had to stand knee-deep in the freezing water, but no one minded when they were fishing for food. On the very first try, a barrel of walnuts floated up. The men cheered. Soon other crates came bobbing up behind it. It was like the arcade game where you moved mechanical jaws to grab a toy from the pile; you never knew what you would get. There was a case of sugar, then one of flour. When they hauled up a case of strawberry jam, the men jumped up and down like kids. They opened a jar right there and passed it around, dipping their fingers into it with sloppy delight. Dried vegetables and lentils were less exciting but still welcome, but when Perce fished out a case of creamed spinach, he was loudly booed. They did not, however, throw it back.

Over the next few days, they made several more holes in the deck of the *Endurance* and eventually brought out three tons of food. Shackleton figured that with a steady supply of seal and penguin, they could eat comfortably for six months, but no one expected they would wait *that* long. It was early November; the Antarctica summer was just around the corner. Everyone was feeling optimistic.

Best of all, as far as Hurley was concerned, was the rescue of his photographs. It was another wet and dangerous job with ankle-holding plunges, but the plates were in good waterproof cases and few were broken. Until that night anyway.

"You know we can't carry them all, Frank," Shackleton said. There were over five hundred negatives. Hurley and Shackleton sat down on some cases and sorted through the plates. They chose a hundred and fifty of the best ones. Then they smashed the rest. Hundreds of glass plates crashed one by one into a pit in the ice. It took hours. Perce found Hurley later, standing by the pit. He could see bits of the broken images still, ghostly and gray against the snow.

"Why did you have to break them?" Perce asked.

"Couldn't we just leave them whole? Maybe someday they'd be found."

"Boss was afraid I might try to sneak them along somehow. And he was probably right!" Hurley laughed. "But you must be happy, Blackie. No more lugging all that gear around with me, eh?"

"No! Of course not," Perce said earnestly. "I liked it."

"I was just kidding, lad."

"Really, I was glad. And I learned something."

"Well, I've got the Vest Pocket left," Hurley said matter-of-factly, patting the Kodak in his jacket pocket. This was the newest, most amazingly small camera invented. It folded up to the size of a paperback book. "Twenty-four shots. Suppose I'll have to restrain myself a bit."

"You'll start over easy when we get back. People will pay to see your lantern shows, and you can buy all the newest equipment," Perce reassured him.

"When we get back." Hurley looked up from the broken glass, out over the endless ice. "Yes, I suppose I can."

chapter twenty-one

After a week of scavenging, Shackleton and Wild decided the sinking wreck had become too dangerous. The raiding parties were ended. Life at Ocean Camp settled into routine. Wake up. Wash your face with snow. Eat breakfast. Do chores. Chop ice for water, shovel snow over the latrines, skin some penguins, cut blubber for the stove, feed the dogs, check the tent stakes. Afternoons: read, play cards. Walk around the floe. Play with the dogs. Eat dinner. Read some more. Play cards. Sleep.

November 18, 1915

We have quite the little town here now and are even comfortable. We have boards for the floor of our tent, which makes it nice and dry. Billy has been curing sealskins, which he knows how to do from his trapping days. When they are ready, we will have soft beds. It is late spring, weather has been mild, usually in the thirties, and the sun shines about half the days. Even blizzards aren't so bad, though, for the wind blows our ice island farther north. It is rather miserable to be squashed up inside a tent for two or three days while the wind howls, and we all shiver all the time, but the miles are worth it. We make bets on how far we will go. When the sky is clear, Worsley can get a sighting and figure our position, just like on the ship. Well, guess we are on a ship, really. Only a ship of ice.

Some nights we have light shows in the sky. Called aurora australis, like the northern lights, all pink and gold and green wavy curtains of light. Shiny, too, like a lady's fine silk scarf. Once Hussey took out his banjo and made up music to go along with the lights. It was different from the singsong tunes he usually plays. Sort of peaceful and dreamy, but a little sad too. Sad in the way when you see something very beautiful and know it will go away. Like a flower will die or a summer picnic day has to end. No one talked or joked around like they usually do. Even the dogs got quiet. After a while, I felt tears filling up my eyes. I think others did too.

The only real work now was hunting. They built an observation tower out of salvaged wood so they could look out over the floe, but with the ice so tumbled up, the seals were often hidden from view. Most days when the weather would allow, the men went out hunting on foot. They went off in different directions in groups of two or three. If anyone spied a seal, he would climb the nearest hummock and wave a flag to the man in the observation tower. Wild carried the rifle, so the flagman in the tower would signal him where to go. Wild was an expert marksman and usually killed the seal with one bullet through the head. Then the men would gut it and wait for a dog sled to come carry it back. If the weather was closing in and the dogs couldn't get there in time, they would hang the guts on a tall ice hummock to mark the place and hurry back to camp.

One evening, almost a month after they left the ship, Perce was lying awake in his sleeping bag after supper. It was light around the clock again, and he sometimes had trouble falling asleep. He knew Shackleton had even more trouble, for

Perce often heard him walking around the camp after the men had gone to bed. Probably it was the only time he really had to himself.

November 21, 1915

I was just drifting off when I heard Shackleton shout. Everyone woke up, some yelling, for they didn't know what was happening. Then we heard: "She's going, boys!" *We all piled out of the tent. Boss said he was walking around when he just had a feeling. He went up the tower and saw the ship starting to go down. We all crowded up on the platform; some hung off the ladder to watch. After so long and so much pressure, our gallant little ship was finally surrendering. Only ten minutes and she was gone. Nothing left at all, no bit of mast, no scrap of sail. Like she never existed. All were silent as we watched the last of our broken ship disappear below the ice. No one talked much after. Everyone is depressed, and not even Shackleton tries to pretend we shouldn't be.*

chapter twenty-two

By early December, they could see from the tower that the ice was breaking up in places, but it still wasn't open enough to launch the boats. The warmer summer weather made a mess of the camp. The black ash from the blubber stove coated the ice and absorbed the sun, making it melt. Their boots were soaked most of the time. At night, steam from their warm bodies and breath would stick to the inside of the tent, then freeze when the temperature dropped. If any man touched the side of the tent, they were all covered in a shower of frost.

The food supply was holding up, but some of the men were pessimistic. Orde Lees was the worst. He spent hours writing up ration lists and keeping a hawk eye on the supplies. He would stand beside Charlie when he made the hoosh, watching him measure out the dried peas, ready to snatch the bag out of his hand if he added even one ounce extra. The men had dozens of nicknames for Orde Lees now. "Old Lady" and "The Belly Burglar" were some of the nicer ones.

Outside of the routine camp chores, the men worked with renewed energy to prepare for the boat journey. McNeish built up the sides of the three lifeboats with salvaged planks from the *Endurance.* He filled the new seams with yarn unwound from a scarf and caulked this with a paste of flour mixed with seal blood. The three boats were named after the three biggest donors to the expedition. The largest boat was the *James Caird,* after a Scottish businessman. The two others were the *Stancomb Wills,* after an elderly heiress, and the

Dudley Docker, after a Birmingham merchant. Crean organized the men into boat crews and drilled them until they could break camp, load the boats, and launch in ten minutes. Shackleton and Worsley had plotted courses to all the nearby islands. The actual destination would depend on the wind and currents.

Hurley built a portable blubber stove. In the most optimistic plan, if everything went perfectly and the weather was good and they hit the nearest island, they would still be in the boats for five days. They could get along without cooking hot food, for they had the dry sledging rations, but they would still have to melt ice for water. They had three little Primus stoves, marvelously compact camp stoves designed for the sledging journey, but there was limited fuel, and Shackleton wanted to save what there was. Even though they all knew an open boat journey would be difficult, they were excited to start. The worst part was just sitting around waiting.

But December wore on, and they were still trapped. The ice would break up a little, then refreeze the next day. Leads would open to tempt them, then close again. They had to ration the ammunition now, so whenever possible, they killed seals with a club to the head and a slit to the throat. It was ugly business. The hot blood poured out of the neck and melted a big puddle in the ice. Perce knew that a good knock on the head was as painless as a bullet, but it was still awful.

"I don't think I'd mind so much if they weren't just lying there peacefully," he said. "It's like punching a little girl in the nose."

The one seal they would never try to club was the ferocious, enormous sea leopard. They preyed on penguins and the other seals and seemed eager to have a taste of man as well. Even with eight hundred pounds of blubber and only flippers to "run" with, the sea leopard could outrun a man. One day, on the way back from a hunting trip, Orde Lees was skiing by himself away from the others. An enormous sea leopard leapt out of a crack and started chasing him. Orde Lees skied as fast as he could, shouting for help. The beast chased him along the edge of the floe, then suddenly, just as fast as it had appeared, it slid back in a pool of water. Orde Lees thought he was safe. But then the same ferocious head poked out of the water in front of him. The seal had been tracking him! It opened its huge mouth and roared, showing long, jagged yellow teeth.

Orde Lees screamed. Wild shouted and waved his arms to distract the beast. When the sea leopard saw Wild, it turned and charged him instead. Wild dropped to one knee and aimed. He was perfectly still as the huge beast charged, waiting for a good shot. When it was only about fifty feet away, Wild fired. Perce saw the bullet hit square in the middle of its chest, but the sea leopard didn't stop. Wild fired again. Again the animal recoiled but didn't stop. Wild never flinched or even moved. He took a breath and slowly let it out. He held steady until the beast was barely twenty feet away, then drilled it with one final shot to the head. It dropped to the ice at last. Wild stood up. He didn't seem the least bit ruffled. He just shouldered the rifle and walked over to the dead sea leopard. It was twelve feet long and had to weigh over a thousand pounds.

"Going to be tough eating that one," Wild said. "Full of lead too. But might as well haul it back. Heavy bugger."

Orde Lees skied over, gasping for breath, looking a shade pale.

"Why, thank you, Frank," he said in a shaky voice, staring at the monster that had almost killed him.

"You're quite welcome." Wild took out his pipe as if nothing much had happened. It took two dog teams to drag the carcass back to camp. When they butchered it, they found hair and bones in its stomach from two other seals it had recently devoured. The jawbone was nine inches across, and Charlie gave it to Orde Lees for a souvenir.

December 10, 1915

Never in my whole life would I have expected my favorite food to be seal liver and seal brains. But it is the truth. They are especially tasty and Doc says most nutritious. Sometimes we find fresh fish in a seal's stomach, and some eat these too. I can't get my mind around eating something that's already been eaten once. Doc still checks us for scurvy every week. Looks at our teeth and bruises. Everyone's healthy, mostly. Some have cuts infected, though, and some dog bites. Cuts don't heal so well out here.

Yesterday I was helping McNeish work on the lifeboats. He has done a knock-up job. He made masts out of scrap wood from the Endurance, *and I was holding one steady while he nailed it into place. I didn't have to pay much attention, just be steady, so I was looking around at the camp and the dogs. Most were curled up and sleeping, but Crean's pups were chasing each other around and rolling in the snow. They go free most of the time, because they were raised gentle. They are full grown now and good strong sledding dogs but also the most like pets too.*

All of a sudden I knew something awful. I looked down at the small boat. Maybe I knew it all along but just wouldn't think about it. Probably all the men know and no one talks about it. But what I thought was, no matter how we eventually get out of here, the dogs will not be coming. I am low now and sick inside to think of it.

chapter twenty-three

By the middle of December, life in Ocean Camp had become pretty dismal. Some days there was open water all around their floe and they thought they would get in the boats the next day. Then the wind would come up and push new ice in, and the escape route would close. Ocean Camp was like a very small town where everyone knew everyone else's business. Men started petty arguments over how loud somebody snored or the way someone chewed. Shackleton had a way of smoothing everything out.

December 17, 1915

I see how life here could fall apart anytime without the Boss. He makes it seem so easy and talks us into thinking his way. Not like hypnotizing, but like when you're a kid and bash yourself up and your mum says it's okay, so you believe her. You don't even have to think about it anymore. I wonder about the men of the Aurora *on the other side. Hope it is better for them and no trouble, for they don't have Shackleton with them.*

It didn't help that Ocean Camp was a slushy, stinking mess. There wasn't much work to do anymore either. The boats were ready, the provisions were all packed, there was just this infernal waiting. Perce was reading *Nicholas Nickleby,* by Charles Dickens. It was a good story about a young man with endless adventures and predicaments. Mostly it was good because it took him far away from the snow and ice. And compared to what old Dickens could come up with, Antarctica sometimes didn't seem so bad.

"Can you imagine his uncle being so mean?" Perce asked Billy. "He wouldn't help him out at all!"

"Nope." Billy was in the encyclopedia, deep into Mesopotamia.

"Which do you think is worse, Billy—stuck here or stuck in the workhouses they had back then?"

"Workhouse."

"Why?"

"You never got out of them workhouses."

"Nicholas Nickleby did."

"Well, that's why the story's about him and not all the ten thousand other fellows died there. Not much of a story otherwise," Billy snapped. Even he was getting to be in a grumbly mood.

The loudest grumbling, however, was in their tent every night. Some of the sailors were starting to talk against Shackleton. John Vincent was always stirring up trouble. He insisted the other tents got more food than they did. He complained the sailors always had the worst jobs around camp. Mostly the others just ignored him, but as the tension of waiting continued, some began to join in. They dragged up old slights. They went on and on about how Shackleton should have turned around. How they'd be nice and warm and eating roast beef and custard pudding right now if he had. Old McNeish, always outspoken, was one of the most critical.

"You know Boss is thinking about another march," McNeish said one morning. "You see him and his cronies out every day, looking around. I'll be damned if I'm going to pull those boats any farther."

"Too right. They can't get anywhere without us pulling the load," Vincent said.

"We can't get anywhere without the rest of them either, so why don't you just shut your trap," Tim sighed.

"And what about pay?" Vincent pressed. "Tell them, McNeish, how once a ship sinks, the crew doesn't get paid. We're stuck here, having to drag his expedition out of bloody hell and not a dime to any one of us."

"'Tis true," McNeish said. "I know the law as it comes for the sailor. A sunken ship has no master. We can't be made to work. Boss can't really make us do anything."

"No, but he could leave you on your arse out here to starve, now couldn't he?" Perce pointed out. He desperately wanted to go off away from them. Just to go for a walk, but there was no place to walk to these days. In a way it was just talk. But in a way, too, such talk could be considered mutiny. Mutiny was the most serious crime aboard a ship. Mutineers could be shot.

"Vincent's just blowing off," Billy said the next day. He and Perce were on cleanup duty, shoveling up after the dogs. "And poor old McNeish is feeling his age. Still hasn't got over Mrs. Chippy either."

"But what if the Boss thinks we're in with them?"

"Boss is smarter than that. And what if he does think that? What's he going to do? Fire us?"

Perce wasn't reassured. He felt like a dumb schoolchild. Not wanting to rat someone out, not wanting to make a big deal out of something that probably wasn't, but not wanting the teacher to think badly of him either.

"Look, Perce," Billy dropped his voice even lower. In the cold air, sound carried far. "The Boss is smart. He knows from looking around what's going on. He comes around to the tents every day like he's just visiting, but you know he's checking on all of us. He knows who's feeling up and who's down. Who's strong and who's getting shaky. We don't spend time with Vincent and McNeish except for meals, sleeping, and blizzards. Boss sees that."

"But if they're planning something and we don't tell—"

"If they're really planning something, we will tell," Billy promised. "But right now, they're just moaning and groaning. It would be different if there was something they could really do. Take over the ship or something. But, well, there sure isn't any danger of that now, is there!" Billy laughed. "The Boss has done right by us so far, and everyone knows it."

"I know, Billy. But don't you think—just, I thought if we could make it smoother for the Boss, you know? He isn't looking so good."

"Nobody's looking so good."

"That's true. But he's got so much on his mind. Don't you hear him shouting at night in his sleep?"

"There isn't much we can do, really," Billy said. "Keep our own heads together, I guess. About all we can do."

That same afternoon, just after lunch, Shackleton called them all together for a meeting.

"I know you've all been keeping a careful eye on our progress out here," he said. "So it won't be too much of a surprise when I tell you that Mr. Worsley's latest sightings haven't put us exactly where we hoped to be. Unfortunately, we're drifting too far to the east. Even if the ice breaks out tomorrow, we'll never make it to Snow Hill or Paulet Island." Some murmuring broke out, but Shackleton went on, ignoring it. "We might beat either the wind or the current, but not both. So I've decided to march west. If we can walk even fifty or sixty miles, we'll be in much better position to drift into the peninsula once we do get into the boats."

For the first time, Perce thought Shackleton's confidence sounded forced.

"We only made a mile a day before," Orde Lees spoke up. "And we know we can't haul all three lifeboats."

"If we keep drifting in this direction, we have no hope of getting *anywhere*," Shackleton said firmly. "Besides, a little march will do us all good."

There was much talk in the tents that night. Some of the men were excited and hopeful, some thought it was stupid and dangerous. But all were going. They would leave in two days. They would travel by night when the ice would be harder. Meanwhile, since it was almost Christmas, Shackleton declared they would celebrate. Next day, most of the delicacies they had salvaged from the *Endurance* were laid out to eat. The jars and cans were too heavy to carry, so the men ate their fill. Pots of jam and cans of peaches, tinned sausages, anchovies, and boiled hams. Their stomachs had shrunk so much, most could only eat a little at a time. They ate, then rested, then took little walks to get ready to eat some more. Even the dogs got a few choice tidbits. While the men were gorging themselves, Shackleton and Wild went out to scout a trail.

The next morning, after almost two months in Ocean Camp, the long march began. Shackleton went first with a few men to chop out a path. The dog teams followed, then the sailors came, relaying the two boats. Once again the smallest lifeboat, the *Stancomb Wills,* had to be left behind.

"Devil's choice," Crean said. "We can have three boats going nowhere or two and surely sink."

This march was ten times harder than their first attempt. Great icebergs had plowed through the floe, pushing up hummocks ten feet high. There were open leads and dangerous patches of thin ice. Still, they went on. Day after day passed in a cold blur of pain, exhaustion, and frustration.

December 26, 1915

Didn't ever think about how there's so many different kinds *of bad times. When the ship was getting crushed and we worked all out for days, it was bad, but you didn't feel it so much. Times like that, when there's a chance you might still fix it, are different. Like back home when the coal mines cave in. Men don't care how hard they work or how long. There's a feeling even if you're dead tired, you keep digging because you think it will come out good in the end. Sometimes it does.*

But this kind of bad is just dull and wet and dragging. Knowing you have to do it. But knowing it won't work. But what else can you do? But no spirit to it. But you're wanting to have the spirit because the Boss does. He's working hard as any man or harder. He believes we'll make it, so you catch on to that. Or try to anyway. Sometimes you just pretend. Sometimes, though, the pretending makes you believe again. Funny how that works.

After six horrid days of marching, they had gone only seven miles. It was to be the last triumph for a while. When Shackleton and Wild went out to scout a trail on the sixth day, they saw broken ice and patches of water, giant icebergs and impossible ridges. Willing or not, there would be no more marching west. Three days later it was New Year's Eve, the last day of 1915. Not much to celebrate. All they could do, once again, was sit and wait for the ice to break up. They called their new home Patience Camp.

Two weeks later, it was time to shoot the dogs.

chapter twenty-four

Everyone knew it was coming. There just weren't enough seals around to feed them anymore. When the ice finally did open, there might not be time enough and it would be too cruel to leave them to starve. But what an awful day. Some men went off as far away as they could. Some sat with their favorite dogs, petting and playing with them until it was time. Only twenty dogs, the two strongest teams, would be spared for now. Shackleton hoped to send them back to Ocean Camp to bring up more supplies if the ice allowed.

Perce walked up and down the rows of kennels, saying goodbye. He knew the little things each dog liked and wanted to be sure their last day on earth was a good one. He knew Lupoid hated having his paws touched and Hackenschmidt loved a scratch just above his tail. Soldier, one of the smartest dogs and usually one of the friendliest, looked up at Perce, then turned away and curled up at the back of his dogloo. It was like he knew what was coming and had decided to accept it with dignity.

Perce worked hard not to cry. He couldn't imagine these friendly faces gone. No matter how bad he was feeling, he could always count on the dogs to cheer him up. As long as they had a hunk of seal, a chance to run, and a scratch on the head, they were happy. A miserable place was going to get ten times worse without the dogs.

The horrible job, as most horrible jobs did, fell to Frank Wild. He and Doc Macklin took the dogs one by one some distance from the camp, behind a large hummock of ice. It was downwind so the waiting dogs would not smell the blood in the air. Even though they had to conserve ammunition, the bullets would not be spared for the animals that had worked so hard and become such friends. Crean and some of the other officers dug a pit. One by one the trusting dogs were led behind the screen of ice. Doc gave each one a little piece of seal meat. Then Wild put the pistol to its head. Thirty shots cracked in the cold air. It was an awful day. Perce tried to read *Nicholas Nickleby* but couldn't concentrate. He was always waiting for the next shot. Finally he gave up and put the book down. He went to the edge of the floe and just walked around, watching the killer whales spout in the open leads.

There, after a while, Perce came upon Wild sitting by himself, behind a hummock of ice. He was smoking his pipe and staring out at the sky. Perce turned to go back, thinking Wild wanted to be alone. But Wild heard him.

"It's all right, Blackie. I'm done weeping like a little girl. Come and sit if you like."

Perce sat down next to him.

"You were good to do it, Mr. Wild. We were all afraid we'd be asked to help."

"Stinking old dogs, weren't they?" Wild said. "Always fighting. And such a racket they'd make."

"Aye."

"Glad to be done shoveling the mess up after them every day, eh?"

"Won't miss that."

"Aye. Won't miss that."

Perce was pretty sure Doc had given Wild a medicinal dose of brandy. They were quiet for a bit, then Wild sighed.

"All the same, I've known many men I would rather shoot than the worst of the dogs."

The next day, a strange blizzard hit. The wind howled low over the ice, spinning around the tents and pushing under the flaps. Tufts of black clouds tumbled across the horizon. There was a weird electrical pinch to the air. Perce felt the hairs on his arms prickle.

"It's the dogs," McNeish said solemnly. "All their poor souls come to haunt us." All night, the blowing snow sounded like the scratch of a thousand paws against the canvas tents. Sometimes the ice trembled beneath them. There were few religious men in the crew, but many prayers were whispered during those terrible three days. The wind never stopped, and the temperature never went above zero.

January 17, 1916

Third day of blizzard. Blows so we can't go out of the tent. Just stay in bag. Bag frozen solid. Like sleeping in a coffin. Bucket by the door for a toilet. At least that freezes too, so the smell isn't much. Charlie out cooking, though. But simple fare. Plain hunks of seal in the pot to cook fast as possible. Peggy goes out on a rope so he can find his way back. Was me yesterday. Snow like a sandstorm on my face. Food is the best part of the day, and it isn't all that good. But it's all we have to look forward to.

Every ordinary day I ever lived now seems exotic and wonderful. What a faraway world that is now. A world of carpets and sofas and curtains. A world where you can have a drink of water whenever you want, a world of chocolate bars and toffees. When I have children, I will buy them candy every day, as much as they want. Just to sit on the stoop on a summer evening when every kid is out playing in the lanes. Mothers drag chairs outside and sit in little circles, some mending the clothes. Dads sit on benches outside the pub, talking football with a pint. And girls, their heads bent so close talking that from behind, their hair all comes together. I like that, all different colors of it, shining like a striped blanket of hair down their backs. Day before I joined my first ship, I saw Anna again. A fair in the town and she in a dress blue the shade of the sea at dusk and her hair with a gold ribbon. She looked at me and smiled and looked at the grass by her where there was room for me. I went and sat there and we listened to the band. Still some red paint around her fingernails.

When the blizzard finally did stop, the men crawled out of the tents, squinting at the sun. They were weak from lying around. They stumbled through the new snowdrifts and fell with jellied knees. The sky was perfectly blue, and the temperature went up to thirty-two degrees. They dragged damp, half-frozen sleeping bags outside to dry in the sun. They rigged lines between oars and hung clothes to dry. Everything was so tattered and gray, it looked like a beggars' carnival.

Hurley got the blubber stove going, and everyone collected ice to melt, eager to drink their fill. They were terribly thirsty. Water had been severely rationed during the blizzard, since it was too hard to melt. Some of the men filled little tobacco tins with ice at night and slept with them, melting the ice with their body heat. In the morning, they would have an ounce of water.

The only good thing about the blizzard was that the winds had blown them seventy-three miles north. When Worsley took the sighting, everyone cheered.

"And look at that!" Hurley stood on top of a lifeboat, looking through the binoculars. "The storm blew the old camp up closer. I can see the *Stancomb Wills*! We can go get it!"

Ocean Camp, with the third lifeboat, was now only five or six miles away. To have all three lifeboats instead of two felt as good as getting rescued. It was a long day of tough work to drag the boat over the bad ice, but no one complained.

"Can't fuss when the weight you're dragging is going to save your life," Crean said philosophically.

chapter twenty-five

Day after grim day passed, and still the ice would not open. The three lifeboats sat ready but idle. Shackleton remained optimistic. He visited the tents and taught the men how to play new card games. One day he dressed up like an admiral, with a shovel for a sword and epaulets made out of sardine cans on his shoulders, and inspected the camp. He demoted Frank Wild for not having proper creases in his trousers and awarded Charlie Green a medal for being the filthiest cook in the Southern Hemisphere.

It was a good bit of fun, but week after week of misery was starting to wear them all down. The killer whales were always prowling. The men could hear them blowing and knocking against the edge of the floe. The wind was always blowing. Sometimes Perce thought that was enough to drive a man out of his mind.

They rationed carefully, but by late January, nearly all the stores they had retrieved from the ship were gone. Shackleton talked with Charlie each day about how to stretch out what was left. He wanted to keep some variety in the meals. Maybe a little curry in the seal today or a few dried peas in the stewed penguin. A bit of cheese or a teaspoon of raisins was a special treat. Once Tim dropped a piece of cheese in the snow. It was no bigger than a button, but he spent an hour looking for it. To make sure the portions were fair, they were always handed out blindly. The day's Peggy sat with his back to the others while he dished out the food. Another man was chosen to call names. The Peggy held up a pannikin and said, "Whose is this?" Then the caller named a man, and the food went to that man. All agreed it was the fairest way to do it, but it was still hard sometimes not to look at the man beside you and imagine his piece was bigger or a more tender cut.

The all-meat diet was causing the men trouble. They called it "squeaky gut." Some were constipated; some had diarrhea. Neither was much fun when your latrine was a hole in the ice and your toilet paper a handful of snow.

February 10, 1916

Patience Camp is wet, ugly, dirty, and cold. And boring. No place much to walk. No more jokes that haven't been told. No more stories—even from Billy, who had years' and years' worth. I know the name of every town he ever stayed, every horse he ever rode, every bar he ever got into a fight in. Same with everybody. Even tired of Hussey's banjo. Seems like every song is the same one. We all miss the phonograph. I liked hearing the orchestra songs. I'd never heard that kind of music before. Hurley says when we get back to London, he'll take me to a real orchestra. They have fifty people or more onstage playing all at once. Imagine that. Hardly any books left and no room to play football, even if we had the energy. Nothing to eat but seal and penguin, and they are growing scarce, migrating, we think. Wish it were so easy for us.

"They'll come back," Shackleton reassured the men. "After all, if everything is migrating, something or other is bound to migrate our way." Orde Lees predicted doom and gloom and starvation. Many of the men grew obsessed with food. The seal blubber that some had first refused to eat was now eagerly devoured. They ate it boiled; they chewed it raw. They drank it melted, even though it looked like engine oil and tasted about the same. Their bodies craved the calories. A scrap of blubber that fell in the ashes would be carefully wiped off and eaten. No one was starving, but they were always hungry. They were also thirsty all the time. They were burning penguin skins in the blubber stove now and needed twenty a day just to melt ice for water.

Just when they were down to a single day's supply of skins, Perce woke one morning to a tremendous noise: squawking, screeching, clattering all around. When he poked his head outside the tent, he could hardly believe his eyes. The entire camp was full of penguins. They chattered and preened and waved their flippers. There must have been a thousand of them. These were Adélie penguins, small, playful birds. They tottled among the tents and practically between the men's legs. Some seemed curious; others ignored them completely. The men came out of the tents and stood around for a couple of minutes just marveling at the sight, then they picked up their clubs. Marvelous or not, the penguins were food.

"All right, men," Wild called. "Let's get to work." He picked up a club. "This is going to get messy."

The slaughter went on all day. After the first hundred or so penguins were killed, they set up an assembly line to clean them. Two men gutted the birds, then tossed the carcasses to others, who skinned them. Charlie sharpened knives and supervised the butchering. If a man left too much meat on the bone, he was banished to the skinning crew. They would eat everything: heart, brains, tongue, liver, and kidney; everything but the beaks and eyeballs. It took about ten minutes to dress each penguin.

"Watch the mess!" Doc Macklin kept reminding. "We have to keep the meat clean." With a thousand penguins waddling everywhere, it was hard to find a bit of ice that was free of penguin droppings. He had them dig a hole to reach clean ice. The men took turns guarding the pit, shooing the penguins away. That was a comical sight. The penguins were curious, so the more the men waved and chased, the more penguins came to investigate.

They packed the meat in empty crates, layered with the clean ice, then buried the crates to keep them frozen. They worked on the edge of the floe, as far away from camp as they could. The killer whales were also taking advantage of the migration. Huge shiny heads lunged out of the water and crunched the penguins. All day the floe was noisy with the sounds of death. A thousand penguins squawking, a dozen killer whales blowing. Men shouting, dogs barking, and always, the soft, dull thud of clubs against small penguin heads. Some of the men seemed almost crazy with the slaughter, swinging wildly and racing after the startled birds. Perce mostly felt sick.

"God—for once I just want to see an animal and not have to kill it!"

"Aye." Crean nodded. "And they just stand there looking at us like we might be friends." He swung his club at the head of another penguin and knocked it dead. The air smelled of blood. Their boots and pants were spattered with it. They worked bare-handed as long as they could bear the cold so as to keep their mittens clean.

Perce clubbed two more penguins with little effort. The feathers shone glossy and bright in the sunlight.

"When I get home, I'll happily live on bread and butter."

"Ach—I'm missing potatoes. Imagine that—an Irishman longing for potatoes." Crean stretched his back and looked out over the carnage. "My grandparents lived through the famine, you know. They ate grass. Dirt sometimes; anything to fill their bellies. I guess I can't complain too hard."

He smacked another penguin and watched it until the last twitches faded away. By the end of the day, they had killed over three hundred penguins. That made six or seven hundred pounds of meat. It was a month's supply of food. Famine was, for now at least, put off. The next day, the enormous flock was gone.

chapter twenty-six

Summer had come and gone, it was autumn now, and the ice had not opened up. The floe that held their camp had melted away to half its size. Every day, gigantic floes drifted by. Sometimes they crashed into each other and crumbled to pieces. Icebergs toppled over as their bases were worn away. By the end of March, food was scarce again. They shot the last of the dogs. They had grown so thin, it was mercy. This time there were few tears shed. The animals that had offered affection now offered meat. With grim humor, some of the dog drivers even stood by while Charlie cooked their teams. It was all so awful, they had to make jokes.

"Be sure to keep Nellie away from Sadie," Crean said. "They never did get along."

Macklin insisted that his own dog would be the most tender. Truth was, only little Gruss, who had been born just two months before, was really tender. The others were as tough and skinny as the men.

Perce took his portion with little emotion.

April 2, 1916

I thought I should feel sad but didn't. Don't really feel hunger either, though. Not regular hunger anyway, like coming home from a long day out fishing and knowing there will be a good soup and fresh bread for tea with the fish just caught frying in the pan. Now it is like I am a machine and the food is a chunk of coal. What does dog meat taste like? I can't really say. Only that it is not seal or penguin. A little bitter. And very tough.

× × ×

It was hard now for even Shackleton to keep up morale. His face was so thin, the ready smile that had always been so reassuring now looked ghoulish. There was no chance of surviving the winter on an ice floe. The tents had been scoured by the wind, so the canvas was as thin and light as a girl's summer dress. The reindeer skin sleeping bags were always wet and beginning to shed, so there were hairs everywhere. On one freakish day, the temperature went up to forty degrees and it rained. The dripping inside the tents was almost as bad as outside.

Several times they had to scramble to move tents and rescue crates of food when the ice cracked beneath them. The smashing, grinding, and grating of the ice got on everyone's nerves. Shackleton ordered "watch and watch," with half the crew on and half off at all times. He also made them sleep "all standing," which meant completely clothed with boots, hats, and gloves on. It wasn't very comfortable to sleep in boots, but since they were always wet, they would freeze solid if left outside the sleeping bags. It could take half an hour to wiggle your foot into a frozen boot.

More weeks passed in tense fear and constant boredom. Their floe was now so small, Perce could walk all the way around in ten minutes. The tents were so close together, he could hear every man snoring, belching, farting. It was dark for twelve hours a day. Billy and Hussey, the smallest men, could not walk alone in a strong wind without being blown over. Perce's shoulder blades protruded so much, they rubbed two holes through the back of his already worn-out jacket.

One day he was lifting a big block of ice onto the sled and the jacket tore.

"You've let us down, Perce, lad," Shackleton said, shaking his head in dismay.

"Boss?" Perce was startled by the rebuke.

"Why, don't you remember what I said? How if things got tough we would eat the stowaway? Well, look at you now—not enough meat on you to do us any good!"

"I'll be glad to take a double ration, Boss," Perce laughed. "Anything to help out, sir."

That night, Shackleton came to the sailors' tent with a jug of hot milk and half a nut bar for each man. The nut bar was the most delicious and filling of the precious sledging rations. He also brought a leg from an old pair of trousers to use for patching clothes. He sat with them and told stories. Nothing about Antarctica, nothing about food or home that would make them feel worse, just funny stories about all the people he had met while trying to raise money for this expedition.

He did imitations of stuffy old businessmen asking long, boring questions at his lectures and of silly young girls hanging around outside the London office, hoping to meet a dashing young explorer. He told about visiting wealthy people's houses full of paintings and gilt mirrors and fine furniture.

"Mrs. Stancomb Wills—bless her heart—she had this very beautiful furniture, all French-style, you see, with silk upholstery. It was the slipperiest thing you ever sat on. There I am, drinking my tea, and so much tea for so long I thought I would burst, but the entire time it was all I could do not to slide off. It was like sitting on a block of ice. And she's a lovely lady, a very charming lady, but oh, I had to press my feet against the floor until my legs cramped up."

"Why don't ladies slide off their own furniture, then?" Perce asked.

"Well, that's what all those skirts and petticoats are for." Shackleton took off his coat and tied it around him in a bunch like a lady's skirt and gave a comical demonstration.

"Now, shouldn't we have brought along some petticoats, then, Boss?" Tim laughed. "They'd make for good sitting on the ice too."

When Shackleton left, Perce lay down feeling almost happy. They were full of hot milk and nut bar and laughter, but most important, they were reminded that there was another world out there beyond this cold, awful place.

April 5, 1916

Mr. Charles Dickens would be happy here for the misery he could write a book about. No workhouses or cruel uncles but plenty of cloudy, wet, gray, and cold. Nothing and more nothing to do. Which is good, because we're too hungry to do much. I can feel all my bones. Didn't ever think Billy could get much skinnier, but he has. We only know from faces, nobody ever takes off any clothes, but faces tell a lot. Tim has the squeaky gut pretty bad. He never complains, but he's built his own seat at the latrine.

Sometimes, though, a day comes up so beautiful. Maybe once a fortnight, but when it's there, it seems a miracle. The day sky is blue like doesn't even exist back home. The sunset is all gold and pink, dark blue shadows on the ice, fiery sparkles where it hits the frost. Then at night you can see the stars, and it's so grand, I do forget all the awfulness and being lost. You can look at stars and go to them in your mind. If a moon, even better. It's so bright and soft. Makes you think things are possible.

chapter twenty-seven

By April, the floe was bobbing like a raft on the currents. Waves washed across it regularly, soaking everything. There was no place to walk. Killer whales circled constantly. The men had their kits packed all the time, ready to run to the boats. Leads of water would open, then vanish as other floes came crashing together. Once a giant iceberg drifted straight for them like a slow-moving freight train. There was nothing they could do. They stood watching helplessly, expecting to be crushed any minute. Some men wept. Some shook hands and said their goodbyes. Shackleton lit a cigarette and stood watching with no sign of worry. At the last moment the huge berg veered a little and rumbled by them. It smacked a nearby floe instead, shattering it into a thousand pieces.

But finally, one evening just after supper, their floe cracked in two.

"The *Caird*!" Wild yelled, and started to run. They were about to lose the biggest lifeboat. It was half in the water, tipping dangerously and shipping water over the side. Perce raced after Wild. Together they leapt up and grabbed hold of the side. Tim and Worsley were right behind them. But the boat was filling with water. The four of them were lifted off the ice as the boat tilted farther. Perce clung to the wooden side. His feet kicked helplessly against the keel. He could feel the vibrations of the creaking wood in his chest. The four of them simply didn't weigh enough to right the heavy boat.

It seemed an eternity of dangling, but then other men

caught hold and pulled. Slowly she started to come upright. Perce felt his feet hit the ice once again. He saw Shackleton, his face red, pulling on the lines with all his strength. In a few terrible minutes, the boat was sitting once again on solid ice. But even as they stood there, gasping for breath, they could see new cracks appearing beneath the sled runners. Then Shackleton's voice rang out.

"Strike the tents, gentlemen. Lash up and stow."

It was time. Ice or not, they would have to take their chances. Every man had been assigned to a boat and given a specific job for the launching. The smaller boats would take eight and nine men, the *James Caird,* eleven. Perce and Billy would be in the *Stancomb Wills* with Crean. It was the least seaworthy boat, but having Crean more than made up for that. Tim was in the *James Caird* with Shackleton and Wild. Worsley would command the *Dudley Docker.*

The water was choppy as the men dragged the loaded *Stancomb Wills* toward the edge of the ice. They cut her loose from the sled and eased her into the water.

"Can you hold her, lad?" Crean asked Perce. "I need all hands to launch the others."

"Aye." Perce took hold of the rope and braced himself to hold the boat. Waves broke over the ice and sucked at his ankles. Even with his feet wet all the time, the shock of the freezing water was awful.

"We'll be needing you now, Blackie," Crean said quietly. "You've grown up rowing, and half these men never rowed their arse across a bathtub. I'm counting on you."

Perce just nodded. He was freezing cold and shaking with

fear, but Crean's words made him feel stronger. "Iron Man" Crean, who had already braved about the worst a man could down here, was counting on him. Perce decided he would do it or die trying. He found his footing and held the boat in the tossing waves while the others dragged the *Dudley Docker,* then finally the *James Caird* into the sea. Finally all the boats were afloat. Everyone jumped in. Chunks of ice crashed all around them. Perce pulled on his oar with everything he had. It was a shock to discover how weak his arms were. The oars were fourteen feet long and hard to manage in the crowded boat.

"Row, you blighters! Row!" Crean shouted. "Billy—" He handed Billy an ice pike. "Go to the bow and fend off!"

The three boats pitched and tossed in the sloppy waves. They were caught in a "cross sea," a place where the wind blew one way and the current ran the opposite. The combination made for big, choppy waves. Within a few minutes, half the men were seasick. The waves were so rough, they couldn't get the oars working together, for one would bite water and the other only air. The men who weren't rowing pushed chunks of ice away. Suddenly shouts erupted up and down the line of boats. Crean looked back over his shoulder.

"Jesus, Mary, and Joseph!" A wall of water two feet high was rushing toward them.

"Row!" Crean yelled. "Row for your bloody lives!" He grabbed an oar from a weaker man and with one powerful stroke got them moving. Some devilish current and cross of wind had stirred up a rip current. It was like a river, pushing up all the ice in its path, racing toward them like an avalanche.

Perce braced his feet and pulled with all his might. His

muscles burned, and his hands became wood. He didn't know how long they raced the wave, minutes or hours. Finally they hit open water and the wall of ice fell away into the sea.

"Well done, men," Crean gasped. "Spell the oarsmen." Billy handed off his pike and came to relieve Perce.

"So how do I work these things?" Billy asked.

"Have you never rowed a boat?"

"Not much need for rowing in the north woods."

"I'll stay on."

"Come on, I need to warm up, and I've got to learn sometime. How hard can it be with all these knuckleheads doing just fine? Go and dry your feet," Billy urged. "Much as you can anyway. Here." He reached in his pocket and took out a precious pair of socks that were only slightly damp. Perce crawled to the bow but didn't have the energy to even undo his boots. It felt strange to be afloat again after so long. How long had it been? They had spent three months in Patience Camp, and was it two before that in Ocean Camp? And before that the months frozen in on the ship. He had to count on his fingers. Fourteen months since he had felt water under a hull.

They rowed all day. Thirty minutes on, thirty off. The *Stancomb Wills* was the slowest boat and stayed in the rear. McNeish had raised the sides of the other two boats, but there had not been enough wood for the *Stancomb Wills:* she had barely six inches of freeboard, and waves broke constantly over the gunwales. Their feet were wet all the time, and they had to bail constantly. It was terrifying at first to be in the water with so much ice crashing around, but after a while, Perce got used to even that. The bow was half covered with canvas and layers of ice built up as the waves washed over. They had to crawl up and knock the ice off. Spray froze on the men until their clothes crackled with ice. It was a wretched day, but spirits were high. At least they were doing something. No longer just sitting and waiting and drifting.

They rowed as long as the daylight lasted. As dusk approached, Shackleton began looking for a sturdy floe where they could camp for the night. He finally found one, and after six difficult attempts, they got the boats landed.

"And see there—dinner's waiting!" Hurley pointed out a large crabeater seal lying on the floe. Life was getting better all the time. Wild got the rifle, Charlie got the blubber stove, and within an hour, the men enjoyed a hot, filling meal of fried seal steaks. They could eat all they wanted. The boats were already too heavy to take more weight. They would carry only some blubber for fuel. As soon as they ate, the exhausted men crawled in their wet sleeping bags and fell asleep.

Shackleton set hour-long watches but still did not sleep himself. The swell was much bigger. The ice creaked and trembled. He was patroling the edge of the floe when there was a tremendous jolt. A crack ripped through the ice right between his feet. Even before he could shout an alarm, the crack raced on through the middle of camp. It split the ice in two, directly under the sailors' tent.

Perce woke when a gush of cold water splashed on his face. He bolted up in shock. It was too dark to see, but he could hear the open water just inches away. Chaos erupted in the tent. Men struggled to get out, kicking and crashing into each other in the dark, shouting and screaming.

"Someone's in!" Billy shouted. He plunged his arm into the black water. Ernie Holness, one of the stokers, had been sleeping right beside him. Now he was gone. Billy felt around in the black water. The breaking ice screeched in his ear. He plunged his arms deeper and finally felt a sleeping bag. He grabbed hold and pulled.

"Billy!" Perce shouted. "Where are you?"

"Here!" Billy gasped. Someone on the other side of the crack also caught hold of the bag, and together they hauled Holness's head above water.

"Hold still!" Billy shouted. Perce reached toward the voice, but the ice pitched up and tossed him back. Then the hoop poles of the tent stretched apart and the canvas fell down on top of them. Perce flailed at the canvas, reaching by instinct in the direction he thought Billy was. Finally he felt a leg and grabbed hold. Perce couldn't move under all the canvas, so he simply hung on, anchoring Billy with his body weight. The ice heaved up again, and Billy slid toward the open water. He was still holding on to Holness and couldn't stop himself. His chin scraped against the edge of the ice. The crack widened, and Holness sank again. Billy's face hit the water.

Then suddenly the canvas was pulled away and Shackleton was there. He plunged both arms into the water, grabbed Holness, and heaved him up on the ice, sleeping bag and all. Perce and Billy rolled to safety just as the crack slammed closed with a force that would have crushed them all.

"All well?" Shackleton gasped.

Before they could answer, another shout rang out—

"Crack!" A new crack had split the floe. The *James Caird* and a dozen men were cut off. Wild grabbed a line and threw it across the open water. The men began to pull from both sides, dragging the ice chunks back together. Shackleton jumped across and helped the men push the *James Caird* over to the main floe. Then one by one, the stranded men jumped across. Shackleton, as usual, waited until the others were safely over. As he was about to jump, water surged up and pushed the pieces apart again. The tiny piece on which the Boss was standing began to drift away. Shackleton was stranded. Wild threw him the rope, but one man wasn't enough to pull against the strong current. The gap was too big for anyone to jump across to help him.

"Can you tie off?" Wild shouted.

"No!" Shackleton replied. There was no hummock or anything he could tie the rope to. He was alone on a tiny raft of ice floating out into the Antarctic night.

"Launch a boat!" Wild cried. "I need hands!" Wild ran toward the *Stancomb Wills*. Perce, Tim, Crean, and some others threw themselves at the boat and shoved it into the water. They jumped aboard and grabbed the oars. Perce's blistered hands hurt with the first couple of strokes, but all he could think about was Shackleton.

"Boss?" Wild shouted into the black night.

"Here," Shackleton replied faintly.

Wild called again, and Shackleton replied and the men tried to follow his voice. It was like a terrible game. They rowed a few strokes and called again. It wasn't more than ten minutes but seemed an eternity. Finally they bumped

Shackleton's little ice raft. Wild pulled him aboard. Shackleton steadied himself on Perce's shoulder, and Perce felt a block of ice brush his cheek. It was Shackleton's coat sleeve frozen solid.

Back at what was left of the camp, Shackleton called the roll. As each man answered, they began to feel relief. Every man alive. Hurley lit the blubber stove, and Charlie boiled up some hot milk. They got Holness slightly warmed by the stove, then for the rest of the night they took turns walking him around to keep him from freezing. The water froze on his soaked clothing and fell off with little tinkles like wind chimes.

Dawn came with little cheer. The wind was strong, and launching the boats was difficult in the choppy water, but within an hour, they were once again rowing. When the wind picked up, they tried to sail, but only the *James Caird* could trim her sails well enough to handle the conditions. Shackleton insisted they should stay together, so he lowered one of his own sails to keep pace with the slower boats. They were eager to be free of the dangerous pack ice, but once they broke out into blue water, they had another cruel surprise. The open sea was far too rough for the little boats. They had to retreat to the shelter of the pack ice. They rowed and bailed and rowed and bailed. For lunch, they each had a piece of cold pemmican, six sugar cubes, and half a cup of water. Everyone was thirsty. Perce's lips were cracked. Shackleton knew the men desperately needed rest. No one had slept more than an hour or two in the past two days. As soon as the weather eased, they would have to go into open water, and then there would be no place to stop. He finally decided to risk camping on another iceberg. Landing was difficult; they had to haul the boats up a five-foot ledge of ice. Dinner was more cold pemmican, barely warm milk, and two lumps of sugar. But after so long with no sleep, hardly anyone cared. They crawled in their wet sleeping bags, and most fell asleep within minutes.

Perce lay awake, shivering. He couldn't tell how much from cold and how much from terror. Cold air seeped into his sleeping bag. No one buttoned up the bags anymore for fear of being trapped. They kept their boots on too, and Perce's feet ached. It wasn't so hard in the daytime, when there was work to do. But now in the dark terrible night, Perce was afraid he was falling apart. He wanted to cry and trembled with the effort not to. Here was the test he had wondered about so long ago on the dock in Buenos Aires. *What if things got tough and he turned out to be weak? What if he was a coward? What if he wasn't strong enough, smart enough, brave enough?*

He turned on his side and buried his face in the wet fur.

"Perce?" Billy whispered. "Are you awake?"

"Yes."

"Are you okay?" Perce pressed his face harder into the sleeping bag, afraid to speak. Billy threw an arm around him. Finally Perce whispered.

"I—I don't think I can do this."

"Don't think, then." Perce felt Billy's arm tighten around him. Billy was shaking too. "Don't think. Just do."

chapter twenty-eight

They rowed through another day and night. Everyone's hands were raw with blisters. Perce could no longer feel his feet. All around them, killer whales circled. One bumped against the boat and surfaced so close, Perce felt the warm mist of its blow.

On the fourth night, a heavy, wet snow fell, soaking through their clothes. Perce made his brain go empty. There was no cold, no sea, no tomorrow. Only this: stroke, stroke, stroke. And terrible, awful thirst. After a while he couldn't remember why they were rowing, but it didn't matter. It was lovely to row. He stopped shivering. He felt warm and peaceful.

"Okay, Perce. My turn." He felt a big hand on his shoulder.

He shook the hand away. Why were people always interrupting when things were nice?

"Perce—take a break."

"No."

"Come on, time to switch off."

Perce was confused. He felt his hands being pried off the oar. This frightened him, for then he would have nothing to hold on to. He struggled and tried to push away the hands.

"Perce—what's the matter? Do you know where you are? It's me, Crean. Get yourself together, man."

Crean shook him. Perce felt a rush of cold air flood over him.

"Sorry. I must have been sleeping."

"Something like that. Now come have a rest."

Crean pulled on his arm, and Perce stood up. Then he stumbled and fell over the thwart. He could not feel his feet at all. Finally the sun rose. The men blinked and looked around like dead men rising from the grave. The winds had dropped, and the sea was calm. It was even warm, almost ten degrees above zero. Within an hour, they found a floe big enough to tie up to. Charlie and the blubber stove were put "ashore." Soon black smoke was chugging up into the sky. There was enough room for the men to get out and stretch their legs.

Perce stumbled around on the edge of the ice. It was so queer to walk and not feel your feet.

Worsley got out the sextant to take a sight. It would be the first one since they took to the boats. Everyone speculated on how far they had come. Twenty miles? Thirty or more? Clarence and Elephant islands were only sixty miles away when they took their last reading in Patience Camp. They might be halfway there. Worsley sat down in the *James Caird* with his little stub of pencil and the tables. He did the math. He frowned. He did it again. The men waited anxiously. Finally Shackleton told them the bad news. They had not done as well as expected. In fact, the little boats had been carried east by the strong currents. They were now farther from land than when they were in Patience Camp.

The news was devastating. Some men wept. Some argued that the sight or math had to be wrong. Perce closed his eyes and pressed his cold fingers against them, trying to feel anything else but this horror.

"We'll check again at noon," Shackleton assured them.

"And the wind is picking up. We'll just set a new course. Meanwhile, finish your drink and let's go on."

They rowed silently. No one even tried to raise spirits; sometimes you just had to feel as bad as you felt. Worsley took the noon sight and did not even bother telling them the longitude and latitude. He just shook his head.

The wind grew steadily stronger all day and they could finally sail all three boats. But that night, the temperature began to fall. Perce could actually hear the seawater freezing around the boat. It was a delicate little sound, like when you sprinkle cinnamon sugar on a piece of toast. It was impossible to row safely anymore that night, so they tied the three boats up again, one behind the other in a line. Worsley made a sea anchor by lashing two oars together in the shape of a cross. As they drifted, the sea anchor would keep their bows pointed into the wind. If they turned broadside to the waves, they would quickly be tipped over. One man in each boat would also have to hold the tiller all night.

The men huddled together and tried to sleep. In the *Stancomb Wills,* there was not enough room to lie down. Waves washed over the side, so their feet were always wet. Shackleton stayed awake all night, checking on the men and constantly testing the lines that held the boats together. Once he called out to the men in the *Stancomb Wills*.

"Are you all well?"

"All well," Crean replied in a croaky voice. "Well, I'll have to go to confession as soon as I get home," he said to Perce under his breath. "For that's the biggest damn lie I've ever told." He had been at the tiller for hours, singing to himself to stay awake. Crean sang all the time he was steering. No one could ever tell exactly what he was singing. He only sang in three or four notes, and those notes were flat. It might have been Irish ballads. It might have been Buddhist chants.

"It could be bloody Mongolian folk songs for all we can tell," Billy laughed.

Even before it got light enough to see, Perce knew something was wrong with the boat. She just wasn't floating right. As the sky lightened, what he saw was terrifying. All three boats were encased in a thick shell of ice.

Crean nudged the nearest sleeping man in the pile of bodies. "Up gently, boys," he said calmly. "Don't anyone move." The *Stancomb Wills* was so heavy, the gunwales were barely two inches above the water. So it wasn't a dream. Perce carefully shifted and reached out his hand. He felt ice a foot thick.

"Boss?" Crean called out.

"Aye," Shackleton croaked. "I see. Let's raft up."

"Easy does it, lads," Crean directed. They carefully brought the three boats alongside each other and tied up for stability. Perce slowly unbent his cramped body. His coat crackled with ice. He looked around for a tool. There was nothing near but a long iron pike. He wasn't sure he could stand to use it. For one thing, the boat was too unstable. For another, his feet felt odd. He tried wiggling them to get the blood moving. Perhaps it was just the awkward way he had been sitting.

The sounds of chipping ice rang out rhythmically.

All the men were stiff with cold and dizzy with fatigue.

Five minutes' work left them shaking. Some could not or would not work at all. Orde Lees lay seasick and moaning, curled up in the only sheltered spot on the *Dudley Docker.* The other men were furious at him. He had pushed another man out to take the place and refused to let anyone else in.

Billy crab-walked down from the bow, keeping his weight low so as not to tip the boat. He had been hammering ice off the bow. His cheeks were flushed from the exertion. He held his hammer out to Perce.

"Go on, have a turn. It's fun. Warms you up nice."

"In a minute."

"What? You joining the slackers now?" Perce turned his face away into the wind. He felt scared and embarrassed.

"Perce?" Billy crawled over and sat beside him. "What's wrong?"

"My feet," Perce whispered. "Something's wrong. Don't tell the Boss, but I don't think I can stand."

There wasn't much need to tell Shackleton anything. He knew his men well. When he saw Orde Lees refusing to work, he wasn't surprised. But when he saw Perce sitting silently doing nothing, he was worried. A little while later, Doc Macklin came climbing across the boats and wiggled into a spot near Perce and Billy.

"How's everyone over here? Doing well?"

"Aye."

"Well, we took the seasick for you up front, I'll say. Bumpy ride, that. Of course, hardest part was trying to restrain ourselves from throwing the Old Lady overboard. Says he can't row, isn't any good at it. And by God, when we gave him a chance, he worked hard to prove he wasn't."

A great chunk of ice fell from the side just then, and the boat rocked in a rebound. They all held on until it settled again. Macklin looked Perce up and down.

"Boss says you were limping a bit on the floe yesterday," he went on in the same casual tone. "Shall I have a look at your feet? Could be a touch of frostbite. Greenstreet has one foot pretty bad. I've had a bit of trouble myself."

"They don't hurt," Perce said. "But I can't seem to get them to work."

Macklin gently eased Perce's left boot off and peeled down the sock. Perce saw him flinch, then look away.

"Is it frostbite?" he asked, worried by the doctor's abrupt silence.

"Well—" Macklin cleared his throat. The foot was frozen solid. He gently pressed on the skin. It was white and waxy, the underlying flesh hard as a piece of marble. He felt in vain for a pulse on top of the foot. He checked the other foot and found it the same.

"Well, the cold has rather got to them," Macklin finally said. "But you'll be more comfortable if we just leave them alone for now. Until we get to some proper shelter." He bit his lip. "As long as they're cold, they won't hurt so much. If we try to thaw them now, we risk more damage when they refreeze." Macklin picked up Perce's wet sock, and little bits of ice crumbled off. "We'll switch you to the *James Caird,*" Macklin suggested. "It's not so wet."

"No!" Perce said quickly. "I want to stay. I can still row." His own voice sounded far off. "And what's the sense if my feet are already gone? They won't get any worse here." He couldn't bear the thought of another man taking his place and risking the same fate. "I can row." Perce stared at his feet with a weird mix of horror and revulsion. They looked like statue feet. There was a buzz in his head and golden sparkles at the front of his brain. He could hear no sound except the clang and crash of ice being smashed off the boats. Then he felt hands on his back and the warm breath of someone speaking in his ear. The voice was faint and tinny.

"There you go, lad. Put your head down a minute. Won't do to faint."

When his head cleared, Perce found he was leaning against Billy, and Tim was sitting across with a handful of nut bars. The smell of peanuts was overpowering. Tim smiled through a mouthful.

"Come on, Perce." He pressed a bar into Perce's hand and raised his own like a toast. "Boss ordered a gorgie. Eat our fill, he said!"

Shackleton had opened a case of sledging rations and told the men to eat as much as they wanted. In the next boat, the Primus stove was hissing and the pot bubbling. Perce took a bite, but his mouth was so dry, he couldn't chew. He carefully spit the bite out in his hand to save for when he got a drink. He looked down at his feet and saw that his boots were back on. That was good. He couldn't bear to look at the horrible white flesh.

"Do you think Doc will have to cut my feet off?"

"Oh, no," Billy said confidently. "Well, a couple of toes, maybe. Not much."

"Bits and pieces," Tim offered. "Hardly nothing at all!"

They were silent for a while. Then Perce took a deep breath. "Do you suppose they'll be any good for eating, then? The bits he whacks off?" Billy stared at him for a minute, then the three friends started laughing. They laughed and laughed until it hurt. What else could they do? They laughed until the tears froze on their cheeks.

chapter twenty-nine

Almost as soon as the boats were chipped free, the wind picked up. By noon, it was almost a gale.

"She's blowing our way, boys!" Crean shouted. "Touch wood." It was hard to trust fortune by now, but the good wind held strong and the boats raced along. Worsley figured the course would take them to Elephant Island, maybe even by nightfall. It was the sixth day in the boats, and the men could not be more wretched. Their faces were cracked, their bodies covered with saltwater boils. Everyone had some frostbite. Empty stomachs growled, but thirst was the cruelest affliction. The pack ice was not very good for water, since there was still a lot of salt in it. Some of the men tried chewing on pieces of raw seal, but it was little help and maybe worse. The seal blood was salty.

Besides that, most were now suffering diarrhea. The only way to handle that was to drop your pants and hang your bare bottom over the side while other men held your arms. The freezing water would splash up on you the whole time. The only relief was the promise of land, and finally, by late afternoon, the mountains and cliffs of Elephant Island came into view. Some dared to believe they would be ashore that very night.

They were wrong.

Around five o'clock, the wind simply stopped. They took up the oars again. They were only a mile offshore now. But hard as they rowed, they got no closer. The currents near the island churned and spun into whirlpools. The wind screamed down the cliffs and held them off. They could not fight these forces. There would be one more night in the boats. At least they knew it would only be one more. For after this, they would either land or die.

All Perce remembered from that long night was a hand in the darkness. It was impossible that he could have seen it. It was so dark, the men in his own boat were only shadows. But he remembered seeing the hand, glowing like the hand of an angel, holding on to the rope that tied their boat to the others. Of course it was not an angel but Shackleton. He didn't trust the worn old rope, so he held it all night. He called to the men throughout the night, trying to keep spirits up. But his voice was so hoarse, he could hardly speak.

"Blackborow? he called once.

"Here, sir," Perce croaked.

"We shall be on Elephant Island tomorrow. No one has ever landed there before, and as you are our youngest member, you will be the first ashore."

Perce knew he should feel honored, but instead he felt strangely annoyed, even angry. *Damn him!* he thought. *That means I'll have to stay alive all night!* He wanted to go to sleep and not have to wake. But Shackleton ordered it, so Perce would have to try and stay alive one more night. *I can't let him down now. I can't let him down.* Perce said it over and over to himself through the endless bitter night.

Daylight came, and all twenty-eight men clung to life. There was no cup of hot milk, not even a sip of water. Those who were still able picked up the oars. For a week, the promise of land had kept hope alive. Now the cruel reality of this land hit them hard. Elephant Island was a rock. A bleak, desolate rock, nothing but cliffs and boulders. There was no beach, no inlet, no cove or bay. No place to land.

"I think when we round the point, we'll have better luck!" Shackleton's voice was almost gone. His eyes were sunken in his blistered face. They rowed on. It was afternoon when they finally saw a narrow fringe of rocks just offshore, with what might be a channel. The spray from crashing waves was high, but it was the best landing they had seen so far.

"Heave to," Shackleton told Wild. He watched the waves for a while, studying the shore. "We might do it. We just might do it," he whispered. "I'll go in with the *Stancomb Wills* first," he directed. "She's lighter and easier to maneuver." The two boats pulled together, and Shackleton climbed over. Crean maneuvered them into perfect position. The men, facing backward, sculled to keep the boat in place until the right moment. Perce saw the perfect wave coming and felt his blood warm and his head clear with the challenge. If they let the boat slip broadside, a wave would crush them into the rocks. The boat surged forward with the swell, then coasted easily over the shoal and into the calm water. One more wave and they felt the hull scrape the rocky beach. Land. No one said a word. They were too stunned to cheer.

"Well, what are you waiting for, Blackie?" Shackleton grabbed hold of his arm. "A red carpet? Off with you now! Claim it for England!" He hoisted Perce over the side. Perce fell to his hands and knees. A wave knocked him over, and he sat in the surf.

"Come on, stand up."

"I—I can't, sir," Perce stammered.

"His feet, Boss—" Billy said as he quickly jumped over and pulled Perce up.

"Oh, bloody hell—I'm sorry, Perce." Shackleton's voice choked. "I'm so sorry." He started to climb out, but Billy stopped him.

"I've got him, Boss." Billy threw Perce's arm over his shoulders and dragged him up the beach. Billy could barely walk himself. The others got out and staggered like drunken men. When Billy set him down, Perce couldn't sit up. The whole world was spinning. He fell back on the stones and dug his hands in, holding on to the earth.

Billy had to leave him and hurry back to the boat. Four other men had to be dragged ashore, too weak to walk. Then they carried the blubber stove up onto the beach. Crean cut up some blubber and got the fire going while Billy filled a pot with ice to melt. Frail little Charlie had collapsed two days ago, but as soon as he had his "kitchen" back, he revived. Still, he could only stand up for a few minutes at a time. He would wobble over to the stove and put in a piece of blubber, then lie back down until he gathered enough strength to stir the pot.

"Have you any more in you, lads?" Shackleton said with as much cheer as he could muster. "I think the *James Caird* is too heavy to get over the shoal. We'll have to shuttle her cargo in first."

"Aye," Crean said. He sat heavily on one of the crates and put his head down between his knees. Billy could only nod. For the few able-bodied, there were many hours of hard labor still ahead.

chapter thirty

Perce lay on the rocks. His head was spinning. For the next few hours, nothing made sense. Boats came and went away again. Some men staggered over the rocks with crates and bundles. Others wandered the beach, screaming, crying, cursing, laughing, stumbling. Someone killed a seal and started hacking off chunks of meat and eating it raw. Then a dozen seals appeared pulling a sled. On the sled were four fluffy puppies. They came up to Perce, and he tried to pet them, but they started chewing on his feet. He tried to kick them off but found he couldn't move. More boats came. Now there were dozens of dark ragged men. It was a crew from a workhouse in *Nicholas Nickleby.* An endless procession of penguins walked past in single file. Each one stopped in front of him and bowed. He had to smash every one in the head. A cup appeared in his hand. It was full of hot, sweet milk. Thousands of white fairies flew from tall black castles. Then, happily, nothing for a while.

When Perce woke, the sun was bright overhead. His head felt clear. Thirst was gone. He sat up on his elbows and blinked. They really were on land. That part wasn't a dream, thank God. There were no fairies, only terns and gulls. He saw smoke rising from the blubber stove.

"Hello, are you back with us?"

Perce turned and saw Greenstreet. "Aye. Was I—was I off my head?"

"Not bad as some," Greenstreet said. "And not so long. We're all taking turns at the collapsing. Only fair."

"Are your feet very bad?" Perce asked.

"Just the one." Greenstreet kicked his good foot around to demonstrate. "And it may be starting to thaw. Hurts a bugger."

"That's good, isn't it?" Perce could still feel nothing in his own feet.

"I suppose it is, yes." Greenstreet laughed. Perce sat up all the way and stretched. He actually felt remarkably good. Certainly better than he had felt in a week. His boots were off, and his clothes were half dry from the sun. He saw two other men lying on the other side of Greenstreet. Both were asleep or unconscious.

"Are we at the infirmary, then?"

"Aye." Greenstreet smiled. "And here's our lovely nurse."

Doc Macklin came over and squatted beside them.

"Food's almost ready, and the stove is warm. You can come sit near if you keep your feet away. We don't want to thaw them until we know we can keep them that way." He put Greenstreet's arm over his shoulders and helped him hop away. Perce tried pressing his feet against the stones. Could he hop? He couldn't bear to be carried. He looked up and cringed when he saw Shackleton coming toward him.

"Can I give you a hand to the stove, lad?"

"I'm fine here. Thank you."

"Come on, join your mates. It's a party."

"I don't really want to go just yet, Boss. If you don't mind."

"Oh, come on—" Shackleton took his arm, but Perce shook it off in a flash of anger. "Perce—" Shackleton said quietly. "Everyone's knackered one way or another. There's no shame in that."

"Can you please just leave me alone, sir?"

"No." Shackleton sat on the rocks beside him. "Look, Perce," he said in a low voice. "Every man here is one tiny step from breaking down. And it's going to get worse. Right now, we're in paradise just because we're on solid ground. Tomorrow, when reality sinks in—well, we're in for a long, rough time of it. I need you to be brave."

Perce squeezed his eyes shut.

"But I'm not brave," he said. He tried to stop himself, but words came tumbling out. "I thought all along I would be. Or that I would try to be, or I would die trying. But I thought it would be like—like Wild was brave when he shot the charging sea leopard. Or like Crean was brave when he saved his mate. Brave where you can do something." Perce wiped his face on his sleeve, and the half-frozen cloth scratched his cracked lips. He was glad for the sting. "What can I do now? I can't carry gear. I can't kill seals. I can't even chop ice for water. I'm useless."

"We have plenty of men to carry gear and chop ice." Shackleton rubbed his hands over his face and looked out at the ocean. "Sometimes being brave is very dull," he said. "Sometimes it's just keeping quiet when you want to fuss or being optimistic when there's no bloody hope. You've done that, Perce. I need you to keep with it now. You're the worst off, lad. If the men see you going on all right, they'll feel they can come through this too."

"I don't know that I can, sir."

"Do you trust me, lad?"

"Oh, yes, sir!"

"Then trust me when I say I know you can. Could that be enough?"

"I don't know. If I lose my feet—"

"You won't," Shackleton interrupted sharply. "Toes, maybe. Maybe a little more. Not much. Just enough for a good story." He smiled. "You'll have a wee bit of a limp, and the ladies will say, 'Oh, poor lad, what happened to you?' And you'll say, 'Oh, 'tis nothing at all. A bit of frostbite, you see. From when I was exploring in Antarctica with Shackleton.' Oh, my—they'll be eating that up with a spoon."

Perce laughed in spite of himself.

"But why am I the only one so bad?"

"I don't know. You weren't exactly sailing in first class, were you? And sometimes it just happens how it happens." Shackleton looked at the men huddling around the smoky stove. "Did you know that on my first trip down here, with Scott in 1901, I was invalided home?"

Perce shook his head, surprised.

"Three of us were out sledding for months: myself, Scott, and Ed Wilson—a great man he was. It was a horrible trek. We were off on what Scott called the Southern Journey, just trying to see how far we could get toward the pole. We had no clue what we were doing. We were out for three months. We had no dogs, Scott didn't believe in using dogs, so we were man-hauling all the way. All three of us starving and with the scurvy. Scott would never say it was scurvy. It was taboo, you know. But then I developed something else, a problem with my lungs. I was coughing up blood. I couldn't breathe. Toward the end, I couldn't pull. I skied alone behind the sleds while Scott and

Wilson pulled. I was so ashamed. Later, when Scott told the story, he said I had broken down. That's how he put it: *broken down. Our invalid,* he called me. It seemed everything to me at the time. That I wasn't man enough."

Perce thought about this for a while. "So when did you know you really were?"

"Really were what? Man enough?" Shackleton laughed. "When *will* I know, you mean." He turned his face from the sea and looked at Perce. The lively blue eyes were so terribly tired. "When we all get home alive. Maybe absent a few toes, but alive."

Shackleton dragged his fingers through his long, greasy hair. For the first time since Perce had met him, Shackleton seemed like an ordinary man.

"I like the glory, lad," he sighed. "I won't pretend I don't. But when the speeches are over and the clapping stops and everyone goes home, it's your own heart you're left with. Your own conscience asking, did I do enough for my men? So. I've little hope of glory after this, but you can save me from failure." Shackleton stood up and held out his hand. "Come on. I'm strong yet. They won't even know you're being helped."

Perce took Shackleton's hand and let him pull him up.

The eating never stopped that day. They kept the fire going and the pan hot. It felt like a picnic, though a very strange picnic. It had been 497 days since they had last stood on land. Some men were silent; some talked without stopping. Billy, one of the few who had worked to the end unloading the boats, finally collapsed on the bare rocks and slept as if on a feather bed. Hurley walked off by himself to the end of the spit and sat watching the birds. McNeish looked over their boats, obsessively examining every crack and split as if he had to repair them immediately. Orde Lees sat at the edge of the circle. He was trying to be helpful now, but some of the men were still mad at him. He had partly redeemed himself toward the end of the terrible trip by bailing for several hours when the boat was swamped by waves. Worsley said Orde Lees had single-handedly saved them from sinking. Others were not so generous. "He was the only one strong enough to bail, for he hadn't rowed a lick all week!" McNeish insisted.

Charlie hardly said a word, for he was either laughing or grinning all the time. He laughed as he sliced up seal steaks and grinned as they sizzled in the pan. Sometimes he stomped his feet a little, as if checking to be sure they really were on dry land. All who could stand stood around the stove, and those who couldn't sat on crates or lay on the rocks nearby. Tim told stories as if he were back home in a comfortable pub. He was making the horrible boat journey sound like a rollicking good time full of comical adventure.

"So there's old Holie— just pulled out o' the water. Soaked through and the floe all busted up and the Boss drifting away on a bit of ice—" Tim waved to an imaginary figure in the distance. "Goodbye, Boss! It's been nice sailing with you! And of course here's McNeish trying to rescue him—" Tim switched to a heavy Scottish accent. "Why, na ya doon't, ya blighter— y'er na gett'n away so easy! Na afore ya sign my paycheck!" The men were rolling with laughter at this.

"While over here—" Tim switched accents again and

mimicked the dunked sailor Holness desperately patting his clothes and looking worried. "My 'baccy!" he said in perfect imitation. "I've lost all my 'baccy! You'd think he lost a million pounds, not his bloody tobacco!"

"I'd smoke the million pounds if I did have it," growled Holness. "Or spend it on one good pipeful."

They made camp slowly. Sleeping bags were spread on the rocks to dry. The tent poles and hoops had been thrown away to cut weight, so they rigged makeshift tents using the oars. Every man had some frostbite, and Doc Macklin was busy bandaging with whatever scraps of cloth he could find. The weather stayed kind. The sky was clear, the moon bright.

"Can you believe we're on good solid earth again?" Billy said. "Do you think we could ever tell anyone how we're feeling right now?"

"Naw. You need words from books, not our own heads. You need one of the Boss's poets to tell it," Perce said.

"Ha," Tim laughed. "Wouldn't you like to see Mr. Byron or Mr. Browning out here just now? With those poetical shirts all flapping in the wind! You think they would've made it this far?"

"And that Mr. Coleridge," Billy added. "Well, that 'Ancient Mariner' was a bang-up poem, but Boss said Coleridge wasn't even a sailor at all! He just walked around the countryside in England, dreaming it all up."

"Aye." Perce stretched out on his bed of stones. "Wish this was something we just dreamed up."

chapter thirty-one

The sky was still clear the next morning, and Shackleton let them sleep late. All morning he simply strolled around and asked how everyone was feeling. Some men wouldn't say anything, as if pretending the hellish journey hadn't even happened. Others wouldn't stop talking, as if that were the only way to get all the bad memories out. Shackleton let each deal with it as he wanted. When they were finally all awake and full again on seal meat, he gathered them all up around the stove.

"I'm afraid I've a bit of bad news," he said simply. "If you haven't noticed the water marks on the cliffs, look around now." Crean and Wild did not look up. Perce looked carefully for the first time and saw the clear signs on the rocks. By the amount of fresh seaweed and debris, it looked like the beach had been covered fairly recently.

"It looks like this place is underwater more often than not," Shackleton went on matter-of-factly. "So we're going to scout out a better place somewhere up along the coast." A horrified murmur of objection rumbled through the ragged group. "Wild and Worsley will take a few men out tomorrow in the *Dudley Docker.*"

Perce glanced at Tim and saw the shadow of fear seize his friend. He was easily the best small boat sailor and among the few men strong enough to go. Tim said nothing, but Perce saw his shoulders slump, his whole body shrinking into itself as if he could vanish before the cruel task. But a minute later, when Wild walked over and squatted beside him, Tim just nodded.

× × ×

April 17, 1916

My mind is dull. So can I even write? But it is about heroes I'm thinking, and duty. It is easy to see Shackleton as a hero, and Wild and Crean as well. And they are, for we would long ago be dead. But isn't Tim just as much today for saying he would go? You could say was only duty. But I think I understand now what Shackleton said yesterday, how hero is not always doing something grand. It's when things get so bad, and you keep on anyway. Like Charlie Green signed on to be ship's cook in a neat little galley with proper stores. Now he whacks up bloody penguins and stands through all evil weather over the sooty fire every day. He could have said bugger that. But he hasn't. Even just Hussey playing music to cheer us up, with his hands so cold. All just doing their duty. But more. And I feel proud of them.

For the men on the beach, the day passed in sunny relaxation. They mended clothes and cut their beards, aired out the sleeping bags, and ate their fill. For the men out scouting, the day was a long, cold struggle. They sailed and rowed along the rough coast of Elephant Island, searching for a better home. The beach needed to be high enough to stay dry in the worst storms. There had to be a glacier for water and enough seals and penguins to feed them for several months. Most importantly, they had to be able to get the boats in and out. No one back at the beach talked about it, but Perce knew everyone was thinking the same thing. What if there was no place?

Darkness fell, and the scouts had still not returned. Shackleton paced the rocky beach, looking anxiously out to sea. He kept the blubber stove going with the door open so the light would guide them in. Finally, a little after eight, they heard Wild hail from the darkness. Shackleton ran down to the shore, waving a bit of white sailcloth to guide them in over the dangerous shoals. All who could walk went down to help pull the boat in. Perce watched from the beach as the shadows approached and turned into men in the light of the stove. Tim sank down on a crate by the stove but tumbled right off it again, too exhausted to even sit up. Even Wild staggered. It was the first time Perce had seen a crack in his unshakable strength. Shackleton quickly handed around mugs of hot milk.

After a few sips, Wild could talk. "We found a place. About seven miles away. No one will mistake it for the Garden of Eden, but I think it will do."

"Good, then," Shackleton said with relief. "Well done. The weather is closing in. We'll leave first thing in the morning."

April 18, 1916

New camp on the bad side of nowhere and through hell to get here. Storm hit just after we started out yesterday morning, kept at us all day. Sleet and wind so we could hardly see. Just getting in the boats to leave was bad. Some men cried, out of their heads with the fear of it all over again. They had to be dragged over and hauled in the boats. I think there is not one of us who is altogether right today. All are wet through, and the storm still raging. Men were fainting and having spells. I could only watch it all, of course. Doing nothing. Trying, as the Boss said, to keep up spirits. But all the angels in heaven couldn't do that here. Now we are lying under one of the boats for shelter. The tents are all torn from the wind. The blizzard won't let up.

It was a long way to get here, seven hard miles and the sea rougher than any yet. I wanted a turn at the oars, but Doc said no, for pressing on my feet would be bad. It would tear them all up, he said, because they are frozen so hard. But it would make me warm too and not feel like a sack of potatoes to be carted around. And a sack of potatoes would be much more welcome here! My boat nearly smashed on the rocks coming in. That was pretty bad. Then the men had to stand waist-deep in the water to unload everything. And carry me ashore.

We were the last boat to land. The first men in killed a sea elephant, and when we landed, some of the men had hands so cold, they ran over and put them in the carcass to warm. Then Rickinson, one of our engineers, fell over with a heart attack. He's still alive, but Doc doesn't know. We set up the tents, but during the night, all were ripped or collapsed from the wind. So we just lay there the rest of the night under the canvas, no one with the strength to move. Today we turned over one of the boats for some shelter, and here we are. No more now.

chapter thirty-two

The men called their new home Cape Wild. It was partly to honor Frank Wild, who had found it, but partly because it was simply the most wild and inhospitable place anyone had ever seen. It was a narrow strip of rocky peninsula, barely a hundred yards long and thirty yards across. There was a cliff and glacier at one end and scattered rock islands at the other. Waves washed from both sides, but the ground in the middle seemed high enough. It was obviously a penguin rookery in the breeding season, and the birds would not nest where they would be washed away. During that first terrible night, the wind was so violent that it picked up one of the boats and spun it around like a toy. The men could do nothing but huddle together under the canvas of the collapsed tents. Daylight brought little relief. The hard wind never stopped. Shards of ice and pebbles zinged around like buckshot.

Finally, on the second day, the wind eased. Slowly the men began to crawl out and have a good look at their new home. Billy and Tim carried Perce to some dry rocks. For a while they all just stood around dumbly. Then Hurley got the blubber stove going. Billy and Tim went to chop ice from the glacier. Crean and Wild examined the torn tents. Everyone was weary and disoriented. A man would start doing one thing, then forget what he was doing, drift away, sit down, and pick up a handful of rocks. Even Shackleton moved slowly, like a deep-sea diver plodding across the ocean floor.

By afternoon, things settled down. McNeish built a

windbreak for the stove, and Charlie cooked up some seal hoosh. He flavored it with the last of the curry powder. It was a rare treat.

"I think I'll move to India after this," Crean said as he devoured his. "Eat curry every day."

"Too hot in India," Hurley said.

"The devil's own kitchen won't be too hot for me!"

"Are you not liking your accommodations here, Mr. Crean?" Shackleton asked.

"Oh, no, sir, they're very fine. Very fine indeed. Why, just like the best hotel in London, the bed won't crack in two or melt away from under you while you're sleeping." They all laughed.

"Well, speaking of our accommodations," Shackleton went on casually. "As I'm sure you all agree, there are not so many attractions here that would keep fine gentlemen such as yourselves entertained for very long."

The laughter fell away, and the men exchanged nervous glances. Was Shackleton thinking of moving them all again?

"You all know that Elephant Island, paradise as it is, was not exactly our first choice of destinations. The whaling ships don't come anywhere near, so we can't count on rescue from them. No one from England is going to be looking for us for another year at best. So I've decided to take a few men and sail up to South Georgia Island." This was not a complete surprise to the men. It was one of many plans they had considered since the *Endurance* sank. But now that they'd had a taste of the open sea, this plan seemed awful. Just one week in the small boats had nearly killed them, and the distance to South

Georgia was eight times as far. Besides that, when they left the crumbling ice floe ten days ago, they had several possible "targets" to hit. Now Shackleton would have only one. One tiny island in the middle of a vast stormy sea.

"It's a bit of a journey," Shackleton went on. "I've asked Mr. Worsley to come along, since he's pretty handy with the navigation, and McNeish, for he can keep us afloat. I'll need three more men."

Several hands shot up immediately, but Shackleton waved them down. "No need to all jump at once. This is something to think about. I don't need to tell you how it will be. We need a few days to prepare the *James Caird,* so there's plenty of time to think about it."

"Will you go, Billy?" Perce asked that night as they tried to sleep under one of the overturned boats.

"If he'll take me."

"I know how you hate sitting around."

"That is the truth," Billy whispered. Sound echoed terribly under the boat. "It's going to be a rotten journey, though."

"Aye. But Shackleton can do it."

If it could be done. No one spoke it, but all thought it. Sailing to South Georgia was all but impossible. Navigating that distance and hitting one tiny island would be like throwing a dart and hitting a tennis ball a mile away. But there was no other option. They could not survive here for long. A tiny chance was better than no chance at all.

Preparations kept everyone busy for the next few days. McNeish didn't have many tools left, but he managed to shore up the *James Caird*. He took the mast from the *Stancomb Wills* and used it to strengthen the keel. With bits of wood from packing cases and the old sleds, he built the gunwales up even higher. An open boat could not possibly make the trip, but there was not enough wood to build a deck unless they took apart one of the other boats. So instead he built a framework of sticks to be covered with canvas. All the canvas had of course been soaked and was now frozen solid. They thawed it bit by bit over the stove. It was still so stiff, they had to use pliers to pull the needle through.

Orde Lees carefully packed up a six-week supply of the sledging rations. Men chipped ice all day and kept the stove burning around the clock to melt it. They filled two casks with water and chopped out some extra blocks of ice to take along. Once they were in the open ocean, they could not count on finding good ice.

Perce sewed sacks for ballast stones. He was glad there were jobs he could help with. He couldn't walk at all now or even bear pressure on his feet. His legs up to the knees were swollen three times their size, and the work kept his mind off the pain. The *James Caird* needed ballast to keep her steady, but they could not just fill her hull with loose rocks. They would roll around in rough seas and be difficult to throw overboard if necessary.

While the *James Caird* was being made ready, the men were also at work building a more permanent shelter. First they dug out a cave in the glacier but soon abandoned that idea. Their body heat melted too much ice, and it was always wet inside. The new plan was to make a hut out of the two smaller lifeboats. They would build walls of stones, then set the boats upside down on top for a roof. It was a grueling job. There weren't many big stones on the beach, so the men had to carry them a long distance. They had to make the walls thick enough to stand up to the ferocious winds. There was no grass or moss or even mud to stuff between the rocks. Elephant Island was only rock and sand.

"There's nothing here to turn the sand into dirt," Crean pointed out. "Nothing living to rot away, no plants, no bugs, no worms."

Throughout these busy days, Shackleton hardly slept. He walked back and forth on the little spit, talking with Wild about how to manage the camp. And always, he kept a watchful eye on the sea. If the bay filled with ice, there would be no escape.

Finally, on the morning of April 23, Tim came and sat beside Billy and Perce while they were eating breakfast.

"Tomorrow's the day," he said simply. "And I'm to go. Boss just told me."

"Oh." Perce felt like he had been hit in the stomach. "Well, of course you are, Tim," he said, trying to sound happy. "Anybody would want you along. You're the best sailor by far, and you'll keep them all cheerful."

"Did he say who else?" Billy asked.

"Crean—"

Crean! Perce thought. *Well, who wouldn't want Crean along when the impossible needs doing. But how will we get by without him here?*

"—and Vincent."

"Vincent? He's taking Vincent?" Billy swallowed hard.

"He's strong yet." Tim shrugged.

"Yes," Billy said in a flat voice. "Well, we'll miss you."

"As well you should." Tim grinned. "But a few months from now, when we're all back home, you'll come up to Ireland for a visit, and what fun we'll have then! I'll take you to a ceili, and you'll dance with the prettiest girls. You'll see, Perce—Irish lassies are the best dancers—" He stopped short. His face went deep red. He couldn't help but glancing at Perce's damaged feet. "I'm sorry—"

"It's all right," Perce said quickly. "When you're good-looking as I am and Welsh besides, you don't need to dance. The girls just come flocking around for your charm and personality."

"That's right!" Tim grinned. "We'll none of us need to dance. We'll just stand around being handsome explorers and fascinate them with our tales!"

After breakfast, everyone went back to work on the shelter. Perce watched Billy walk far off by himself. He said he wanted to look for big rocks at the bottom of the glacier, but Perce knew Billy was upset at not being chosen. He couldn't help feeling glad that one good friend would be staying. Still, Perce remembered how bad he felt so long ago when he had been passed over for a place on the *Endurance*. A few minutes later, Perce saw Shackleton leave his boat preparations and go off in the same direction. Billy was chipping out a good-size rock when Shackleton came up behind him.

"Could I give you a hand with that, Billy?"

"It's almost out, Boss," Billy said, still knocking at the ice. Shackleton picked up a rock, squatted down beside Billy, and began chipping anyway.

"I want to thank you for offering to go with me, Billy. It meant a lot, and I'm sorry I couldn't take you. Sorry for me, not for you. I'd be proud to have you along."

Billy was startled. "So why don't you take me, Boss?"

"Because I can't leave Vincent behind," Shackleton said bluntly. Both men stood up. "He'd be trouble here," Shackleton went on. "I need good men here more than I need them in the boat. I wanted Crean to stay too, but he pleaded so hard, I finally gave in. And to be honest with you, Bill, I'm too much of a coward to try something like this without Tom Crean. Wild begged for him too and may never forgive me, but he'll rest easier with you here. And so will Perce. He'll be needing a good mate."

Billy didn't know what to say. He felt half proud and half embarrassed.

"You're a good man, Bill. Especially for a Yank."

"What?" Billy grinned. "How'd you know I was American, Boss?"

"How could I not know a thing like that after all this time! Mind you, we may keep you Canadian for the books. Can't very well have a rebel on the queen's expedition," Shackleton laughed. "Well, that's an awful big rock we've dug out," he said, squatting down by one side. "Take that end and I'll help you carry it back."

April 23, 1916

This is it, then. The end of our crew after so long together. We can't make much fuss of them going. We only talk about when we will see each other again and how it will be. And of course all the things we will eat. We pretend there isn't death waiting out there. I know they should die on this trip. Odd, I don't think about the rest of it, that if they die, then we die too. Only that I will lose my friends, Tim McCarthy, Tom Crean, Captain Worsley, poor old Harry McNeish, who is still missing his Mrs. Chippy, even John Vincent, for he is not so bad, really, just is the way he is. But Shackleton, well, we shouldn't lose him. I think, honestly, the rest of the world will always go on fine without most of us, but sometimes there is a man like Shackleton, that when he is gone, the whole world is less and feels a broken heart and is lost.

The way life is, I would never have met Shackleton, or only to see him give a lecture, maybe, or in the newspaper. I would not have talked with him about my brothers and his sisters and what tricks we did to them. Or about books and poems. Some of his poems, I have to say, I did not understand until he explained them. In real life, a man like Shackleton does not explain poems to a man like me.

Tomorrow they will sail off. Maybe they will make it. Many times I didn't think we would ever get here, and here we are. I don't know what to feel right now. No matter what happens, everything in my life from now on will be different. I do want this to be over. But I also don't. That is crazy but true. I know this for sure, that I would rather die being one of these men than otherwise live my whole life without knowing them.

That night, the stars shone bright in a rare clear sky. Hussey's banjo had miraculously survived the journey, and he played as they all gathered around the blubber stove. The waves beat a gentle rhythm to the music. Flickers of firelight gleamed on worn, dirty faces. No one made any speeches or said any prayers. Shackleton just walked around, talking to his men. He told them how impressed he was with the hut and promised to bring back a proper doormat and some potted geraniums. Charlie boiled up some hot milk and used half the amount of powder instead of one quarter, plus lots of sugar. It was thick and sweet and delicious. They drank toast after toast: to the success of the *James Caird;* to Frank Wild; to Charlie, for feeding them so well; to the dogs, may they have lots of penguins to chase in heaven; to the *Endurance,* the finest little ship there ever was. Finally Hurley stood and raised his mug and toasted Shackleton.

"To a great leader," he said simply. "And a greater friend. Safe home!"

The men stood. The firelight glinted on their metal cups as they cheered.

The next morning, a ragged band of forlorn men stood in the cold wind on the desolate beach and waved goodbye to six of their own. Shackleton took the tiller, Crean and Tim hauled up the sail, and the tiny boat sailed away on an impossible mission.

chapter thirty-three

Perce heard Charlie clattering his pans on the stove and knew, with a mixture of relief and dread, that it was morning. Another long, sleepless night was over, another grim day on Elephant Island had begun. It was one week since Shackleton left. Throughout the little hut, dark shapes began to move. In the dim light, they looked like wiggling grubs. Then shaggy heads appeared, and the men began to crawl out of their sleeping bags. The smell of frying seal steaks cut through the smoky air.

Perce heard rustling overhead and immediately turned over on his side and put his arm over his face. Ten men slept above in the "attic," and when they got out of their sleeping bags in the morning, a shower of loose reindeer hairs fell on the men below. If they didn't warn Charlie to cover the pot before they started moving, breakfast was full of hair. The attic was simply boards and makeshift hammocks built across the thwarts of the overturned boats that made the roof of the hut. It was nice because it was the driest place, but there was barely a foot of headroom and no place to move around. Billy slept up there, in a sort of net he had woven for himself out of the wires they had used to stake out the dogs.

Perce lay in his sleeping bag and listened to the usual morning sounds: groans, farts, coughs, sniffs, yawns. He heard men stumbling toward the entryway, the swearing of those they stepped on to get there, and the swish of the canvas door as they crawled out to relieve themselves.

"Hoosh, oh!" Charlie called. Perce listened to the other

men rolling up their sleeping bags. The damp hides made peculiar squelchy noises. Then there was the dull thump of wood against gravel as they moved the crates into seats around the stove. There wasn't enough room for everyone to sit close to the heat, so each day they rotated one spot. Whoever sat across from Charlie each day was the one to turn his back and call the names for each portion, the way they had done since Ocean Camp. Today the namer was Hurley.

"Whose is this?" Charlie said, holding a pannikin of fried seal.

"Hussey," Hurley replied, and the pannikin was passed around to Hussey.

"And whose is this?"

On and on it went. Perce listened to all this with detachment, almost like he was listening to a daily radio program. He didn't care much when or even if he got his share. He did not join the group on the crates around the stove. He was stuck in his sleeping bag day and night now. As Macklin had warned, once his frostbitten feet began to thaw, they began to hurt. The pain had started as a dull ache, then grew to constant hammering that jolted his whole body. There was no morphine left, not even an aspirin to treat it. Sleep was his only escape, and that did not come easily. He woke many times throughout the night, shocked that anything could hurt so bad. It was sharp, hot, cold, throbbing, stabbing all at once.

Sometimes he was oddly impressed by the pain, as a fighter might be impressed by a strong and clever enemy. But mostly he was just miserable. Any movement sent daggers up his legs. He could not bear the lightest touch. The weight of the reindeer hide was crushing, so Macklin had cut open the bottom of his sleeping bag, then put a crate over Perce's feet to protect them. Sometimes Perce imagined it was the box itself sending out waves of pain, like from a ray gun in a Jules Verne novel. It was easier to think of pain coming from outside.

Greenstreet was also suffering. His toes were a horrible purple color. There were four men in the "hospital ward" at one end of the hut. One had a huge boil on his hip and suffered from general collapse. Rickinson's heart was still weak, but he was getting better.

Billy brought Perce's breakfast over. The "ceiling" of the hut was only about four feet high, so even little Billy had to walk hunched over. Some of the men were still smacking their heads regularly, but most had developed the necessary stoop. With their ragged clothes and bearded faces, they looked like trolls.

"How are you?" Billy asked as always.

"Fine," Perce answered as always. "Did you sleep well?"

"Like a baby," Billy replied. "I woke every two hours wanting to be fed!" There were no jokes that everyone hadn't heard a thousand times by now, but sometimes they told them anyway. Billy put the pannikin down on the crate that covered Perce's feet, being careful not to jostle it. He helped Perce sit up and stuffed one of the rolled-up sleeping bags under his shoulders.

"Here." Billy handed him the pannikin. "Special treat—see what you think." Perce peered into the mug. On top of the usual brown lump of seal meat was what looked like a tiny chicken breast. "What is it? A baby penguin?"

"A paddy!" Billy told him. "Little birds about the size of a pigeon. They've been pecking on our garbage pile, so yesterday I made some snares and caught three. Going to set some more snares out today. And the ice is out from the bay again, so we might have some penguins come up too."

"That's good." Perce took a bite of the little bird. It was tough and dry, but at least it was something different. Meals on Elephant Island were already dreadfully monotonous. Breakfast was fried seal or penguin. Lunch was a thin gruel made from crumbled biscuit and weak milk. Supper was a seal or penguin hoosh. There was no curry powder left, no spices at all. Even the salt was carefully rationed now. Each man got three sugar cubes a day and one precious nut bar on Sundays and Thursdays.

Billy finished his breakfast and wiped out his pannikin with his fingers. "I'm going out now while the weather holds, but I'll come see you later, okay? Do you want an encyclopedia?" Only two volumes of *Encyclopaedia Britannica* had made it this far. They were all getting to be very knowledgeable about subjects beginning with *L* through *P.* Though Billy tried hard to preserve them, the pages were used more often for toilet paper than for reading.

"Later, maybe," Perce replied. He felt too sick to hold up the heavy book. "I've a very busy day planned, you see."

"Right, then." Billy jumped up. Perce knew he was eager to be outside while the weather was good. "I'll see you later."

× × ×

"Morning, Boss!" Tim croaked cheerfully as Shackleton crawled out from under the canvas. "Another grand day it is, sir!"

"Aye," Shackleton replied hoarsely. The cold and constant salt spray had scraped their throats raw. "Hoosh is hot. Need a pull?"

"Aye, thanks." Tim was at the tiller, and as usual, his clothes were frozen to the seat. Shackleton took his hand and helped pull him free, then took his place. Tim slid down into the cockpit, ducked under the canvas decking, and folded himself up in the cramped space. Crean handed him the hot mug. Tim pulled his spoon out of his pocket and began to eat fast, trying to get as much as he could inside himself while it was still warm. Breakfast today was the usual. Every meal, in fact, was the usual: crumbled sledging rations and hard biscuit mixed with water and a little milk powder.

Even if there had been more interesting food, cooking aboard the *James Caird* was a tricky business. It took two men to prepare a meal, three in rough seas. They sat scrunched under the low decking, facing each other, backs pressed against the gunwales, feet together like toddlers playing ball. One man had to hold the Primus steady, while the other held the pot. Whenever the boat moved, they had to lift both stove and pot. In bad weather, a third man stuffed himself beside the other two to steady them as they steadied the pot. Their hands were now painfully blistered from burns as well as frostbite.

Tim held the pannikin in his shivering hands. He was so cold, he could barely open his mouth. His teeth chattered against the metal cup. It was hard to swallow in such a contorted position. The space belowdecks was hardly bigger than a coffin. It was seven feet long and five wide at the cockpit, growing even more narrow as the boat tapered toward the bow. It was dark and fetid and horribly closed in, with barely two feet of headroom. The sacks full of ballast rocks made an uncomfortable "floor."

"Can you wait up with us a bit?" Worsley asked Tim. "The sky's clearing. I might be able to take a sight."

"Sure." Tim nodded as he choked down the last of his hoosh. A few more minutes before "bed" hardly mattered, and all hands were needed to take a sight. Worsley had barely finished eating when Shackleton called out.

"Blue sky, Skipper!"

Everyone scrambled. Worsley had only taken one sighting since they left. All his navigation since then had been dead reckoning, which was basically guessing. Worsley tucked the sextant inside his jacket and crawled forward to the mast. They had to be careful to put weight only on the wooden frame so as not to poke a hole in the canvas. Tim and Vincent each took hold of one of Worsley's legs so he would not be tossed overboard. He needed both hands for his instrument. Shackleton went below with the chronometer to watch the time. McNeish and Crean kept the boat under control. It seemed like hours. Worsley had to see the horizon through the sextant, and the little boat pitched so wildly, he had trouble. There were a hundred possibilities for error. Any one of them could mean they would miss South Georgia by miles. They waited anxiously as Worsley did the math.

"Two hundred thirty-eight miles!" He grinned. "If I've figured right." It was a big *if.*

"Well done, lads!" Shackleton said. They were almost a third of the way. Six days into it. And still alive.

chapter thirty-four

The wind screamed down the cliffs, blowing a hail of small rocks against the hut. Perce tucked his head down between his elbows and squeezed as hard as he could, trying to shut out the noise. It sounded like an avalanche. His "bed" was in the corner, where the gunwales of the boat rested on the stone wall. Perce shifted, trying to find a comfortable way to write. The pages of his journal were warped from being wet so often, the pencil was just a stub, and the light was so dim, he could barely see. But it gave him something to do, filled a few precious minutes in the endless boredom.

May 3, 1916

Sometimes this is the worst thing, the noise of the wind. Never stops. Sometimes I think that will make me go crazy. But ha! Maybe crazy would be a good thing stuck in here! I can feel the vibrations of the wooden hull inside my chest. There are still cracks all over, so the wind screams through. Like a hundred children with new tin whistles and no lesson yet.

Billy is out to get ice for us. It seems like his turn always falls on the worst days. But then, on Elephant Island, every day is the worst day. Plus sometimes he trades others food to do their work. He would rather do almost anything than sit around in here. Hurley also is bad at idleness; he has got moody. When he is in a good mood, he comes to visit me, but that is not often. I think I know why. Because when I was strong, I felt that way around invalids. Like I was mad at them for being invalids. Which is strange, because you know they can't help it. (Though some here are thought malingerers.) But I think it's more that everyone is afraid how easy they could go bad too. They don't like to be reminded, and I remind them.

Hurley has fixed up the stove again. He built a box around the chimney out of an oilcan, so now we can cook in two pots at once and use half as many penguin skins. Still, the hut is always smoky and sooty and dark. I wonder, can a man just turn into dirt if you're in it enough? And dirt inside too, for there is always grit and dirt and hair in the water. I remember at home, getting the little ones' hands washed for tea, thinking how dirty they were, and now I laugh. They were clean as newborn babies compared to us!

Perce heard the flap of canvas open, felt the burst of cold air as Billy crawled in.

"Are you the last in, Billy?" Wild's voice came from a dark corner.

"I saw Hurley and Doc on the spit but coming this way. They've seen the weather. Let's hope it's better out at sea."

Shackleton had been gone for ten days now. He could be landing on South Georgia right now. If there was a ship available and fair weather, he could be back for them in another week. No one talked about this, though. Realistically, they were anticipating two months, even three. Billy scooped out a cup of water, drank some, then carried the rest over to Perce, stepping over huddled bodies along the way. Stormy days were long and monotonous. Many men simply lay in their sleeping bags all day.

"Perce?" He didn't answer. Billy peeled back the soggy flap. "I have some water for you."

"I'm not thirsty."

"It's specially flavored with three kinds of gravel."

"I'm tired. I just want to sleep."

Perce pulled the flap back up over his head. This time, writing in his journal hadn't made him feel better but much worse. He was afraid he might start crying.

× × ×

The sea is an enemy without malice. The waves don't care what they smash about. A bit of driftwood is the same as a boat, a man no more or less important than a moth. Human enemies will tire, but the sea is inexhaustible. For the men aboard the *James Caird,* every minute of every day was so beyond endurance that it all became a blur. Every peril of the first voyage hit them ten times over. For those on watch, the four hours were an endless torture of cold. For the men trying to sleep below, it was not much better. At the change of the watch, they had to creep out one by one as the others crawled in. The reindeer skin sleeping bags were slimy with rot. Clumps of hair stuck to their clothes and skin. When Tim did manage to fall asleep in the tiny space, he often woke terrified, thinking he was buried alive. The boat pitched violently day and night.

"I'd be bruised considerable if I had any flesh left to bruise," Crean remarked.

They were wet all the time. McNeish took off his boots one day, and his feet were white and swollen, pasty and soft as bread dough. Shackleton had everyone check their feet, and all were the same. The flesh was not quite frozen, but it had a creepy, half-dead feel to it. The worst blow came when Crean opened the second keg of water. It had cracked and let in salt water. Now it was brackish, hardly better than drinking straight from the sea. Alone in the vast Southern Ocean, the men's hope grew fainter every day.

"Well, Tim," Shackleton said as they huddled in the cockpit. "If you knew what we were in for, would you still have volunteered to come?"

"Especially if I knew," Tim laughed. "You see, I can't think of anyone I hate enough to wish this on instead."

× × ×

On Elephant Island, sleep was the only escape, but few slept solidly. They were so crowded that any man's movement could wake his neighbor. Orde Lees snored so loudly, the ground shook. Wild came up with the idea to rig a line all along the side of the hut, like the line you pull to signal a bus to stop. At night, they tied a piece of string to Orde Lees's hand and tied the other end to the line. Whoever was awakened by his snoring could pull the line and jiggle his hand. It usually did make him stop, but soon enough he rolled over and the rumbling would start up again. Perce never pulled the line. Partly he didn't care about the snoring since he couldn't sleep anyway, partly it was more interesting to listen and guess which of the others would be first that night to complain. Perce had many night games by now.

The best, and one everyone else surreptitiously shared, was listening to the piss can.

Since it was usually below zero with howling winds, going outside at night was a disagreeable task. This problem was solved by placing a two-gallon can by the entryway. The only condition was that whoever filled the can to within two inches of the top had to take it outside and empty it. This was even worse than just pissing outside. Soon enough, everyone learned to recognize the sound as the level rose in the can. When a man woke up and felt he had to go, he would lie in his sleeping bag, waiting for someone else to go first. If the can sounded too full, he would try to hold on until morning. There were other tricks as well. Some men could aim skillfully against the side of the can and make no noise. A man would get up and find the container too full even though he never heard anyone use it. This usually resulted in both cursing and laughter. It was annoying for the one stuck but generally respected by all as a good trick.

Perce had an old saucepan for his own use. After a couple of weeks, he was almost used to the embarrassment of being an invalid. But he would never get used to the smell of his own flesh rotting. The toes on his left foot were black and shriveled. Both feet were swollen and dark purple. Blisters had broken open and oozed pus. Awful as the thought was, Perce was starting to wish Doc would go ahead and amputate and get it over with.

× × ×

Tim lay in his wet sleeping bag on the bed of stones in the hull and tried to stop shaking. Worsley had just fallen asleep beside him, the first time in two days, and he didn't want to wake him. A gale roared on. The sound of the waves pounding the hull was like a drum inside his brain. For two days, they had sailed blindly through sleet and snow, steering only by the feel of the wind on their faces. It was mostly just four of them working now. Vincent had all but given up and lay belowdecks most of the time, crouched on his side, one arm over his head. McNeish's strength was crumbling, and he was barely able to move.

Up on deck, Shackleton's fur mitt was frozen to the tiller. Crean was sitting hunched beside him, the two trying in vain to shelter each other from the relentless wind, when Shackleton heard a strange sound behind him. He turned to look and saw a broad line of white across the horizon.

"Tom." He shook Crean and shouted in his ear. "Look there, the sky is clearing!"

Crean looked up and turned. Shackleton saw his face change rapidly from puzzlement to horror.

"No, Boss," Crean croaked. "That isn't a clearing at all."

"What do you mean?" The two men stared at the horizon. Then Shackleton realized the white line wasn't clear sky, but the foaming white crest of a gigantic wave. Not even a wave, but a giant wall of water, wide as the earth, high as Jupiter, rushing straight toward them. There was not a thing in the world they could do to escape it.

"For God's sake, hold on!" Shackleton shouted. "It's got us!"

The wave slammed into them. It lifted the boat up so violently, Shackleton was thrown into the cockpit. Crean grabbed the tiller and hung on for his life. The giant wave caught the little boat, surged completely over it, and tossed it like a cork.

Belowdecks, Tim was half asleep when the world crashed in around him. First he was thrown in the air, then slammed down hard on the rocks. Something smacked his head. His ribs crunched against the rocks; then his face was mashed against the canvas decking. He couldn't tell up from down. Rocks, boxes, and equipment flew everywhere. Then the water poured in. The boat was filling, and he was trapped! A body slammed into him. Tim grabbed for it. A hand grabbed back. It was Worsley. The water swirled over their heads. Something hit him hard in the ribs. Tim lost his breath and started to choke. Then hands caught hold of his jacket. He felt himself hauled up. Up into air. Shackleton dragged him out of the flooded hold.

Crean pulled Worsley free. Vincent lay dazed on the deck. Tim coughed and struggled for breath. The boom swung wildly, inches from his head. Something strangely warm ran down his face. He thought, quite absurdly, that it must be melted blubber. He saw Crean's face inches from his own, saw his lips moving but couldn't hear what he was saying. The warm drip ran down his face and into his eyes, and Tim realized it was blood. Then with a sudden rush, sound returned.

"Bail!" Crean shouted, and thrust a bucket into his hands. "Bail for your life!" Tim dragged himself to his knees. The cockpit was full of water. More water poured over the gunwales. The *James Caird* was flooded and sinking fast.

chapter thirty-five

May 8, 1916

I feel lucky in one way. I don't have to worry about how I might be—would I be slack and lazy or mope around like some. As bad as I feel, all I really have to do is keep quiet. Sometimes I feel like I'm invisible. I like that. I do long to go outside, though. I forget what fresh air is even like. This is like being in a dungeon. Back on the ship, I read a book called The Count of Monte Cristo. *Cracking good book. The count was in a dungeon for years. I think I don't have it so bad as that.*

Greenstreet's foot is getting better and probably will come through whole. But the frostbite on his face won't heal. A lot of men have sores that won't heal. On wrists where the cuff rubs or elbows, hips, knees. Anywhere that rubs against cloth. Because of lacking in our diet, says Doc. It isn't the scurvy, thank God. Just being weak. I have sores from lying the same way all day. Now Doc makes me turn different ways for a while.

The days passed slowly. It was dark by six now, so supper was at four-thirty. After that, the men unrolled their sleeping bags and settled in for the long night. A few blubber lamps were lit, but no one read much anymore. There was nothing new to read. Besides the encyclopedias, which were growing thinner every day, there was only a penny cookbook and a copy of a Shakespeare play called *Henry the Fifth*. Sometimes Hussey played his banjo. Sometimes they recited poems. Sometimes

Wild held debates. He usually chose ridiculous topics so no one could get into a real argument. If a man who was proportionally strong as an ant (which was, according to their biologist, Clark, very strong) was in a fight with a gorilla, who would win? What about a tiger? But sometimes the topic did get serious. They talked and wondered about the war. Who had won? What would Europe be like when they got home? Some thought the war could still be going on. Most thought that was ridiculous. It was almost two years.

"With the weapons we have now, the artillery and the tanks and airplanes dropping bombs, you couldn't go on with a war this long," Wild said. "All of Europe would be in rubble."

Hurley argued the opposite. "It's because everybody has so much firepower now means they're going to use it. If I build a new kind of bomb or U-boat or tank, I'm sure as hell going to want to use it." The debates went on and on. Anything to pass the time. Boredom put everyone on edge. Many just wanted to lie in their sleeping bags all day. When the weather was tolerable, Wild would drag them out, physically if he had to, and make them do something. But when everything was just too miserable to bear, he tried for some kind of relief. An extra half a nut bar, a cup of hot milk, or a lump of sugar.

Food was not yet a worry, but some of the men worried anyway. If there was bad weather or ice in the bay, penguins didn't come ashore. Orde Lees, always obsessed with the food situation, was becoming a maniac. He argued with Wild over everything. If Charlie served three penguin legs per man,

Orde Lees thought there should be two. He rationed the sugar so tightly, it would have lasted until Christmas. When Wild discovered this, he changed the ration to six lumps a day and decided to put someone else in charge of storekeeping.

"Well, that's very good," Orde Lees said. "Very nice indeed! I will be happy to give up such a huge responsibility! Now let someone else see how much work it requires to keep track of everything!" Then he went off to his corner and wrote with angry scratches in his journal for three hours. Orde Lees never ate all of his food at once but saved bits of it in a tin box to eat later. He cut his nut bar into pieces and ate one tiny piece each day. His bed was near Perce's, and Perce could hear him crunching on hoarded sugar cubes or chewing on the piece of nut bar late at night. Sometimes he just opened the tin and counted the pieces. He might do this ten times a night. It was kind of creepy, but Perce knew that every man made up his own way to deal with life out here.

"There's none of us quite right in the head by now," Macklin pointed out with generosity. "How could we be?" Still, the Old Lady was especially annoying.

"That's good in a way, though," Billy said. "When everybody hates one fellow, they don't go around messing with each other as much. And you know what's funny, the Old Lady doesn't seem to mind."

"Maybe he doesn't notice," Perce laughed. "He's too busy counting up the penguins and scheming how to trade for nut bars."

While no one was starving, they were always hungry and sick to death of meat. They generally had half a penguin per man per day, about a pound of meat each. It would keep them alive a long time but never satisfied. They craved the precious nut bars. Even the hard biscuits were more popular than another chunk of penguin or seal. The nut bars and sugar cubes were like gold nuggets. Everyone bargained and gambled for these. They would bet on how many penguins would come ashore during the week, whether a seal would be killed on an odd or even day, or how many chunks of ice would fall off the glacier that day.

"I'll give you half my penguin steak every day this week for your nut bar on Wednesday," Orde Lees offered Billy.

"Half my nut bar, maybe!" Billy scoffed.

"I'll let you cut the steak and choose the piece?"

"Half a bar plus two lumps of sugar," Billy countered. Orde Lees went off huffily in search of a better bargain. Sometimes he dealt in future portions: two seal steaks and one nut bar today for one piece of sugar every day until the rescue ship came. It could get very complicated.

They traded food for chores too. The only thing Orde Lees feared more than starving was having to work. When it was his day for chores, he traded someone half a penguin steak to take his place. As the days wore on, the tensions, quarrels, and conflicts settled into a routine until they seemed normal. It was like old married couples who have the same arguments every single day for fifty years.

Fifteen days had passed since Shackleton had gone. He could already have landed or very soon. Some insisted they would see a ship any day now.

× × ×

The *James Caird* was sinking fast. Tim felt the cold water rise up around his knees. The water crept over the cockpit and washed a pair of fur mitts off the deck. Tim didn't stop bailing long enough to grab them. They would have been nice to have because his hands were freezing cold. But if he stopped for even one second, they would all die. He saw Crean and Shackleton bailing as well, but still the boat kept sinking. Then Tim realized what was wrong. His bucket had no bottom.

"Boss! Boss! The bucket!" he shouted. Shackleton was covered in ice, frozen in place like a statue. The water swirled up around Tim's neck. Then with a final creak and groan, the *James Caird* drifted out from under him. Her bow tipped down, and she sank out of sight. Bubbles trailed up after her like pearls from a broken necklace. Tim struggled to stay afloat, but his clothes were dragging him down. Icy water closed over his head. Then, out of the dark water, he heard Shackleton's voice.

"Tim? Tim? Come on, lad, wake up now!"

Tim bolted up. His heart pounded. His whole body was shaking. He took a deep breath. He was on the boat. The boat was still floating. They were all still alive.

"Steady now—it's a dream you're in. Only that."

"Sweet Mary, mother of God," Tim gasped. He sat up, then recoiled. "Could you at least comb your hair before waking a man from the dead of sleep, Boss? You look like the bloody devil."

Shackleton ran his hand through his hair, trying to press down the oily mass that was indeed sticking up like horns.

"I'm sorry about that, Tim," he said with a weak laugh. "But come have some milk while it's hot."

Tim uncurled himself slowly. Since the monster wave hit, he could not sleep in the hold. Instead, he tucked himself up just inside the edge of the decking, where they did the cooking. It was much easier to escape from here. It was terribly uncomfortable, and he knew it wasn't even logical. If the boat sank, he would die just as fast, whether trapped belowdecks or free in the water. Still, he could not make himself crawl down there in the dungeon. His feet were numb, and he wiggled the toes until he felt the pins and needles that told him they weren't frostbitten. Shackleton handed him a cup of hot milk, and Tim took it gratefully.

"You were dreaming of the wave," Shackleton said.

"Aye."

They all had nightmares of the huge wave. They had gone through a hundred more dangers in the week since then, but none haunted them so badly. Tim took a sip of the warm, salty milk. The little bit of water they had left was so foul, they had to strain it through a piece of cloth before drinking. Even then, they were never sure if it was doing more harm than good. But the ration was only half a cup a day now, so it probably didn't matter much one way or another. Tim drank his down.

"I'll go spell Worsley," he said as he pulled his hat down.

"He's just gone out, but Crean would do with a break," Shackleton said. They had abandoned the structure of formal watches. With two men down all the time, the remaining four slept only in catnaps whenever one man could be spared.

Tim crawled out and unfolded his body into the cold wind. Standing up made him dizzy. His heart was still racing from the nightmare. He closed his eyes and held on to the mast until his head stopped whirling. When he opened his eyes again, Tim thought he was not just dizzy but hallucinating. He thought he saw a mountain. He blinked a few times, squeezed his eyes tight, then opened them again. It was still there.

"Land!" Tim cried. His voice cracked in his dry throat. He swallowed, then worked up every bit of spit he could and tried again. "Land! Land!" he shouted. This time everyone heard him. No one said anything, and Tim thought for a long, dreadful minute that it was only illusion. Then a break appeared in the clouds. They all saw it now, as clear as could be. The dot in the middle of the ocean was theirs. There were no hugs or handshakes. They simply stood there, staring at the prize, swaying with the motion of the little boat.

"Well, congratulations, Mr. Worsley," Shackleton said quietly. "That was a pretty fair bit of navigation."

chapter thirty-six

Macklin lifted up the blanket and slid the crate back from Perce's feet. He put two sardine can lamps on the crate and held another in his hand, but the light was still too weak for much of an examination. He tapped a finger lightly along the top of Perce's foot, feeling for the change that told him where the dead tissue began. Perce stared silently up at the thwarts of the overturned boat.

"The right foot's looking a little better," Doc Macklin said encouragingly. "How do they feel?"

"Fine."

"Tell me honestly, Perce."

"Honestly, Doc." Perce managed a weak smile. "However they might feel, what could you do about it?"

Bad enough they had to see him lying there day in and day out. At least with all the other stink in here, they probably didn't mind the rotten flesh all that much.

"I think it's about time, Perce," he said. "Maybe another week or so. I want to be sure there is a good separation between the live tissue and the dead." He felt Perce's forehead. The fever was no worse.

"How far up will you—cut?" Perce asked.

"Here—" Macklin gently drew his finger across Perce's foot, just above the blackened toes. "Hopefully at this joint where the toes join the foot. I won't know for sure until—until then. I may not be able to give you much notice either," Macklin explained. "We need a mild day so I can send all the others outside. And a warm day will make it easier to heat up the hut so the chloroform will vaporize. So I might just come to you one morning and tell you it's time. Would that be all right?"

"I'll try to keep my schedule open."

"There you go!" Macklin squeezed his shoulder. "And who knows, one more week and Boss could be back anyway. I wouldn't mind a proper operating room with a nurse or two around—what do you think?"

Perce thought about butchering penguins—the sound the knife made when it cut through a gristly joint.

× × ×

Two awful days later, South Georgia Island was still out of reach. A hurricane was raging and night was closing in. The ocean was like a horrible child unwilling to give up his toy.

"Make any landing!" Shackleton shouted in Worsley's ear. Worsley nodded. The whaling station was on the opposite side of the island, but there was no way the *James Caird* would make it that far. Another huge wave smashed over the side, knocking both men down. The sails flapped as the little boat lurched off the wind. Tim slid across the cockpit and slammed into Crean. With hardly a second's pause, they untangled themselves and resumed bailing as if nothing had happened. By now they were so numb and exhausted, they could not think or feel. Only move. Just keep moving.

Their little boat was falling to pieces. It was almost as bad as Tim's nightmare. The planks in the hull were beginning to splinter. The sails were torn, and the mast shook with the strain. The canvas decking was split in a dozen places.

There was no shelter now at all. They had to bail all the time.

Shackleton slid down into the cockpit and flung an arm around Tim's shoulders.

"Won't be long now!" he croaked encouragingly.

Tim nodded. "I'll keep her dry, then."

"A fine idea—why didn't we think of that sooner!" Shackleton laughed. They might as well try to empty the ocean. Shackleton took the bailing bucket from Crean. Even the Iron Man was looking frail right now, but Shackleton knew he would never rest, even if ordered. Distraction was the best he could offer. "Find us a landing, will you, Tom? You have the keenest eyes."

They had been at sea for seventeen days. They would not survive one more. No one but Vincent had slept in over thirty hours. The last of the brackish water was long gone, and they were all crazed with thirst. McNeish huddled in a corner, working the little hand pump with all the strength of a ninety-year-old grandmother.

Crean crawled up on the shattered remains of the decking and scanned the rocky coast. They had to land tonight or die of thirst. They didn't really know where they were, for this side of South Georgia was hardly mapped, and most of that by Captain Cook 150 years ago. The mountains that might have been landmarks were hidden in the clouds. Just like on Elephant Island, the coast was so rocky and the waves so rough, they might never get through at all.

Tim couldn't feel his arms or legs anymore. He no longer shivered. He felt nothing but a mild relief. He knew the long, cruel journey would end in the next few hours. One way or another. He didn't care anymore. He just wanted it over. They had done all they could. Even Shackleton's iron will couldn't blast a channel through the rocks.

× × ×

"Lash up and stow," Wild called out. "The Boss may come today!" The wake-up call didn't sound so reassuring these days. It was late May, and Shackleton had been gone for almost three weeks. Some of the men were starting to lose hope.

"Come on, who really thought he'd be back so soon!" Wild tried to reassure them.

"Once he gets to South Georgia, it might take a while to find a ship. He might have to go on to the Falkland Islands or even Chile. There aren't many ships that can handle the ice," he reminded them. "He might have to get the *Aurora* sent out from New Zealand. That alone would take a month. And she will have just come back herself, so she might need some repairs first."

Most of the men had forgotten entirely about their sister ship, *Aurora,* and the other half of the Imperial Trans-Antarctic Expedition. Wild would never forget, for his own brother was among them. The Ross Sea, on the other side of Antarctica, was easier to navigate, but there were still a thousand ways to get into trouble.

"It's a shame for them," Billy said. "Must have been hard work laying the supply depots and now for nothing."

"Shackleton could still come back and do the crossing," Perce offered optimistically. "Sledging rations won't go bad, after all."

"Because they start out bad!" Billy laughed. "But really, it would take years to put together a new expedition. He'd never be able to find the depots after all that time."

"He could," Wild said. "They'll be well marked."

"How?" Perce asked.

"Snow cairns ten feet high built out from both sides of the depot," Wild explained. "Like a line of pawns on the chessboard. Even if the tracks are gone or the men are off course, they'll find the depots. My brother knows what he's doing there."

Perce studied Wild's face and saw that the man still guarded Shackleton's dream in his own heart.

× × ×

Tim woke up with an oar in his hands. That was strange. He didn't remember rowing. Then he felt the crunch of rocks against the wooden bottom of the boat. The boat jolted, and he bumped against Crean. Everyone was silent. No one moved.

"All right! Come on, then," Shackleton said. Tim turned, puzzled. Shackleton was standing behind him. Standing on a beach.

"Go on, Tim," Worsley whispered. "We're in the surf." Tim nodded dully. But for some reason, he couldn't remember how to get out of a boat. Worsley put a hand under Tim's knee and lifted one leg over the side. Then Worsley heaved him up and Tim tumbled over. Somehow he crawled a few feet up the beach. Crean was on his feet now, but barely. He leaned on Shackleton, both reeling. Tim crawled another few feet, then collapsed flat on the beach. He felt cold stones against his belly, cold stones against his cheek. He smelled grass and dirt. Suddenly everything was real again.

"Oh, Jesus, Boss! Did we land on something?"

"Aye. Something all right."

"You bleeding dimwit, we made it!" Crean cackled. Worsley, McNeish, and Vincent staggered out now, and all six tried to pull the *James Caird* farther up the beach. They managed only a few inches, then a big wave pushed the boat up a few feet, tumbling the men like bowling pins.

"Leave it," Shackleton gasped. "I hear water." The six men crawled and stumbled across the beach and found water pouring out from the rocks. They pressed around the tiny stream, drinking the cold, sweet water. Tim had never tasted anything so good in all his life.

chapter thirty-seven

"What shall we do when we get out of here?" Billy said, settling down on a crate beside Perce. "What do you think we should do first?"

Perce groaned to himself. They had this conversation almost every day now. It was almost like a play with a script they both knew by heart. It was fun at first, making up stories, but now it seemed stupid. He didn't really feel like playing anymore. *Why can't Billy just go away and leave me alone?*

"When we get home?" Perce took a deep breath and sat up a little more. "Well, first of all, we'll eat for a month without stopping. We'll have raspberries and cream, cake and cream, cream and cream," he said wearily.

"Yes." Billy closed his eyes, smiled, and sighed contentedly. *How can I even think like that?* Perce chided himself. A little fantasy was the smallest thing anyone could ask out here. And hadn't Billy kept him going more times than he could even count?

"Then we'll have cake again and chocolate bars," Perce said with more enthusiasm. He went on through every dish he had ever tasted or heard of. They would eat bread and butter, sweet peas from the garden, and fresh pineapples. Neither had ever seen a pineapple, but Worsley ate them all the time in the South Pacific and said they were very good.

"After we've eaten for a fortnight, we'll go off and see some more of the world." Perce moved on to the next scene.

"Where will we go?" Billy said his part.

"China first, and then Africa."

"I'd like to see China," Billy agreed. They had the usual talk of China. This part could last twenty minutes. The food they would eat there, walking on the Great Wall.

"I hear the Chinese girls are beautiful," Billy sighed.

"But not as lovely as my Welsh girl back home." And here Perce had to tell Billy all about his sweetheart. But it was getting harder and harder to remember what Anna looked like. It was hard to remember what *any* girls looked like.

"She has a beautiful smile and a laugh like music," he said. "And every day she wears a different-colored ribbon in her hair."

They went on with the fantasy: sailing to Africa and going on a safari, visiting those Masai, who drank blood out of the necks of their cows. They both agreed they probably wouldn't try that.

"And then? When you're done with the world? What'll you do, then?" Billy asked.

"When I'm done with the world, I'll go home and marry my girl. I'll buy a snug little house with a garden in the back."

"And what will you have in the garden?"

"Strawberries and flowers. And chickens."

Billy frowned. "What chickens? You never said chickens before."

"Well, now I think I'd like chickens." Perce was surprised. He thought Billy would enjoy a little embellishment in the imaginary garden. "What's wrong with that?"

"Nothing, I suppose." Billy looked sulky.

"Wouldn't you like a nice fried egg?"

"Yes, in butter, with the edges crisp." This idea brought

Billy around. "Okay, chickens, then," he said, back to his cheerful self. "What else?"

"I'll have two nice comfortable chairs right in front of the stove for me and my wife. And a pretty little hearth rug there, and buy a new one every Christmas so it never looks tatty."

Billy liked this part. Perce went on describing his house. There was a shelf full of books and a gramophone. Curtains on the windows, new dresses for his wife, good shoes and plenty of chocolate and toffee for his children. Finally Perce could think of no more for the fantasy. "And we all live happily ever after," he ended.

"Aye," Billy said. He looked away. The dark had come. Wild lit the blubber lamps. The weak flames cast a cruel glow on reality. Filthy, ragged men huddled together against the cold, balanced on the last thin edge of hope.

× × ×

Tim tottered out from the cave and squinted at the morning. It wasn't a real cave, just a rock overhang, with giant icicles for a front wall, but it was shelter enough last night. The beach was fringed with grass. Real grass! It was the first living plant he had seen since they were on this same island waiting for the ice to break up in the Weddell Sea. Eighteen months ago—it felt like a lifetime. He walked clumsily down to the beach, where Crean was sitting by a roaring driftwood fire. Crean handed him a mug.

"Cheers."

"It's scalding," Crean warned. "Watch out."

Tim took a cautious sip. For the first time in a week, the milk wasn't salty. Crean had made a little cooking ring of stones on the edge of the fire. He raked some coals into it with a piece of driftwood, then put the pot on top. He dropped in a lump of seal blubber. When the fat began to sizzle, he threw in what looked like two little chickens.

"What are those?" Tim asked.

"These? Why, they're South Georgia pheasants." Crean grinned wickedly. Tim looked around the beach, then up on the nearby cliffs, where dozens of albatross mothers sat on their nests. Killing an albatross was taboo for a sailor, but the sizzling meat smelled delicious. "It's just the chicks," Crean explained. "We've decided the bad luck doesn't come till they're fully grown."

"And if it does come, how would we know it from the regular bad luck anyway?" Tim laughed. They saw Shackleton climbing down the little bluff.

"What's he doing off on a hike first thing in the morning?" Tim said. "I can barely walk."

"Scouting," Crean said simply. Shackleton stiffly eased himself down beside them and held his hands out to warm by the fire.

"Good morning, Tim, did you sleep well?"

"Never better," Tim replied. He didn't ask Shackleton how he slept. They had all been awakened by his shouts from the nightmares.

"I thought we might have another try at the boat after breakfast," Shackleton said. The battered *James Caird* bobbed slowly in the water, half full of water. They hadn't strength enough to pull it up on the beach last night. The mast had fallen; the rudder was gone. "If we cut the decking off and knock down the gunwales, it might lighten her enough."

"Are there nails enough to put it all back together, then?" Tim asked. Shackleton paused, then chose his words carefully, like a doctor delivering bad news.

"She's not sailing anywhere else, Tim. I'm afraid the best we can expect from the *James Caird* now is a bit of shelter here on the beach. Crean and I have been talking. We're going to hike across. Worsley too if he's fit enough."

"Hike across the island?"

"That's where the whaling station is."

"But it's all mountains, Boss! And we don't have a map."

"I didn't have a map to the South Pole either." Shackleton smiled wearily. "And the mountains aren't so high. They just look bad."

"There's all this driftwood, though," Tim said. "McNeish could shore up the *James Caird*."

"It's a hundred and fifty miles around by sea," Shackleton said. "And bad sea all the way. We might patch the *Caird* up. We might even make a new rudder, but we can't exactly weave new sails out of grass. There isn't another way. It's across or nothing."

"Then I'll go with you, Boss. I'll be fit in a day or two."

"I've no doubt, Tim. But I need someone to stay and look after McNeish and Vincent. Worsley has done some climbing in New Zealand."

"They'll do all right for a few days here alone," Tim protested. "We'll make a snug shelter, gather lots of wood and seal meat—they'll do fine."

"Tim, my friend," Shackleton interrupted. "You know it might be more than a few days." He looked Tim straight in the eye. Tim didn't want to see the truth in his gaze. He looked away, but there was more terrible truth in those mountains.

"Men could live here for months if they had their wits about them," Shackleton went on. "You're the only one with wits to spare. Come summer, a whaler might pass near enough to see a signal fire. It isn't just the three of you either. It's possible . . ." Shackleton's voice broke. He looked down and struggled to compose himself. "It's possible the others could hold out too."

Tim understood. Shackleton, the supreme optimist, was also a realist. If there was a way across the island, he would find it. If not, he would die trying.

"Aye." Tim nodded. "I'll stay, then."

chapter thirty-eight

June 15 was a mild warm day, with the temperature in the low thirties. Doc Macklin came and sat on the crate by Perce's bed. Perce knew by his face what he had come to tell him.

"I don't want to wait any longer, Perce," Macklin said gravely. "It seems a good day; what do you think?"

"Good as any," Perce said. Shackleton had been gone almost two months. There wasn't going to be any nice clean operating room. The news spread through the hut, in the hushed way bad news does. The other men pulled their boots on and crawled out one by one. Some stopped to wish Perce good luck, some tried to pretend nothing was happening. Billy and Wild pulled the crates together for an operating table. Hurley began to stoke the fire. Wild would assist Macklin with the operation. He had no medical training, but they all knew Wild could be counted on to do whatever needed to be done. Once the hut was ready, Billy came over. Perce was writing in his journal.

"Are you taking back all the bad things you've written about me there?"

"I haven't enough pages left for that." Perce put the pencil down.

"Perce." Billy looked down at the ground. "I want you to know I'd do anything for you in the crunch."

"Aye. I do know. And you have already. A hundred times over."

"But—well." Billy looked up, saw the operating table,

and quickly looked back at the floor. "Well, would you mind if I didn't stay here for the—operation?"

"Good Lord, Billy!" Perce forced a laugh, though he wanted to cry. What a good friend he had in Billy. "Why would I want you in here crowding my operation? I'm going to sleep through it anyway. And what would you do? You don't even have the *S* encyclopedia anymore, so you can't look up *surgery* or *A* for *amputation.*"

Billy smiled with relief. "Well, I thought I might hold your hand and say, *'There, there'* and *'Poor little thing.'*"

"And look at you! You haven't had a bath in a year," Perce went on. "Get your stinking self out with the others."

"Thanks, mate! I'll see you soon, then."

Hurley began to light the blubber lamps. Macklin took off layers of filthy clothes until he wore only an undershirt. He dipped some warm water out of the pot and began to scrub his hands with a tiny sliver of soap.

"Water's boiling," Hurley said. Macklin dropped the instruments into the pot. The clink of metal gave Perce a sick feeling.

"Are you ready, then?" Macklin asked.

"Yes, sir," Perce said quietly. Macklin looked around at all the flickering lights and the roaring stove, then at the little bottle of chloroform. If he worked quickly, there should be enough. Hurley and Wild carried Perce over to the table. It was covered only with a thin blanket, and the boards were hard against his bones. His feet hung over the edge. Wild tucked a sweater under his head for a pillow. Hurley fished the sterilized instruments out of the pot with a piece of wire.

Macklin carefully unscrewed the lid on the bottle of chloroform. This was actually the trickiest part of the operation. Too much chloroform could kill Perce. Excess vapors in the air could ignite from the open flame and set them all on fire. He poured a few drops on a piece of gauze and held it over Perce's face.

"Just close your eyes and breathe deep," Macklin said.

The vapors smelled sweet. Perce felt dizzy and a little bit panicked. He grabbed the sides of the crates. He felt Wild's hands on his chest and heard Macklin's soothing voice.

"It's all right; just go to sleep now. . . ." Perce remembered nothing more.

Macklin picked up the scalpel. Then he put it down again and took a deep breath.

"You all right, mate?" Hurley asked.

"All right?" Macklin wiped sweat off his forehead with the cleanest bit of his discarded shirt. "This was my first posting, you know, straight out of medical school. Now I'm on a godforsaken island in the frozen middle of nowhere, crouched under a boat, about to do practically the first surgery I've ever done in my life, with little more than a scalpel and tin snips."

Wild and Hurley looked at each other, then back to Macklin.

"Well, good luck, then," Wild said calmly.

Billy climbed as high as he could up the cliff and sat on a rock. He could hear the other men laughing and talking in the ice cave below. They were cutting each other's hair. Thick black smoke poured out from the chimney of the hut below. The bay was full of pack ice, and a dense fog hung low over the water. There would be no rescue today. Not unless a spaceship landed from Mars. And they would have to be pretty stupid Martians to land in a place like this.

Macklin picked up the scalpel and lightly made a cut across the top of Perce's foot. The hut was silent except for the sizzle of the penguin skins. He peeled the skin back and cut away the dead flesh until the joints were exposed.

"Can you give me more light?" he asked Hurley. Hurley tried to maneuver one of the sardine can lights close enough to shed light without risk of dripping blubber into the open wound. "Good," Macklin whispered. He picked up the tin snips and cut neatly through the joints. The toes fell one by one with a dull clink into a can. Wild watched without flinching. Macklin went on cutting and scraping until only healthy tissue remained. Then he cut away the excess flap of skin, trimmed the edges, and neatly sewed up what was left of Perce's foot. The whole operation had taken just under an hour.

Billy watched an albatross soaring along the edge of the island. Maybe he could make some wings out of penguin feathers and fly away like Icarus. No chance of melting in the sun down here. He looked down on the hut, but there was still no sign of anyone coming or going. Wild would call for them when the operation was over. Billy stared out into the fog but couldn't see more than a hundred yards. He certainly couldn't see eighteen miles offshore, where a small ship crept slowly along the edge of the pack ice. He couldn't see the small, forlorn figure of a man standing on the bow, binoculars pressed to his eyes, desperately looking.

× × ×

"Boss." Crean came up beside Shackleton and touched his arm. Shackleton slowly put the binoculars down. He had pressed them so hard against his face, they left deep red rings around his eyes. But no matter how long and hard he looked, he could not see anything except the tallest peaks of Elephant Island sticking up out of the clouds. It was only eighteen miles away, but it might as well be a thousand. They could not get through the ice.

"Captain says we can't stay any longer," Crean said gently. "It's time to turn the ship around."

"Yes. Of course. I just hoped to see something. A bit of smoke." Shackleton cleared his throat. "Please tell the captain to go ahead. I'll come down in a minute."

Twenty-five days ago, when they had staggered into the Stromness whaling station, the rescue seemed so close, he could smell it. He had sailed the impossible ocean, crossed the forbidding mountains, and conquered a thousand devils—all that was left was to find a ship and return to Elephant Island. This was his second attempt and his second failure. The ice was crushing his hopes as surely as it crushed his ship.

"They'll be fine, Boss." Crean spoke as if reassuring a child. "We'll find another ship; we'll make another try." For twenty months he had been by Shackleton's side through every danger and hardship and never seen him as despondent as this. "Our boys are strong, you know. And our Frankie's there. What could go wrong with Frank Wild around?"

Shackleton just nodded. What could go wrong was madness, violence, death from starvation or despair. A hurricane washing away the fragile shelter. Ice fall from the glacier crushing them. But there would be no rescue today. The little ship he had borrowed was running out of coal. There was only three days' supply left. They had to turn back.

"Tell the captain I'm going to fire a few shots," Shackleton said. "Perhaps they'll hear and at least know we're alive and coming for them." Crean went below with the message.

× × ×

Perce woke slowly. His head ached, and he felt sick to his stomach. His foot felt heavy with the bandages.

"How are you, Perce? All right?" Macklin smiled.

"Never better," Perce replied. "Though I'd dearly like a cigarette."

"You know smoking is bad for you, lad!"

"It's Antarctica that's bad for me, Doc!"

Macklin laughed. "Oh, well, then, has anyone got any tobacco left?"

"A bit," Wild replied. "But I'll have to take a page from your encyclopedia to roll it in. What would you like to smoke, Perce?" He opened the encyclopedia. "Linotype? Lemurs of Madagascar? Poland?"

"How about Polar Exploration?"

Perce tried to sit up, but his head was spinning too much. Everything felt queer—all his senses turned up loud but only noticing one thing at a time. He could hear the stove door clattering but not what anyone was saying, or he heard words but no other sound. Then the words faded away, and he heard a crack, like fat popping in the fire.

"Is the fire all right?" he asked worriedly. "It's snapping so."

"Fire's gone out," Hurley said.

"I heard something. A cracking sound," Perce insisted. "Like a gunshot."

"It's probably ice falling off the glacier," Wild reassured him. Ice was always breaking off, and it sounded just like gunshots. Then they all heard it. Macklin crawled outside, still in his undershirt. The sweat on his forehead quickly vanished. His neck was cramped, and his legs trembled. He looked up at the glacier but didn't see any chunks falling or the white plume that indicated an avalanche. Hurley came out and stood beside him. The two men stared out into the fog.

"Probably just floes crashing in the bay," he said. "It sure is thick again."

"Aye." They stood listening for several minutes but heard nothing else. Macklin shivered, then crawled back inside to tend to his patient.

× × ×

Shackleton looked out the window and watched the wake carve a foamy arc through the dark sea as the ship turned around. The mountains of Elephant Island quickly faded out of sight, shrouded in the fog.

"Have another, Tom," Shackleton said despondently as he picked up the bottle of whiskey.

"I've had enough, Boss," Crean replied gently as he took the bottle away.

"It's all right, Tom. We've nothing to do now," Shackleton protested mildly. "Just ride along." If the weather was fair, it would be a three-day trip back to the Falkland Islands.

"Will you eat something now?" Tom asked. "Whiskey isn't good on your stomach like this."

Shackleton shook his head. He was too upset to eat. How odd that was! When they had stumbled into the whaling station on South Georgia Island, he thought he would do nothing but eat for a year. Now he could not take a bite of the sandwich on his plate. The very sight of the soft white bread was a physical pain as long as his men were still stranded. He lifted his glass and drained the last drops of whiskey. He looked around the empty table.

"Tom, have you taken away my only solace?"

"Aye."

"You're a rotten friend."

"Aye."

A steward came in with a pot of tea, and Crean poured a cup for Shackleton. His hand shook as he picked up the teacup.

"We'll find another ship," Crean said reassuringly. "Somewhere, Buenos Aires, Montevideo—we'll have another go. You know what they say, Boss, third time lucky."

"The ice—"

"The ice comes and the ice goes."

"I can't—"

"Boss—" Crean interrupted sharply. "You wouldn't let any man under you talk like this, so I won't have it now. You're sounding like the Old Lady. Drink your tea and go on to bed."

× × ×

That same night, aboard a ship bound for England, Tim was also sleepless. He couldn't stay in his bunk. He had strange spells where it seemed unbearably hot and he couldn't breathe. His heart raced, and he felt trapped. It was very odd. For nearly two years when he should have been afraid every day, he wasn't. Now, for no reason at all, when he was perfectly safe and going home, every little thing made him jump.

He felt out of place and very alone. He was sailing back to England with Vincent and McNeish, but they had never been good friends like Billy and Perce. Vincent and McNeish played cards and joked in the mess room with the other sailors, but Tim stayed to himself. Sometimes it seemed like nothing was real, like he had forgotten how to be a person. He missed his friends. The world was upside down. The war was still raging, and it was like no other war in history. The Germans were using poison gas on the battlefield. Millions were dead. It was ridiculous, but he found he was longing for the days when they were camped on the ice floe. Life was so simple then. All you had to do every day was stay alive.

chapter thirty-nine

"Lash up and stow. . . ."

Nine weeks had passed on Elephant Island. Every day Wild's wake-up call sounded more hopeless. Half the men paid no attention. They didn't even stir in their sleeping bags. Wild didn't press them. Each day was a struggle against despair. Every night they crawled into bed thinner, colder, and more despondent than ever. The boredom was crushing, and some of the men were barely holding on to sanity. Orde Lees challenged Doc Macklin to a duel over some petty offense. Broken oars on the beach at sunrise.

They had not killed a seal for two weeks. Penguins were scarce too. If the bay was full of ice, they couldn't come ashore. Sometimes five or six days passed with none at all. There was enough meat stockpiled for a month at least, but it was a painful way to last. There were still two cases of biscuits and two of sledging rations, but the precious nut bars and milk powder were gone. There weren't enough skins to keep the fire going all day, so Charlie could only cook in the morning. The evening meal was cold penguin hoosh.

July 1, 1916

I never knew what it was like to really be hungry before. There were times I thought I was: times Mum would thin out the soup to make it go around, times there was only bread or porridge for supper, but we never starved. This is like your whole body is caving in. Like everything inside you has grown sharp edges.

You feel a little bit crazy too. Shaky and nervous and like crying. We have a penny cookbook, and every night someone takes a turn at reading a recipe out loud. It's like church service. We've heard them all ten times or more by now but still listen. My favorite is plum pudding because the recipe is very long. I would actually rather eat an apple pie, but the recipe doesn't have many ingredients: apples, sugar, piecrust. Plum pudding has nineteen ingredients and many lines of directions. After we read, we talk about the recipe. How we might change a thing or two. Would it be good with custard or cream. (Everything would be good with custard or cream!)

One night we went around and named the one food we would have if we could have anything at all. Hurley wanted cream horns. Clark named sweet dumplings with cream. Almost everyone longed for sweets: apple pudding, doughnuts with syrup, blackberry tart. But Doc wanted scrambled eggs on buttered toast, and Billy asked for baked pork and beans. When it came my turn, all I could think of was bread and butter. Endless slices of warm white bread and sweet butter. But soon, any day . . .

Perce dropped the pencil. It was only a stub now and hard to hold. It was too dark to see, so he felt around for it. All he felt was stones. Just as well. Writing made him tired. He felt sick again. A different kind of sick. His feet didn't hurt so much, but he ached all over. He was hot even as he shook with chills. He was thirsty, but it was too much trouble to ask for a drink of water. His notebook slipped off his lap. He could write more later. There was always plenty of time for that. Maybe he would sleep. That would be so nice. Just to go to sleep and not wake up again.

× × ×

Halfway back to the Falklands, Crean saw the old Shackleton come back to life.

"We'll go to Chile for a new ship." His eyes sparkled again; his voice was confident. He had a plan. "There's a British community in Punta Arenas. Sheep ranchers mostly, but there's money there." He paced the small wardroom. "We can't count on any help from England. Even if they do decide to send a ship, it will take too long to get here."

In a series of stern telegrams, the British government had made it clear that it had more important things to do with its ships during wartime than rescue a bunch of wayward explorers mucking around the South Pole. No ship could leave England for a month at least. Then it could take up to another month to reach Chile. If Shackleton were to save his men before that, he would have to come up with his own ship.

"There must be something we can charter in South America. I can raise the money," Shackleton explained. "Lecture, you know? I'm a bit rusty, but God knows I've had enough experience. We go around to their parties, be charming, and give talks about the expedition."

"We?" Crean frowned. "What do you mean, we? Do you see me chatting up the swells at a fancy party? You're daft now, Boss."

"Oh, Tom, you won't have to talk. You just stand there and look the part. Who looks the part more! Better if you don't talk. I'll tell them how the iron pike bent around you—there's a fine story." Shackleton lit another cigarette and went on, talking rapidly. "You'll see. People want a taste of it. We get them all stirred up for adventure. Tell about our boys rowing day and night even as the sea froze around them!"

Crean was glad to see the Boss shake off his depression, but he had not seen this side of Shackleton before. He sounded like a sideshow barker.

"I'll get us another ship. By God, I will if I have to steal it and shanghai a crew. Will you come, then, Tom?"

"If you steal a ship?" Crean leaned back in his chair as if deep in thought. "Well, if she's a good ship, I might."

The *Emma* was not a good ship, but they didn't have to steal her either. Shackleton was indeed a success at fund-raising. The British community in Punta Arenas welcomed him with open arms. Shackleton took Worsley and Crean around to an endless assortment of dinners, luncheons, and teas.

"Aw, not more bloody champagne!" Crean growled. The dainty little glass always looked comical in his big, rough hands. "Damn froggy fizz. Don't the swells ever drink a good pint?" But Shackleton was true to his word and did most of the talking. Crean just had to stand around looking like an explorer. He was starting to get a little flesh back on his big bones, so he was convincing. Shackleton did have some magic about him when he gave his talks. People listened to every word. Women wept. Men opened their checkbooks.

In no time he raised fifteen hundred pounds. There was little choice of what to spend it on, however. Few ships were built to work in the ice. Fewer shipowners wanted to take the risk. Finally they found the *Emma*. She was built of wood, but otherwise a terrible vessel for an Antarctic voyage. She was a small schooner, only seventy feet long, and depended almost entirely on sail. There were many yachtsmen who wouldn't trust her to cross the English Channel. She had a light diesel engine, but it wasn't built for long voyages. And diesel engines were so new that it was hard to find an engineer who could repair them. Shackleton scratched together a crew of six, and on July 12, he set off with Crean and Worsley on the third attempt to rescue his men.

Storms hit the second day out and never stopped. One horrible week later, *Emma*'s engines were dead and her sails torn. Heavy layers of ice snapped spars and rigging. Half the crew was too seasick to stand. They were still over a hundred miles from Elephant Island when the pack ice threatened to trap them fast. Once more, Shackleton had to turn around.

He had no time for despair on this return. The *Emma* was in constant danger. For two weeks, they fought simply to keep her afloat. They had thirty-foot waves and almost constant gales. With only nine men aboard, it took everyone's energy just to keep her floating. Once again, Shackleton, Crean, and Worsley were on a desperate voyage. No one slept for days at a time. They rarely had a hot meal. When they finally arrived back in port, Shackleton's hair was streaked with gray. He could barely walk. Crean had to help him ashore like an old man.

× × ×

"Lash up and stow, for the Boss may come today."

"Oh, shut up," someone muttered from a dark corner of the hut.

August 19, 1916

Billy is restless these days. Hurley as well. They can't stand to be inside the hut. I don't even think about it anymore. It seems that I have always been here and always will be, on a bed of rocks in the dark and cold. They are hammering bent nails on a rock outside. I can hear. The plan is to fix up the Dudley Docker *and send another party out for help. It is four months since Shackleton left. They will sail out closer to the whaling grounds and hope to see a ship. It is impossible, and everyone knows it. All the best bits of the three boats already went into the* James Caird. *There isn't a scrap of sail left or a mast to hang it on. There are only five oars and no canvas for decking. No compass, no sextant, or navigational tables. Nothing to carry water in.*

But I want them to go. It is better that way. Some are talking now. . . .

Perce scratched out those last words. What was he doing? He couldn't write that down! He shivered. It was so hard to keep his mind focused. But he certainly would never write that down. He shut the journal and tried to calm himself.

"Hey!" Billy suddenly squatted by his bed. "Look at these!" Billy shook a can, then reached in and pulled out a flat shell. It was about the size of a bottle cap. "They're called limpets. They're all over the rocks now that the ice is melting back. Charlie's going to make us a bully-base. That's French for fish soup, you know."

Perce stared at Billy. His face seemed underwater. His voice was far away.

"Perce? Are you all right?" Billy felt Perce's forehead. "Your fever's up again." He looked around for Macklin, but most of the men were outside.

"Look here," Billy went on with forced cheerfulness. "Something new to eat. We got them off the rocks. There's loads and loads."

Perce felt even more confused. There was a strong fishy smell from the can. He tried to focus; there was something urgent he had to tell—oh, yes—he remembered.

"You need to go away, Billy." It was such an effort to talk, but he had to warn Billy. "You need to leave."

"Of course I need to leave." Billy frowned. "We all do! What's wrong, Perce? You're acting strange."

"They were talking—" Perce dropped his voice to a whisper. "Some were talking."

"Who was talking?"

Perce grabbed Billy's arm. He tried to pull himself up but was too weak. Still, his grip was tight from fear.

"They want to draw lots. They talked of drawing lots! This morning. After Wild went outside. I heard them."

"Oh, Perce! What are you talking about?" Billy laughed uneasily. "Come on, you were dreaming."

"No. I heard them."

"How many times have we joked about that? Oh,

Greenstreet, you're the sweetest one, so you'll go first. Or wouldn't the Old Lady taste good with a little curry and sweet relish."

"It isn't a joke."

"Or what if we just cut one leg off each one at a time, and do you think a man could eat his own leg. . . ?"

"They're serious now."

"They're not serious!" Billy yanked his arm away "Shut up. I'm going to get Doc. I don't think you're well."

chapter forty

The *Yelcho* was the most unsuitable boat yet.

"Achhh, Boss, you can't be serious." Crean frowned when he saw her. "She's a tugboat!"

Tugboats were not even designed for open seas, let alone the most stormy seas on the planet. They were meant for towing bigger ships through harbors. No metal ship was good for ice, but the *Yelcho* was particularly bad. Ancient paint peeled off her dented hull. She was rusty from bow to stern. The engines chugged and wheezed. The boilers made alarming noises. She was the worst possible choice.

"She's the only choice left," Shackleton pointed out. "And I had to beg to get her."

While the British government was stalling about sending a ship, the Chilean people were eager to help. They had come to love Ernest Shackleton. Everyone in Punta Arenas had fallen under his spell. They thought of the stranded men as their own brothers and sons. So after receiving Shackleton's solemn promise not to take the *Yelcho* close to any pack ice, the government agreed. The *Yelcho*'s regular captain, Luis Pardo, offered to command. Sailors from the Chilean navy rushed to volunteer as crew. On August 25, with Crean and Worsley still at his side, Shackleton sailed south once again for a fourth attempt at rescue.

× × ×

Billy stood outside the hut, waiting for Macklin to come out. When he did, his face told little. They walked down the spit, heads bent into the wind until they were out of earshot.

"So what's the matter? Is he very bad?" Billy asked. Macklin hesitated.

"The wound has gone septic."

"Blood poisoning?"

"I'm afraid so."

"How bad is that?"

"We'll have to wait and see."

"Would that make him delirious?" Billy asked. "He was talking all crazy." Billy picked up one of the smooth stones and rubbed it nervously. It was a habit he had started now that there was no pipe to smoke.

"What do you mean, crazy?" Macklin frowned.

"He said some of the men were talking. Talking about drawing lots." Billy didn't look at Macklin, reluctant to say any more, as if speaking the idea were devil enough. "You know how we've all joked about it. But now, after so long and so little food left . . ." Billy dropped his voice so his words were almost lost in the wind. "It's happened before. In America, there's a terrible story of these pioneers called the Donner Party. They got trapped in the Rocky Mountains over one bad winter and half of them ate the others."

"I've heard of that." Macklin sighed and pulled his worn coat tighter around his neck. "It won't happen here, Billy. Wild wouldn't let it. I wouldn't let it, nor would you or Hurley or most anyone else. And the penguins will be back any day now anyway."

Neither offered the suggestion that Shackleton would come. Few really believed that anymore.

"It's a few men with too much time to fret talking that way. Though I'd like to smack the sod who talks like that around a sick man," Macklin said with disgust. "Besides, it isn't even practical! Take the fattest man among us and you might get two days' worth of meat at best. Stringy meat at that. No fat to any of us. And without blubber or penguin skins, how are you going to cook the poor bugger anyway? It's one thing to eat your mate all nicely stewed; it's quite another to gnaw on him raw."

Billy stepped back, his eyes widening. Macklin gave a short laugh. "Oh, probably not the sort of thing you like to hear your doctor say." He took a deep breath and steadied himself against the wind. "Look, Billy, we may have become savages, but we're not stupid. And the larder isn't empty yet by far. We have biscuits and penguin for another week at least. It's only the weather keeping them away, and that has to turn soon. Remember, just two weeks ago there were seals and penguins all over the place!"

It was true. In just one week they had killed three seals and ninety-three penguins. Then the ice came back to choke the bay, the weather turned bad, and all wildlife vanished.

"Think of how many times we've been down to the wire and a seal shows up. We haven't come this far to fall apart now. Perce heard some idle talk, that's all. We're all of us a bit crazy, and the fever makes it worse for him. I'll talk to Wild."

× × ×

The sea was calm, the wind good. After four days, the *Yelcho*'s engines were still chugging along well. Most importantly, there was no ice. They saw the occasional bergs, but the dreaded pack ice that had surrounded Elephant Island was gone.

"What did you do, Boss?" Crean joked. "Light a hundred candles or sacrifice a virgin?"

"Sixty miles to go, Boss," Worsley said, making no effort to control his excitement. "And no pack in sight. Finally some good luck."

"Luck? Ah, you know what good luck is?" Shackleton said with a note of bitterness in his voice. "It's being too bloody stubborn to die through all the bad luck that's come first."

× × ×

"He can't die," Wild said. "Not now." Frank Wild's voice caught in his throat. He turned into the wind and rubbed his face. "After all we've been through?"

Doc Macklin said nothing. He could give Wild a medical answer—that Perce's body simply could not keep fighting the infection much longer—but Wild was not asking a medical question. He was asking the question of all men in all horrible times: God—why? Macklin had no answer for that.

"I'm sorry," Wild sighed. "I know you're doing everything you can." The two men sat on some rocks at the far end of the spit. It was a rare sunny day, and with most of the men out walking, that was the only place to talk privately.

"Are you sleeping at all these days, Frank?" Macklin asked.

"I must be, for I keep waking up in this godforsaken place."

"How do you do it? How do you make your mind go quiet? Do you have some trick?"

Wild smiled and looked a little embarrassed. "I paint icebergs. I tried counting sheep, but they kept turning into juicy chops. Now I picture myself on a ladder with a bucket of paint, like I'm painting a house, only it's a great huge iceberg. I dip the brush and paint in these long, slow strokes. The color runs down the ice. It's really quite lovely. I work my way through the spectrum. Start with ultraviolet, you know, then purple, blue. I'm not sure I get them in the right order, but if I'm lucky, I fall asleep by orange or yellow."

The trick was not working much lately. The only color he could see was red. *Keep them alive.* That was all Shackleton had asked of him. Wild's hands began to shake. He tucked them under his arms so Macklin wouldn't notice.

"Doc," Wild whispered, staring out to sea. "Doc, we can't even dig a grave out here."

chapter forty-one

The fog dropped suddenly at midnight. It swallowed the *Yelcho* like a python swallowing a rat. Captain Pardo stood beside Shackleton on the bridge. Neither said anything for a long time. It would be dangerous to keep going when they couldn't see. No ship should sail in a fog this thick when there could be icebergs around, let alone a little metal tugboat. The memory of the *Titanic* was still fresh. But the pack ice could close in again anytime. The decision was Captain Pardo's to make, but Shackleton couldn't help pressing his case.

"We haven't seen any icebergs for a while, Captain Pardo," he said casually. "What do you think about going on?"

"I think I would be very irresponsible to do that, sir," Pardo said gravely. Shackleton tensed. "However, I wrote a letter to my father before I left on this voyage. I told him I would come back with your men and there would be a great party. Or I would not come back at all, and there would be a great funeral. Either way, they will have plenty to eat and drink, eh?" He gave Shackleton a wicked smile. Shackleton laughed with relief and clapped Pardo on the back.

"How is our course, Worsley?"

"Steady as she goes, Boss."

× × ×

Billy plunged his hand into the icy water and scraped another handful of limpets off the rocks. The good thing about the water being so cold was that it numbed his hands. His fingernails were scraped and split from prying the tiny shellfish off the rocks.

For a week now, limpets and seaweed had been their main food. In the past twenty days, only twelve penguins had come ashore. All had been killed, but still made only two meals. Charlie cooked the limpets up with old seal backbones and other bits of carcass dug out of the rubbish pit. They hadn't used the backbones to begin with because they took too long to cook and there wasn't enough fuel. Now there still wasn't enough fuel, but the men were much less particular about how tough the meat was.

But now even the supply of limpets was fading. They had stripped the rocks bare as far as they could walk or wade. Billy sat on a rock and shelled his catch, then carried his can up to the hut.

"You ready for the little guys, Charlie?" he asked. Charlie lifted the lid. The pot was already bubbling, and big green gobs of seaweed floated to the top. The seaweed didn't taste like much but thickened the broth a little. Billy tipped the can into the pot. He warmed his hands over the steam while Charlie stirred. The limpets only needed a few minutes to cook through, and soon Wild was dishing out portions.

Suddenly they heard Hurley shouting from outside. No one could tell what he was saying. For a few seconds, they stared dumbly at each other. Then it was like being hit by lightning. What else would anyone be shouting about? There was a mad rush for the entryway. Mugs of soup went flying. Men got stuck in the narrow entry flap and soon tore it to pieces. The whole pot of limpet stew was toppled. The blubber stove went out with a hiss and cloud of soot. Perce listened to the chaos from his dark corner of the hut.

"Look!" He heard Hurley's voice outside. "Out there. I thought it was an iceberg at first."

"Can it see us? Has it come for us?" Orde Lees said.

"It's not a proper ship," someone said. "It looks like a tugboat!"

"Proper or not, if it floats, it's a ship," Hurley insisted. "Look, you can see it's under power."

Shackleton! Shackleton had come for them.

"It's going away!" Orde Lees said nervously. "Look!"

"It isn't going," Wild said calmly. "They're searching. It's been some time since Shackleton saw this place. How about a signal fire?"

Perce threw open the sleeping bag. A ship had come! They wouldn't forget him, would they? Pulling with his arms, pushing with his better foot, and energized by hope, he dragged himself to the entryway. If his foot hurt, he didn't notice or care. The bright daylight hurt his eyes, and he ducked back into the shadows to let them adjust. When he could look, he saw Doc Macklin on the hill, raising an old shirt on the flagpole. He saw Billy and the other sailors frantically gathering up all the old blankets, sennegrass, fur mitts, socks, anything that would burn. Hurley ran to the larder and got a crate of blubber. Wild put a pick through a tin of paraffin and poured it all over the pile. He lit it and it practically exploded.

"Get all the sail scraps," Wild ordered. "Shirts, coats, anything to wave." The men raced back to the hut. Some tore the old tent canvas off the roof. Beams of light flooded in like spotlights. Perce thought his heart would beat right through his chest. Was it all a dream? He squeezed his eyes shut, then opened them again. He looked around the small dungeon that had been their home for these endless months. Dirt and reindeer hairs floated in the sunbeams.

"It's turning!" He heard the shouts, nearly hysterical now. "It's coming! They see us!"

The men cheered and waved and hugged each other. A few just knelt on the beach and wept. Wild stared out over the calm water as the mysterious little ship turned and made straight for their bay.

"It's a Chilean flag!" Orde Lees cried out.

"Gentlemen, I assume your gear is lashed up." Wild smiled. "Let's bring it down. And can someone go fetch our young stowaway?"

Now Perce couldn't hear anything but excited babble. Of course they hadn't forgotten him. And there really was a ship. Shackleton had to have made it. He was alive! Tim and Crean, all of them had to be alive. Macklin popped back inside and grinned at Perce. "Well, what are you waiting for, lad! Don't want to miss the boat, do you? Have you got your things together?"

"My things?" The only things he had were the clothes he was wearing and his journal. He stuffed the little notebook in his pocket. "Yes, I've got all my things."

Suddenly the hut was a flurry of activity as men squeezed in and scrambled around for their meager possessions. Hurley still had three tins of the precious photographic plates. Greenstreet had saved the log from the *Endurance*. Perce watched the old sailor McLeod climb into the "attic" and carefully take a bundle out of the bow. It was the queen's Bible that Shackleton had dumped to save weight. McLeod had smuggled it along.

In a very few minutes, the hut was emptied of everything worth keeping. Macklin carried Perce outside and propped him against some rocks near Wild so he could see the ship. The fresh air felt wonderful. The ship had anchored about two hundred yards out and now was putting down a rowboat. They still had no idea where the boat was from. It certainly didn't look like any ship they had expected. A battered metal tug! Who would bring such a thing down here? They all watched as the rowboat came nearer. When it turned to work through the shoals, all at once they saw the broad, square shoulders of the man they knew so well.

"Oh, God, 'tis him," Wild murmured. The men cheered. Perce saw Wild's shoulders tremble and his eyes tear up. Their unflappable leader, the champion stoic, was working hard not to cry.

A few more oar strokes and they could see Shackleton's face.

"Are you all well?" he shouted.

"All safe! All well!" Wild replied.

"Thank God!"

"Are you all well?" Greenstreet called.

"Don't we look all right now that we've washed?" Shackleton laughed. There was no good landing on the beach, so Wild guided them up alongside some rocks. Shackleton threw him the line. Everyone stood still as if paralyzed.

"Well, come on, then, no time to lose," Shackleton said. "Let's have seven men and whatever baggage is ready."

"Baggage is always ready, Boss!" Billy said. "Mr. Wild made us stow it every morning."

"But you must come see the hut, Boss!" Orde Lees said. "See what a good job we've made of it."

"I'm sure it's a palace, but we have no time to spare. The ice might come back any minute. Let's get away while we can. Come on, men, any takers?"

Wild waded into the gentle surf. Shackleton leaned over, his face beaming, his eyes shiny with tears.

"Good to see you, Frank." He took Wild's hand.

"Aye, and you're looking well, Boss."

Now both men had tears in their eyes. Shackleton looked at the ragged group of men waiting on the beach. Every one alive. "Thank you, Frankie." Shackleton's voice broke with emotion. "Thank you for this."

One hour later, they were all aboard and the *Yelcho* was under way with the engines at full speed. Most of the men went below immediately, eager, of course, to start eating and drinking. Perce didn't want to go below just yet. He hadn't seen the sky for four months.

"I haven't even seen the island since we went into the hut."

"I would like to watch it disappear in our wake," Billy said. "Otherwise I'll think this is just another dream." They sat on a deck locker at the stern. It was hard for Perce to even sit upright; his muscles were weak from lying down so long. Billy sat close beside him and kept him from toppling over.

They watched the hut grow smaller and smaller. What a desperate, forlorn little shelter it seemed now, with its patchwork cover of sealskins and torn tents.

"Do you suppose anyone will ever see it again?" Perce asked. "And what would they think?"

"First they would think they had never smelled anything so foul in all their lives." Billy laughed. "I guess you can't leave anyplace that's been home without some sad feelings, but I won't be missing that place anytime soon." Billy shuddered. "Shall we go inside and warm up?" He looked around to see who might help him carry Perce. He saw Wild and Shackleton walking alone along the port-side rail. They stopped at the stern. Wild leaned against the railing, his arms crossed tightly across his chest. Shackleton bent close, talking quietly but with some urgency.

"Hey." Billy nudged Perce. "Doesn't look like a happy chat there. Wonder what's up?"

Wild frowned and nodded. Shackleton touched him on the shoulder. There was obviously some bad news. When Shackleton left, Wild took out his pipe and tobacco. His hands shook as he filled the pipe. Only then did he look up and see Perce and Billy. He came over and leaned on the locker beside them.

"I didn't think anyone would still be out here."

"We were just admiring the scenery," Billy said. "Admiring it disappear, that is!"

"Is everything all right, Mr. Wild?" Perce asked.

"Aye, for us," Wild sighed. "But the *Aurora*'s had a bit of trouble over in the Ross Sea." Perce hadn't even thought about the *Aurora* in months but now realized why Frank Wild would be upset at the news.

"Is your brother all right?" Perce asked.

"Boss doesn't know. He only got the bare bones of it from the telegraph before he left Chile. The *Aurora* dragged anchor in a gale. The men were ashore when the ice came in. The ship couldn't get back to them. She got frozen in, then lost her rudder and barely made it back to New Zealand. They're trying to repair her now to go back for the men."

"But there is a hut there, right?" Billy said. "So they have shelter."

"Aye. And they landed half their supplies. Boss says there was plenty left there from earlier expeditions too. Probably enough for a year. They should do fine. He's going after them himself as soon as we get back and he can find passage to New Zealand."

The three fell quiet then. It was no use offering reassurance. They knew too well what the crew of the *Aurora* was facing. Having a hut and stores made it a little easier. And at least the men there knew that others knew where they were. As far as getting stranded in Antarctica went, they had it pretty good. But nothing could take away the horror of this awful place.

chapter forty-two

As soon as the *Yelcho* cleared the pack ice, the men began to celebrate. Finally the rescue was real. They had escaped the ice at last. The ordinary dangers of crossing the ferocious Southern Ocean seemed small. Doing it in a rusty little tugboat that should never have left the harbor only made it better.

"Finally we get to give old Neptune a good punch in the face!" Billy laughed.

The boat was crowded, and some were already seasick, but they were safe. They were going home. They were warm and dry. Charlie Green, who had worked more hours than ten other men put together, went immediately down to the galley with the *Yelcho*'s cook. Soon the men were feasting on roast lamb and potatoes, fresh bread, peaches, and twelve pounds of macaroni and cheese. There was coffee and wine and sweet, thick fruit juice. Macklin told them to go easy, but no one listened. Everyone ate their fill. Everyone was soon sick.

There wasn't enough water for anyone to take a proper bath, but just having clean hands and faces made them feel like new men, even in their grimy old clothes. Shackleton asked them not to shave yet.

"The good people of Punta Arenas helped us out so much, I think they deserve a look at genuine castaways."

No one cared. That first day passed in giddy confusion. There was so much to catch up on. Conversations started and stopped and zigzagged all over. Shackleton told them a little about the war. He had brought along papers and magazines but didn't hand them out right away. It was shocking enough to discover the war was still going on. They could learn the particular horrors later.

Shackleton had also brought along a box full of medical supplies. To Macklin, it was like Christmas morning. There was alcohol and iodine, carbolic soap for cleaning wounds, sulfur and bichloride of mercury for infection, and miles of clean gauze bandages. Some of the *Yelcho*'s crew gave up their bunks for the invalids. Crean and Billy carried Perce down to have his foot cleaned up, but Perce was not about to spend the day lying around belowdecks.

"Come on, Doc, it's not like I could sleep anyway!"

"Perce, you can barely sit up now, and believe me, once the first excitement fades, you're going to feel weaker."

"So I'll lie down then."

"I'll fix him up a chair and a footstool in the mess room," Billy offered. "He can't miss the party, Doc!"

"Go on, then," Macklin finally agreed. "Set it up in a corner, for I'm sure there'll be drunken fools dancing around the place by day's end crashing into everything." Once Billy and Crean left, Macklin started to unwrap Perce's foot. The bandage was soaked with blood and pus. The smell filled the tiny room. Perce bit his lip to distract himself. The lightest touch was a lightning stab of pain.

"You might not want to look, Perce," Macklin warned as he pulled away the final layer. Perce stared at the ceiling and counted the rivets. The more he tried to hold still, the more his body trembled. This was the first time since the amputation that Macklin had seen the wound in good light.

"I think we could do with a shot of morphine first," he said, trying not to let any worry come through his voice. "I'm going to give it a good cleaning, and that will hurt." He filled the syringe and injected the painkiller into Perce's arm. Almost immediately, Perce felt relief. His whole body relaxed, and the pain simply vanished. What a wonderful sensation! He felt peaceful and dreamy and relaxed. Even as Macklin cleaned the open wound and cut away dead tissue, Perce didn't feel a thing.

"Don't touch it," Macklin said after he bandaged the foot. "Don't try to walk or hop around. Just sit and keep it up."

"Okay, Doc." Perce felt so good right now, he would go around with a live duck on his head if Doc told him too. It was so nice not to hurt. Macklin gave him some aspirin to bring his fever down, then released Perce to join the rest of the crew. The party went on well past midnight. Shackleton wanted to hear all about their time on Elephant Island. He praised their skills and ingenuity. He laughed at the songs they had made up.

In typical fashion, he made light of his own journey in the *James Caird*. It was "a bit rough now and then," he said. The monster wave "gave us a fright and needed some bailing to put things right again." He made the whole journey sound like an endless picnic.

"So there we were," Shackleton said. "Perfect navigation—only wouldn't you know it, some fool had decided to put the whaling station on the opposite side of the island! Well, we weren't too keen on another sail, even if the poor old *James*

Caird hadn't sprung a leak in every plank by then. So we rested a few days, then Worsley and Crean and I just walked across. And here we are today!"

The men played along. They could guess the truth, of course, but the truth was just too awful to think about right now. Despite all his casual talk and endless cheer, Perce could see that Shackleton was a different man. Even now, after four months of regular eating, he looked gaunt. His hair had gone gray, and his eyes were sunken in a weary face. He looked old, Perce thought. Old and damaged.

Perce and Billy learned more of the truth, for Crean gave them a letter Tim had written while he waited on the beach.

Dear Sailors,

Did you ever think to get a letter from yours truly? But I have plenty of time to write and not much else to do, for this is the land of plenty. We have fresh water bubbling right out of the rocks, and seals come over every day and lay their head down on the block for us. Water is the best thing. Sometimes I just sit there and look at it, coming out all clear and sweet. Well, it was a hard trip, I will tell you that. Now Boss and Crean and Worsley are going across the mountains on foot. I wish I could go, but someone had to tend to these here.

There is wood on the beach from shipwrecks over the years. I wondered if any was from the Endurance *yet. A strange thought. But it makes a good fire. I won't say I wish you were here because that would be rotten for you, but it is kind of gloomy by myself. It will be no more than four or five days, though. If they don't make it across by that time, then they plain don't make it and neither do we. Then I suppose you won't get this letter, right!*

No one has ever gone across South Georgia Island before. (Why would they?) Oh, well, how many other things have we done by now that were never done before or even possible? It will be chancy, though. All they have is some bits of rope tied up together and Chippy's adze for an ice ax. That adze is good for everything, I will say. We pulled nails out of the boat and put them on the bottom of their shoes for walking on the ice. They took no sleeping bags, for they are too heavy, only the Primus and a little fuel. They will just go straight without stopping. Worsley figures it is around twenty-five miles. That would be a hard walk on flat ground for the way I'm feeling now. And of course they don't know the way. But that has never stopped Shackleton before, right? I will tell you, I was not feeling so happy to see them leave. But if you read this—well! Then we came out fine! If we don't, then hello to whoever might find this someday.

The second page was on letterhead from the Stromness whaling station. It was scribbled in huge joyous writing with exclamation marks everywhere.

May 23, 1916

We are all right now! Here at the whaling station and plenty to eat. Boss came through again! I don't know how. You remember how big and sharp these mountains are. The whalers all

275

look at him like he must be one of their old Nordic gods from legend. I know how he will tell it. Like it was a walk in the park. But don't believe that. It nearly killed all three of them. I don't know why it didn't. Don't know why any of us has lived when you think about it! Maybe we're meant to do something big, do you think? I will go home on a ship from here. The war is still on, and I think to join. The Boss leaves today to fetch you all, so I will finish now. He is eager to be off, though he is in a bad way and Crean and Worsley too. But see you all in Ireland someday soon.

Cheers,
Your shipmate, Tim McCarthy

Late that night, after Crean had enough whiskey in him to loosen his tongue, Perce got a little more out of him.

"Aye, I have to say, many a time I thought we wouldn't make it. We would go up a mountain, then find no way down, so we'd retrace our path, go down again and up another way," Crean explained. "That first night, we were up on a ridge with the cold closing in fast. We had no hope to last up there, and it was too steep to climb down. I thought, well, that's it, we gave it a good try. But then Shackleton decides we'll slide down!" Crean rubbed his big hand against his face as if he still couldn't quite believe it. "It was crazy, but we could see there was no other way down. We coiled up the rope and sat on it one behind the other like on a toboggan. Then we just pushed off and flew! I shut my eyes. We were going too fast to see anyway and couldn't very well steer even if we wanted to. We had no idea if we would shoot off a cliff or slam into a rock. But we made it. Aye, by God, we made it."

Perce didn't remember being carried to his bunk. He woke in the morning with a strange sensation. He was warm and dry. No blubber smoke, no stones poking him in the back, no reindeer hairs in his mouth. So it was true. They were safe at last.

September 1, 1916

After living so long how we did, it is hard to adjust to real life again. No one really knows how we should feel or what to do. Some men will not stop talking. Some hardly talk at all. Like they are pretending nothing ever happened. I am unbelievably happy most of the time, then suddenly, out of nowhere, I am so sad, I think I will break apart. And though I have food now and medicine, I sometimes shake all over. Wild paces the deck at night, can't sleep at all. Those who can sleep wake shouting with the nightmares.

Only Charlie Green seems right, for he has a job to do again. He is feeling right at home in the Yelcho's *galley with a proper stove and real pots and pans! He made dumplings and pies, yeasty white rolls, and Shackleton's favorite jam tarts.*

We mostly sleep and eat and read the papers. It is hard to make sense of the war. Three million are dead. All of Europe is a battlefield. The whole world has changed seems like overnight. There is a place called Gallipoli, where officers sent their troops straight into machine-gun fire. A passenger ship was torpedoed and sunk. It is impossible to make sense of it all.

It took four days to reach Punta Arenas. As they got closer, Perce saw a change come over Shackleton. He seemed anxious and distracted. On the third day, Perce was sitting by himself in a sheltered corner of the side deck. Shackleton came out and began to pace. He did not look like a man who had just pulled off a triumphant rescue. He looked old, Perce thought, old and lost and terribly sad. When he finally noticed Perce, his face changed abruptly back to the calm, genial leader, confident and unruffled.

"Are you ready for civilization, Perce?" Shackleton said. "We'll be there tomorrow." He sat down and lit a cigarette. "You know, I'm actually very good at it. Civilization. You can't get anywhere in this game if you're not. But it never quite fits me somehow." He stopped abruptly and shook his head as if ridding himself of the gloom. "So what are your plans now, lad?"

"I don't know, Boss."

"Macklin says you'll be in hospital here for a while. I'll make arrangements for your passage home whenever you're fit."

"Thank you." A petrel soared alongside the ship, coasting effortlessly. It turned its head with quick little darts to examine the two odd creatures sitting there.

"Sir—" Perce said after a while. "Even how things turned out, I'm glad I did it."

"Good God, Perce—don't think like that!" Shackleton

snapped. "Don't let it get hold of you. There's nothing but ruination in this game!" Shackleton looked as angry as when he had first discovered his stowaway. Perce was startled by the response.

"Oh, I don't think I'm ruined, Boss," he said. "I said I was glad I did it. Not that I'd want to do it again."

Shackleton relaxed. "Aye, all right, then."

"But it's like in that play by Shakespeare," Perce went on. "Henry the Fifth, when he's sending them off into battle. How all the men in England lying abed would wish they were there."

"Ah." Shackleton nodded. "*And gentlemen in England now a-bed shall think themselves accursed they were not here, and hold their manhoods cheap whiles any speaks that fought with us upon St. Crispin's day.* So you read *Henry the Fifth*, did you?"

"Aye. On Elephant Island. Billy read it to me mostly. But I would read that part over sometimes. *We few, we happy few, we band of brothers.* That seemed right for us too: how we were, a band of brothers. Bad as it got sometimes, well, I don't know how to explain it. Bad as it got, I wouldn't trade it back. I don't think a lot of men ever get to know how that feels."

"Just us and Shakespeare?"

"Aye," Perce laughed.

A cloud came over Shackleton's face. "Well, at least I'm not sending you into war like King Henry. You'll be one less dead soldier on some bloody field."

"But I mean to sign up, Boss! As soon as I get back."

"They won't take you, lad. Not missing your toes."

"I want to do my duty!"

"Your duty, Perce," Shackleton sighed. "Your duty is to find a pretty girl and give England lots of fine sons and daughters. Teach them what grand things they can do and what places there are out here in the world." He looked out to sea, where the bird still glided along beside them. "If there's anyplace left after this madness."

chapter forty-three

The next morning brought the glorious sight of land. The mountains of southern Chile were bathed in a golden sunrise. The wind smelled of grass and trees. As they neared the harbor, the men lined the rail, exclaiming over each sight of civilization. As the *Yelcho* got near the harbor, dozens of boats came out to escort her in. They were decorated with flags and flowers and streams of bunting until the entire harbor was bright with color and noisy with horns.

"Holy Christmas—will you look at that!" Billy laughed. "They've got the whole town out and every flag flying. You'd think we went to the moon and back! All we need now is a brass band and dancing bears."

The brass band was waiting on the dock. The entire city of Punta Arenas had turned out to welcome Shackleton and his rescued men.

"I don't know whether I'm happy or terrified!" Billy exclaimed.

"Both, I think," Perce said. "A whole lot of both." It had been almost two years since they had walked on a street, entered a house, or seen a woman. Even Frank Wild looked nervous. He kept fiddling with his pipe, tugging at his coat sleeves, and brushing back his thinning hair.

"Steady now, boys, remember we've been through worse!" Shackleton understood the men's nervousness. He walked among them, putting them at ease, straightening a torn collar, pretending to brush a bit of lint off a tattered jacket. They still wore the same filthy clothing they had worn for the past year, soaked through with blubber, soot, and penguin blood. The *Yelcho* eased up alongside the dock, and the crowd pressed in tight.

"Don't worry," Shackleton reassured his men. "As soon as they smell the lot of you, they'll stand back!"

The crew scrambled to secure the mooring lines. Shackleton came over to Perce.

"The Red Cross has a car here for you, Perce." Shackleton pointed to the dock, where a nurse in white uniform was waiting with a wheelchair. "They'll take you right to the hospital."

Perce hadn't thought about how he would get off the ship. He didn't want everyone to see him carted off like an invalid.

"We'll get the others off first; how's that?" Shackleton said as if reading his mind.

"Thank you, sir."

A sailor opened the gate, and Shackleton, with Frank Wild once more by his side, stepped up to the top of the gangplank. The crowd went wild. Shackleton waved, then turned back to his men and winked. Then for one final time, he led the way. A group of officials greeted them at the bottom, and photographers pressed in close to snap pictures. Then the men began to file off. A shabby, skinny, dirty group of triumphant men. Everyone wanted to shake their hands, kiss them, take a photograph. Billy stayed behind with Perce until the crowd got distracted, and the Red Cross nurse came to fetch him. She was a tall woman who walked like a general. The crowd parted in front of her, and she wheeled him through so quickly that Billy got lost in her wake. She and the driver bundled Perce into the car. Perce felt suddenly very strange. He was shaking all over. He tried to control himself but couldn't stop it. It wasn't just the fever. It was like fireworks inside him shooting off every which way. It was all over now. Nothing to worry about anymore. They were safe. But Perce felt like he was falling into a million pieces. The car began to move slowly through the crowd. Suddenly hands pounded on the roof.

"Hey!" Billy's face appeared at the window.

"Hey, Blackie!" Greenstreet was right behind him. There was a knock on the other window. Perce saw Crean's craggy face, grinning through the window on the other side. Other bearded faces crowded behind him. They had broken away from the official welcome to see him off.

"See you soon, Perce!"

"Hey—I'll trade your share of champagne for a nut bar! What do you say?"

"Leave us some nurses, lad!"

"We'll come see you tomorrow!"

Perce's eyes filled with tears, but he didn't care. His hands stopped shaking. He waved at his friends as the car slowly pulled away.

The men were taken to a hotel to wash and given new clothes and a bin in which to put their old ones for burning. They hardly recognized one another with clean, beardless faces and new clothes. Without the layers of underwear, sweaters, and jackets, it was clear to see how painfully thin they all were. That night was the first of many banquets and parties. Macklin had warned them not to go crazy eating and drinking too much, but no one listened to his advice, not even Macklin himself.

Billy slept very soundly that night and late the next morning. It was late afternoon when he went to the hospital, but the doctors wouldn't let him see Perce.

"No see," a nurse explained in broken English. "Too sick."

"He can't be any sicker than he's been for months," Billy protested. "He's in a hospital now!"

The nurse did not understand. "Too sick," she repeated. "And too many come here, want to see poor boy with Shackleton."

"But I'm his friend," Billy explained. "I was on the ship. I was with Shackleton." Just then Billy saw Doc Macklin come through the hospital lobby. Billy ran over to him.

"Doc, what's going on? They won't let me in to see Perce."

"Not yet, Billy." Macklin frowned. "He's still groggy. We operated on him this morning, and he's recovering from the chloroform."

"Operated for what? You didn't cut his foot off, did you?"

"No. Just a little more tissue and bone. The bone is infected."

"But he'll be all right now, won't he?"

"I don't know, Billy."

"What do you mean you, don't know? Come on, Doc,

after all this? He can't—it—it would be—" Billy couldn't even say it. *Perce can't die now.* It would be ridiculous, cruel, ungodly.

"I know, I know." Macklin was even more frustrated. It was over a hundred years since scientists first discovered bacteria. They could look at them under the microscope, they could grow them in a dish, they just couldn't kill them.

"You can see him tomorrow." Macklin rubbed his tired eyes. "Just remember he has a way to go yet. I'll tell the nurses to let you in. He's become a bit of a celebrity, you see. There were a hundred people here yesterday wanting to see the *poor frostbitten lad.*" Macklin gave him a weary smile.

chapter forty-four

As Macklin promised, the nurses let Billy in the next day. They were much more friendly now that they knew who he was. Perce's bed was in a corner of the ward near a window. In the bright sunlight, Perce looked as pale as the bedsheets. A wooden hoop held the blanket off his feet.

"Well!" Billy laughed. "You're looking so good, I don't think you'll get any sympathy out of me now!" In truth, Perce looked terrible, but they had spent enough time with Shackleton to learn the value of optimism. "Though a proper barber would do you some good."

"I wouldn't have recognized you at all!" Perce smiled. "Tell me everything—are they treating you grand?"

"We're drinking champagne like water and eating like kings. And we're famous, you know! Look here." He brought out a stack of local newspapers with photos and stories about them. Neither of them knew Spanish, but it was clear from the size of the headlines and the bold type that they were making for a good story.

"They've got us all farmed out in folks' houses now," Billy explained. "Sleeping on great soft beds and food all over. How about you? Are they feeding you up all right?"

"Aye." Perce pointed to a table beside the bed that was heaped with tins of cookies and chocolates and all manner of delicacies. "All the English have been sending baskets over!" He picked up a scone from one of the baskets and tapped it on the bedside table. It sounded like a rock and didn't even crack. "But Charlie could give out a few baking lessons, if you know what I mean!"

"Oh, Charlie," Billy laughed. "He's quite the celebrity now. Some writers for a ladies' magazine came to interview him. Asking for his recipes. So Charlie goes on, you know how he can go on about cooking, goes on about how many ways there are to cook a penguin." Billy imitated Charlie's squeaky voice. "Oh, well, the legs is tasty fried, you see, and the breast, well, depends on if it's a gentoo, you see, or an Adélie, for the tenderness, eh? Of course the emperor has the most meat, but I rather think the gentoo is sweeter."

Perce laughed until he was too weak to laugh anymore and a clucking nurse chased Billy away. Over the next week, others came to visit. They brought him more cookies and chocolate than he could eat in a year. When Crean came, there was a great buzz among the nurses, for the story had spread throughout all of Punta Arenas about how he bent the iron pike across his chest. At least six different nurses found some reason to walk by Perce's bed during the visit, each one slowing to glance at the handsome Irish Giant.

Wild, by contrast, was barely noticed by anyone. The strongest, most stalwart member of the expedition never looked the part of an explorer unless you took the time to look into his eyes. Perce thought those eyes looked a little red and tired these days. Unlike most of the men, Wild's responsibilities had not ended upon arrival here. He was busy helping Shackleton with a thousand details and arrangements. There was still no news about the fate of his brother and the other men in the Ross Sea Party.

"I've brought you something." Wild glanced around to see if anyone was near enough to eavesdrop, then he took out a brown envelope. "Hurley's photos. He went in the darkroom the day we got back and hasn't come out much since. No one's supposed to see them yet," he explained. "The rights were all sold years ago to finance the expedition, so we have to ensure the exclusive, but Hurley said you could take a look."

Perce took the photos. There was one of the men eating at the wardroom table aboard the *Endurance* and one of Crean holding Sally's four puppies in his big hands. There were several pictures of the dogs. Perce felt a new stab of loss for them.

"They're brilliant." Perce was amazed. There was a grand picture of the *Endurance* stuck in the ice that Hurley had taken at night. That photograph had taken hours to prepare for. Perce remembered setting up a dozen pans of flash powder all around the ship.

"She was a beautiful ship," Wild said quietly.

"Aye." The entire ship was frosted in ice. The ice in her rigging looked like diamonds.

"Look here." Wild handed him another print. "Now, that's a fine-looking cat. Very fine. Too bad he's posed with such an ugly mug." Perce looked at the photo with astonishment. There he was himself, with Mrs. Chippy sitting on his shoulder, just outside the galley. Perce had never seen himself in a photograph before. And that long-ago self looked nothing like the person he was today. The man in the photo was healthy and muscular. He stood with the easy confidence of untested youth, looking very sure of himself. Off on a jolly lark. Perce felt tears creeping into his eyes. When he came to a picture of the hut on Elephant Island, he couldn't bear to look anymore. The tears flowed down his cheeks.

"Happened to me too, lad," Wild said reassuringly. "All of us are still a bit tender, I think."

chapter forty-five

After two weeks in the hospital, Perce was well enough to sit up in a wheelchair. Billy wheeled him outside to the hospital garden. It was spring, and the air was sweet with the scent of flowers.

"I've got some good news!" Billy grinned.

"You've met another beautiful Chilean girl and danced with her all night."

"Well, yes, but besides that. I got a job."

"On a ship?"

"On a ranch in Patagonia!"

"Patagonia? Where the heck is that?"

"South of here. I got to talking with an old Scottish fellow who owns a big sheep ranch. His nephew was running it but got killed in the war. I told him I'd done a little ranching, and I guess he took a liking to me. It'll be good to get back in a saddle again," he said. "Sleep out on the ground under the stars."

"Don't you want to go home? See your family?"

"Yeah, sure, but the job needs someone now. You wouldn't think it after all this, but my wandering feet aren't ready to settle down just yet."

"Congratulations, then." Perce forced a cheerful smile. "That's grand. When do you leave?"

"Well." Billy looked down and picked at a torn fingernail. "Actually, my boat leaves in a couple of hours."

"Today?"

"Yeah. I just met this fellow two days ago, and it turns

out the boat only sails every other week. The others are all leaving in a few days, and I can't just keep living off hospitality here, so, well, time to move on."

"Well," Perce repeated. He couldn't imagine not having Billy around. But somehow it also seemed perfectly right. Billy had breezed along onto the *Endurance* and now was breezing off into his next adventure. "Come see us in Wales when you get tired of the sheep," he said. "We'll go to Ireland and find our Tim."

The bell rang to announce the end of visiting hours.

"Shall I take you back?" Billy stood beside the wheelchair.

"No, I'll stay here a while longer."

"It's a nice evening."

"Aye."

"Well, goodbye, then."

"Goodbye." They shook hands.

"Thanks for bringing me out, Billy," Perce said quietly.

"It is a lovely garden." Billy sighed and looked around at all the flowers.

"I didn't mean the garden," Perce said.

"I know. But if you say any more, you'll get me blubbering."

Shackleton came to visit the next morning. He was still dealing with an avalanche of bureaucracy, telegrams back and forth to England and arrangements to get everyone home. Some of the men had already left, eager to return to England and join the war. The rest would sail north tomorrow on the

Yelcho to Buenos Aires and from there to England. Shackleton and Worsley were about to leave for New Zealand, then back to Antarctica to rescue the other stranded men.

"There's a chap from the British Club who will look after you here," Shackleton explained. "He'll arrange your passage home when you're fit to travel. Macklin says the doctors here know what they're doing, so you should be up soon."

"Yes, Boss. I'll make out fine."

"Good. Very good. Here's a few pounds in advance of your wages." Shackleton put an envelope on the bedside table. "You'll want to buy clothes and a few things."

"Thank you, sir. I'd like to bring some presents home."

"I expect you'll find something."

Their conversation was stiff. Shackleton clearly did not like hospitals and seemed ill at ease. Perce finally gave him mercy by pretending to be tired. Shackleton got up with relief.

"Well, it was good to have you along, Perce." They shook hands. It was oddly formal.

"You did well, and I'm proud of you," he said. Then he was gone. Perce leaned back on his pillow and smiled. He didn't mind the abrupt goodbye. He understood this man's heart by now. In the grip of disaster, Shackleton had inspired his men with words. Faced with ordinary sentiment, he stumbled badly. Perce didn't care. Mr. Shakespeare would have had a grand flowery speech to say. But Mr. Shakespeare would not likely have gotten them home.

chapter forty-six

December 1916

Perce sat on deck, watching the night slip slowly into morning as the sky changed through a hundred shades of blue. It was odd to be on a ship as a passenger. Perce wasn't really sure what to do with himself. They were two days out from Buenos Aires now, and the weather was fair. He could hear dolphins swimming and blowing alongside the ship, though it was still too dark to see them. He had been up all night as usual. Partly because he still had trouble sleeping, but mostly because it was just more peaceful then. He liked to watch the stars circle overhead and listen to the familiar sounds of the sea. He liked to be alone. The other English-speaking passengers had been suffocatingly kind. Perce could not sit on a deck chair without someone running over with a blanket or have a simple cup of tea without plates full of food being pressed on him. He was shy enough to begin with, but especially so with people so far out of his class. Night gave him the solitude and peace he craved.

He walked along the side deck toward the stern, only occasionally holding the railing for balance. The special shoe still felt awkward, but Perce was determined not to show a limp by the time he got home. Day by day, he felt stronger. Every night, he went to one of the ship's fire stations and lifted buckets of sand to build up his muscles. The shirts he had been given in Punta Arenas were getting tight in the shoulders. He walked a lap of the ship and returned to the bow. It was a little brighter now. The dolphins were silvery shadows.

Andres, the ship's steward, came out with a basket of

folded blankets. He began to put them out on the first-class deck chairs. He was a small, cheerful Argentinean boy of fifteen. He liked talking to Perce. Perce liked Andres too because he didn't talk too much. Andres spoke very little English but was trying to learn. He asked Perce for five new words every day, then practiced them in sentences.

"Mister Blackborow, sir. How are you doing this fine morning?" he said with careful precision.

"I am well, thank you."

"I have for you English news!" Andres said, taking a folded newspaper from his towel basket. "Paper is from Buenos Aires. Only three day—ah—of time?"

"Three days old."

"Yes! I find in the trash of cabin. And always you are reading. So I save for you."

"Thank you, Andres." Perce took the papers. He was puzzled. Passengers usually left papers in the salon for others to read. It was strange that any of the English would throw away a newspaper, especially the *Telegraph,* which carried the very latest news, sent at great expense from London by wire.

The sky wasn't quite bright enough to read by yet, so Perce sat in a chair to wait for the sunrise. He felt peaceful. The bad memories were starting to loosen their grip. The cold and pain and terrible fear were fading. He had good memories now too: dogsled races and football games; the crazy, raucous singsong nights; playing in the snow with Sally's puppies. He smiled as he remembered Charlie frosting a brick as a joke for Crean's birthday. He had seen a thousand things that few other people in the world would ever know:

crystal green icebergs in an azure sea, the shimmering gold of the aurora australis blazing across an endless sky. He had friendships that no one else could even imagine. Slowly the sky grew lighter. Perce's eyes fell on the newspaper in his lap. At the bottom of the front page, a few paragraphs were set off in a box with a small headline.

ENDURANCE SAILOR DIES IN CHANNEL BATTLE
Sailed for Rescue with Shackleton

Timothy McCarthy, a crew member on Sir Ernest Shackleton's Imperial Trans-Antarctic Expedition, was among the brave sailors killed in battle when his ship was torpedoed by a German U-boat. McCarthy, twenty-eight, of Kinsale, County Cork, Ireland, had only recently returned from the expedition, which has already become a legendary story of heroism and survival. After their ship, the *Endurance,* was crushed by ice, Shackleton and his twenty-seven men spent seven months camping on an ice floe before escaping in the ship's three small lifeboats. A week's harrowing boat journey took them to a desolate scrap of land called Elephant Island. Once there, McCarthy was one of five men chosen to sail with Sir Ernest across another eight hundred miles of open ocean to obtain rescue. Sir Ernest, en route to New Zealand, could not be reached for comment.

Perce shut his eyes. He couldn't breathe. The paper had to be wrong. How could it be true? Every day for months, they had walked with death. They had slept beside death, swallowed it whole, laughed at it, cowered from it, taunted it, sometimes longed for it. But death had proved to be no real match for twenty-eight ordinary men. Perce read the story twice more. He opened the paper and searched every page, looking for a different story, one that would change this, have it all be a mistake. But there had been no mistake.

Perce got up and threw the newspaper overboard. The pages came apart and fluttered gently in the wind. Death was such a coward. *You had a fair chance!* he thought angrily. *You had your chance at all of us! In the worst place in all of the world, with a thousand knives in your bag, you failed. With the cold dagger of Antarctica, you could not take even one of us, so with a dull thump of war you have taken the best of us.*

Perce slumped to the deck and buried his face in his hands. All the tears he hadn't cried for the past two years came pouring out of him. He wept and wept as the first golden edge of the sun broke out of the calm sea.

chapter forty-seven

A light snow was falling as Perce walked down the street. He did not huddle against the cold. His coat was unbuttoned, and he wore no hat. The cold felt good to Perce after riding in an overheated train from London. The street was empty, and his were the only footprints. He saw Christmas decorations hanging across windows and wreaths on some of the doors. It was strange how everything looked and felt exactly the same, as if no time had passed. He stopped outside his home. The house was dark and empty. Perce glanced up and down the street, then walked up to his own front door for the first time in three years. It squeaked as he pushed it open, just like always.

The first thing he noticed was the smell. There was no one thing that marked "home" for him, no one smell he could even identify, but it smelled exactly like home. It was just the mix of bread, soap, wet shoes, lamp oil, and the lavender water his mother put on for special occasions. There was a little extra soap smell right now, and the parlor was very tidy. He walked back toward the kitchen and saw the table full of food and laid for a party. There were meat pies and ham sandwiches under tea towels. Cups and saucers were lined up on the sideboard beside plates of cookies. Perce put his bag down and picked up a cookie. He had dreamed about his mother's cookies so many times on Elephant Island. He took a bite. The cookie was nothing like he remembered. It was tough and dry. *Guess some things do change!* he thought.

He went into the kitchen. Everything there was the same. Same tea cozy, same flowered curtains, same worn oilcloth. Perce pushed back a curtain and looked into the backyard. Now there was something different. Hanging on the clothesline, in his very own backyard, was a row of white cloths. Smaller than tea towels, bigger than handkerchiefs, it took a little while for him to realize what they were. Nappies! He turned away in surprise. There was a saucer of pins on the kitchen table. A teeny tiny spoon was in the dish rack and a bib hanging off the back of a chair.

Just then the front door crashed open and the house exploded with noise.

"Perce! Perce, are you here?" Five pairs of stomping feet thundered down the hall. Perce braced himself as a herd of brothers tackled him. They weren't so little anymore. Everyone was shouting and screaming and talking at once.

"Harry!" he exclaimed, pushing himself free enough to have a look.

"I'm not Harry, I'm Jack."

"You're not!" It took Perce some time to figure them all out. Before he could begin, though, the boys were thrust aside by the more formidable force of his mother. She saw Perce and immediately burst into tears. She threw her arms around him, weeping with happiness, then just as quickly reared back, cocked her middle finger against her thumb, and thwacked his skull just above the ear.

"Ow!" Perce laughed.

"What do you mean by sneaking out the back of the train?" She hugged him again, tears streaming down her face. "Stealing home when all and everybody were waiting for you at the station!" She thwacked him again.

"I'm sorry, Mum." Perce was dizzy from her embrace. "I

saw the huge crowd at the station. It looked like the whole street turned up."

"The whole town, more like!" The real Harry, his next-down brother, threw an arm around Perce's neck. Little Bill, who wasn't so little anymore, grabbed him around the waist. Everyone was talking at once, and the little house was suddenly bursting with people as the neighbors came flooding in.

"Of course they were there! They all wanted to welcome you! Oh, don't eat that." His mother snatched the cookie out of his hand. "I made a good batch for you." She dropped her voice to a whisper. "These are for the neighbors. The butter is rationed now, you see, because of the war. These are made without. Oh, you gave us such a scare when we didn't see you!" She hugged him and thumped his skull a few more times. "We thought you missed the train! Are you all right? How are you? You're too thin, boy! Teddy, fetch Perce's cookies down. Up top behind the flour. Don't touch a one or I'll turn you inside out! Harry, put the kettle on."

"Did you bring us a penguin?" Charlie tugged at Perce's coat. "I'm doing a report on penguins now for school."

"Come sit down by the fire."

"I'm not cold, Mum," Perce said.

"Bill, let go of your brother! Where's Father?" She craned her neck and looked down the hall. "All of you out now!"

"Mum?"

"Where's your poor father? Pushed out! Dad?"

"Mum? There's nappies on the line." Perce felt Teddy push a cookie into his hand. He saw Charlie slither back down the crowded hallway and fling open the front door.

"Hey!" Charlie shouted up and down the street. "He's here! He's here, everybody!"

"Saw what? Nappies? Oh, goodness yes, the baby." His mother smiled proudly. "Oh, God, how many times did I wonder if he would ever get to meet you!" She burst into full-blown tears now, snatching a tea towel up to her face.

Then Perce saw his father, standing in the back of the parlor. He looked almost exactly the same as Perce remembered. Solid, strong, quiet, he rarely showed his emotions. But now heavy tears ran down the lines in his weathered face. Perce unwound his mother's arms and waded through the tangle of his brothers.

"Hello, Dad," he said quietly. They shook hands. His father was holding a wiggling fat baby. The baby looked at Perce very seriously, then burped and slurped up a big smile.

"Hello, Perce," his father said. "Welcome home."

"It's good to be back."

"This is your new brother, Reggie."

"Hello, Reggie. You're a fine big lad, aren't you?" The baby squealed and grabbed at his face. Perce took him in his arms. He weighed about as much as a gentoo penguin. Perce sat down. His head felt spinny. The baby smelled so baby. Perce felt wonderful and awful at the same time.

"Come on, Perce!" Charlie and Bill wiggled through the crowd and flung themselves against his knees. "Tell us everything! Tell us all!"

Baby Reggie smacked his face as if he too were demanding the story. This little baby—all these little brothers—Perce wanted to protect them forever, to keep them here by the warm stove in the safe swarm of friends and neighbors, always. Never for them the ocean's terror, never the desperate hunger, the endless fear. The baby's little feet were soft and smooth and plump as bread rolls. Yes, everything should just stay like this forever.

Your duty is to teach them what grand things they can do and what places there are out here in the world.

"Come on, Perce! Tell. What's the South Pole like? Is it awful?"

"Not so much." Perce smiled and stretched his feet out toward the stove. "Mostly it was grand."

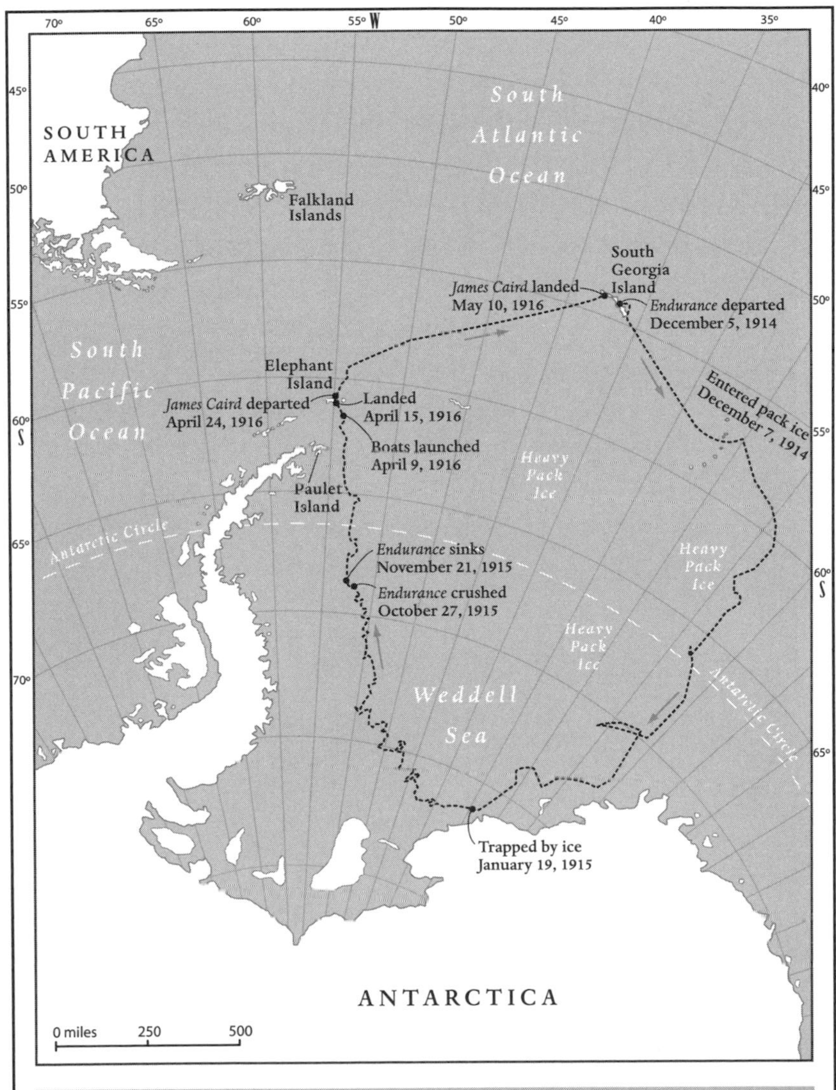

The *ENDURANCE* EXPEDITION

1914–1916

AUTHOR'S NOTE

The story of Ernest Shackleton's *Endurance* expedition is one of the great true adventure stories. All of the main events in *Shackleton's Stowaway* actually happened as they do in this book. I have used my imagination to develop some scenes, but these are always based on actual historical information. I have combined some events (there were actually three different times when the pressure ice squeezed the ship before it was crushed) and occasionally nudged time around a little bit (Shackleton's second attempt to rescue his men actually occurred two days after Perce's operation, not the same day, and Tim McCarthy was really killed three months after Perce got home). I have made up conversations and thoughts for the characters, and this makes for a novel, but the story is all true.

All of the characters were real men, and I have tried to present them as honestly as I could, based on published accounts, interviews with their descendants, and, whenever possible, their own journals or memoirs.

There was a total of twenty-eight men, including Shackleton, on this expedition. It was impossible to put them all in this book, but I am sorry to have left any of them out as they were all remarkable men. I feel that I have come to "know" some of them very well, and I have tremendous respect and admiration for all of them. No one has ever gone through an ordeal as long and difficult as this one, and no one should ever think to judge the hearts of these men.

There were six sailors on the *Endurance*, but very little is known about them. All of the published accounts come from Shackleton himself, the officers, and the scientists. Perce Blackborow probably did not keep a journal. He never spoke of one, and no one in his family ever found one. Billy Bakewell did write his memoirs, but he had so many adventures that this one takes up just one-fifth of them! Perce's thoughts, his conversations with Billy, and his feelings are all my own creation.

EPILOGUE

When he returned home in 1916, **Perce Blackborow** tried to enlist in the British navy but was rejected because of his missing toes. Instead, he joined the merchant navy and spent the rest of the war working on transport and cargo ships. After seeing much of the world, he returned to his hometown and married a young Irishwoman named Kate. They had six children, two of whom died young. He never talked about his experiences on the *Endurance,* but his daughter Peggy remembered sitting on his lap in the 1930s listening to a special BBC radio program about the expedition. The lights were low in the living room, so she couldn't see his face clearly, but when the story came to the part where they had to shoot the dogs, she knew he was crying.

Perce never walked with a limp, and no one but his wife ever saw his foot. He worked hard all his life as a dock boatman in the harbor, rowing out to bring in the mooring lines for big ships. It was hard physical work and often very cold. Perce would come home at night and sit with his feet up in front of the stove. He treasured his shelves full of books and encyclopedias. He liked nature and took his daughter Joan for long walks in the woods on Sunday afternoons, where he told her the names of plants and birds. Every Christmas, he bought his wife a new hearth rug, and every Saturday, he would bring home a bag of candy for his children.

Perce died in 1949, probably of a combination of chronic bronchitis, pneumonia, and a heart condition.

William "Billy" Bakewell worked for almost a year on the sheep ranch in Patagonia. In 1917, when the United States entered the war, he decided to return and join the navy. However, since he did not have a passport, a birth certificate, or "some other papers that I had never heard of before," he could not get aboard any American ships or even enter his home country. Instead, he talked his way into a job on a British merchant ship. He spent the rest of the war working on supply ships, crossing the Atlantic many times. Twice he was on ships that were sunk by torpedoes, making a lifetime record of four shipwrecks! When he finally went home to Joliet, Illinois, around 1920, he had been away from home for twenty years. Billy decided it was time to settle down. He got a job with the railroad, fell in love, got married, and had one daughter named Elizabeth and three granddaughters. He remained an avid reader all his life and was never without an open book nearby. He died in 1969 at the age of eighty-one.

Perce and Billy never met again in person, but remained lifelong friends through letters. In 1964, Billy's daughter, Elizabeth, traveled to Wales and met Perce's family. The two families remain friends to this day.

Tim McCarthy was killed in action on March 16, 1917, when his ship, the SS *Narragansett,* was torpedoed by the Germans in the English Channel. He died at his post and went down with the ship. His body was not recovered.

Ernest Shackleton, after rescuing the stranded crew of the *Aurora,* gave a series of lectures in the United States, then served out the remainder of the war in northern Russia. After the war, he went on a world tour, giving slide-show lectures about the *Endurance* voyage. He hated doing this, but he still had lots of debt to pay off from the expedition. He also hated writing books and dictated his book *South* to a collaborator. The writer said that Shackleton could hardly talk about the terrible walk across South Georgia Island.

Shackleton never really felt at ease in civilization. In a way it was true when he wrote in a letter to his wife that he went exploring because he "wasn't good for much of anything else." In 1920, he organized another expedition to Antarctica with a ship called the *Quest*. He didn't have a very clear mission this time. He planned to circumnavigate the continent, updating charts and looking for uncharted islands. He also thought they might stop off in the South Pacific and look for Captain Kidd's pirate treasure and investigate early Polynesian navigation methods.

Many of the *Endurance* crew went with him again. Frank Wild, Doc Macklin, Worsley, and several sailors were on board. Hussey was there, with the same banjo that had kept everyone going for so long. Charlie Green was once again the cook. Macklin knew that Shackleton was ill. He suspected that he had serious heart trouble for many years and had probably suffered several small heart attacks while on the *Endurance*. But Shackleton would never let doctors examine him or even listen to his heart. On January 4, 1922, the *Quest* stopped at South Georgia Island. That night, Shackleton called Macklin into his cabin at two in the morning. He was suffering a heart attack. A few minutes later, he died. He was forty-eight years old. Wild was going to send the body back to England, but Shackleton's wife, Emily, sent a telegram and asked that Shackleton be buried on South Georgia Island. She knew he was always happiest in the Antarctic.

Tom Crean returned to Ireland and his job in the navy. He spent the rest of the war working on patrol ships along the coast. In September 1917, he married a woman named Nell, from his hometown of Annascaul. They had three daughters, one of whom died at age four.

Shackleton wanted Crean to come along on the *Quest* expedition in 1921, but Crean did not want to leave his family. (He told Shackleton, "I have a long-haired pal now!") He had also been injured in a fall aboard a ship and suffered damage to his eyesight. Although he never mentioned the suffering he had endured during his three expeditions in Antarctica, there were some visible signs of lasting damage. His ears had been frostbitten so often that his daughters described them as feeling like planks of wood. His feet were badly discolored and probably often painful. He had special boots made.

In 1927, Tom and Nell opened a pub and named it the South Pole Inn. The locals always called him "Tom the Pole" and his wife "Nell the Pole." Like so many of the crew, he rarely talked about his experiences in Antarctica. He didn't give any interviews, and when people asked him questions, he usually changed the subject. He lived out his life just enjoying quiet times with his family. He remained very fond of dogs and named one Toby after one of the pups he raised on the *Endurance*.

Tom Crean died in 1938, just a week before his sixty-first birthday. He had appendicitis and had to travel several hours to get to a hospital for surgery. His appendix burst, and he died from infection.

Frank Wild worked for the British navy in the Arctic for the rest of the war. He helped supply ships navigate through the ice for the Russian army. (The Russians were allies of the British and Americans in World War I.) Then he served with Shackleton in Russia. His brother Ernest, who had survived his own ordeal with the crew of the *Aurora*, died from typhoid fever while serving in the war. Frank Wild went with Shackleton on the *Quest* voyage and helped bury him on South Georgia Island. He took over command of the *Quest* and finished the journey but never seemed to recover from the loss of his best friend. He moved to South Africa and tried cotton farming but was ruined by years of drought. After so many years as an explorer, he never seemed to be able to find another passion or a place for himself in the world. Some shipmates from earlier expeditions tried to help him out, but sadly, he became an alcoholic and died in 1939.

When **Charlie Green** joined the *Endurance* in Buenos Aires, he sent a letter to his parents in England, but they never received it. They eventually thought he was dead and were very surprised when he returned home. They had cashed in his life insurance policy, and his girlfriend had married someone else. Charlie enlisted in the British navy as a cook and served until the end of the war. He married in 1918. He went with Shackleton on the *Quest* expedition as a cook. Shackleton gave Charlie a set of slides from Frank Hurley's photographs, and Charlie gave illustrated talks about the *Endurance* expedition for the rest of his life. Charlie continued to work as a cook and baker and died in 1974 at age eighty-five.

Frank Hurley went back to South Georgia Island in February 1917 to take more photographs and film of scenery and wildlife for a movie about the *Endurance* expedition. His film was first shown in December 1919 and was very popular. He became an official war photographer for the Australian armed forces and continued to pioneer photographic techniques all his life. In 1918, he met a French opera singer named Antoinette in Cairo, Egypt, and married her ten days later. They had three daughters and a son. He traveled the world as a photographer for the rest of his life. He died of a heart attack in 1962 at age seventy-six.

Dr. Alexander Macklin served as a medical officer for the rest of the war and was awarded several medals. He had become very close to Shackleton and helped him sort out all the financial affairs of the expedition. He went along on the *Quest* and was with Shackleton when he died. He settled in Aberdeen, Scotland, married, and raised two sons. His dream of a pill to cure infections was finally realized in 1940 when penicillin, the first antibiotic, became available. (It was discovered in 1928 but was not really developed as a drug until 1940.)

Thomas Orde Lees returned to his position as a fitness instructor with the British Royal Marines, then joined the Royal Flying Corps. At forty, he was too old to become a pilot and was put to work on observation balloons, where he learned to use a parachute. He got very interested in parachuting, which was a new thing at the time. He began a crusade to give parachutes to airplane pilots. The military believed that if pilots had parachutes, they would become cowards and jump out anytime they got in trouble! Orde Lees performed several public demonstrations of parachute jumps. He divorced his first wife and moved to Japan, where he married again and raised another daughter. He died in New Zealand in 1958 at age seventy-nine.

Frank Worsley was captain of a ship during the war, and a German submarine was sunk under his command. After he returned from the *Quest* expedition, he went on to pursue more adventure in the Arctic and the South Pacific. He tried to return to service for the Second World War but was rejected when it was discovered he was almost seventy years old. He died of lung cancer at age seventy in 1943.

Harry McNeish continued to work as a ship's carpenter. When he retired, he lived with his son's family for a while, then decided to move to New Zealand. He had a drinking problem and eventually wound up homeless, living on the docks in Wellington. The other sailors there respected him for having been on the *Endurance,* and all chipped in to take care of him. They finally got him into a rest home, where he died in 1930 at the age of fifty-six.

The Crew of the *Aurora* (The Ross Sea Party), under the command of Aeneas Mackintosh, succeeded in laying the depots of food and fuel that Shackleton would have needed in the crossing of the continent. They endured many hardships and suffered the loss of three men. Much like his brother Frank, Ernest Wild was a quietly heroic figure who many considered responsible for their accomplishments. "There are some things that have great value but no glitter," another expedition member wrote about Ernest in the *Report of the Ross Sea Party*. "Consistent . . . long-suffering, patient, industrious, good-humoured, unswervingly loyal, he made an enormous contribution to our well-being."

ON THE *ENDURANCE* EXPEDITION

Alexander, Caroline. *The Endurance: Shackleton's Legendary Antarctic Expedition.* New York: Knopf, 1998.

Bakewell, William. *The American on the Endurance: Ice Sea and Terra Firma Adventures of William L. Bakewell.* Munising, MI: Dukes Hall Publishing, 2003.

Huntford, Roland. *Shackleton.* New York: Carroll & Graf, 1985.

Hurley, Frank. *South with Endurance: Shackleton's Antarctic Expedition, 1914–1917.* New York: Simon & Schuster, 2001.

Hussey, L. D. A. *South with Shackleton.* London: Sampson Low, 1949.

Lansing, Alfred. *Endurance: Shackleton's Incredible Voyage.* New York: Carroll & Graf, 1959.

Shackleton, Ernest. *South: A Memoir of the Endurance Voyage.* New York: Carroll & Graf, 1998.

Smith, Michael. *Tom Crean: Unsung Hero of the Scott and Shackleton Antarctic Expeditions.* Seattle: Mountaineers Books, 2001.

Worsley, Frank. *Endurance: An Epic of Polar Adventure.* London: Philip Allan, 1931.

GENERAL BACKGROUND

Cameron, Ian. *Antarctica: The Last Continent.* Boston: Little, Brown, 1974.

Gurney, Alan. *Below the Convergence: Voyages Toward Antarctica, 1699–1839.* New York: Penguin, 1998.

Kamler, Kenneth. *Surviving the Extremes: A Doctor's Journey to the Limits of Human Endurance.* New York: St. Martin, 2004.

Murray, George, ed. *The Antarctic Manual for the Use of the Expedition of 1901.* Johannesberg: Explorer Books (Facsimile Edition), 1994.

Stoner, George W. *Handbook for the Ship's Medicine Chest, 1900.* Washington, D.C.: U.S. Government Printing Office, 1900.

UNPUBLISHED SOURCES

The Antarctic Chef: The Story of the Life of Charles Green. 1999. Compiled by Green's nephew, Roy Cockram.

Diary of H. McNeish, Carpenter with Shackleton's Expedition, 1914–1916. 1916. Transcribed by Shane Murphy from microfilm G512, National Library of Australia, Canberra, courtesy of Robert Stephenson.

Diary of Thomas Orde Lees. 1916. Transcribed by Margot Morrell, from the collection of Robert Stephenson.

Shackleton's Photographer: The Standard Edition. 2001. Composite of the diaries of Frank Hurley, Frank Worsley, Thomas Orde Lees, and others, edited by Shane Murphy.

WEB SITE

www.Antarctic-Circle.org

TIMELINE

1914

Aug. 8	The *Endurance* leaves England.
Oct. 9	The *Endurance* arrives in Buenos Aires.
Oct. 26	The *Endurance* leaves Buenos Aires.
Nov. 5–Dec. 5	Shackleton waits at South Georgia Island for the pack ice to open.
Dec. 7	First sight of pack ice.

1915

Jan. 6	Sally delivers puppies.
Jan. 19	The *Endurance* trapped by ice.
Jan. 24–Feb. 14	Open leads appear, and the men make several attempts to free the ship.
Feb. 24	Shackleton declares the ship is now a winter station.
May 1	The sun sets for the winter.
June 22	Midwinter's Day—longest night of the year.
July 26	The sun peeks above the horizon again.
Aug. 1–3	Ice begins to move—first major attack of pressure ice.
Aug. 26–Sept. 2	Second major attack of pressure ice.
Oct. 17	The *Endurance* floats in a small open lead but cannot break out.
Oct. 18–27	Pressure crushes the ship; the men work valiantly to save her.

Oct. 27	The *Endurance* is abandoned.
Oct. 30–31	Attempt to march toward Paulet Island, hauling two lifeboats and all supplies.
Nov. 1–Dec. 23	"Ocean Camp"—the men make scavenging trips to the wrecked ship for more supplies and the third lifeboat.
Nov. 21	The wrecked *Endurance* sinks completely.
Dec. 23–29	Second attempt to march—covers only about ten miles.

1916

Dec. 29, 1915–April 9, 1916	"Patience Camp."
April 9	Set off in the three lifeboats.
April 15	Land on Elephant Island.
April 17	Sail to safer location on Elephant Island, set up camp on "Cape Wild."
April 24	Shackleton and five men leave in the *James Caird* for South Georgia Island.
May 10	They arrive on South Georgia Island.
May 19–20	Shackleton, Crean, and Worsley walk across the mountains to the whaling station.
April 17–Aug. 30	Remaining men live under two lifeboats on Elephant Island.
May 23–28	First rescue attempt from South Georgia in the *Southern Sky*.
June 15	Perce Blackborow's toes amputated.
June 17–25	Second rescue attempt from Falkland Islands in *Instituto de Pesca No 1*.
July 12–Aug. 3	Third rescue attempt from Punta Arenas aboard the *Emma*.

Aug. 25	Fourth rescue attempt aboard the *Yelcho* departs from Punta Arenas.
Aug. 30	Shackleton rescues all men on Elephant Island.
Sept. 3	The *Yelcho* arrives in Punta Arenas, Chile.
Oct. 8	Shackleton leaves for New Zealand.
Dec. 20	Shackleton sails for Antarctica aboard the *Aurora* to rescue the Ross Sea Party.
Dec. 22	Perce Blackborow arrives home in Wales.

1917

Jan. 10	The *Aurora* arrives in McMurdo Sound. Three of the men in the Ross Sea Party have died.
Jan. 17	After several searches for the bodies, the *Aurora* leaves Antarctica.
May 29	Shackleton arrives home in England.

1921

Sept. 17	Shackleton sails from England aboard the *Quest*.

1922

January 5	Shackleton dies aboard the *Quest*, which is anchored by Grytviken whaling station on South Georgia Island.
March 5	Shackleton is buried in the whalers' cemetery at Grytviken.

Members of the 1914–1916 Imperial Trans-Antarctic Expedition

Name	Position	Nickname	Birthplace
Sir Ernest Shackleton	Leader	Boss	Ireland
Frank Wild	Second in command	Frankie	England
Frank Worsley	Ship's captain	Skipper, Wuzzles	New Zealand
Lionel Greenstreet	First officer	Horace	England
Thomas Crean	Second officer	Tom, Irish Giant	Ireland
Alfred Cheetham	Third officer	Alf	England
Hubert T. Hudson	Navigator	Buddha	England
Louis Rickinson	First engineer	Rickey	England
Alfred J. Kerr	Second engineer	Krasky	Scotland
Dr. Alexander H. Macklin	Surgeon	Mack	England
Dr. James A. McIlroy	Surgeon	Mickey	England
James M. Wordie	Geologist	Jock	Scotland
Leonard Hussey	Meteorologist (banjo player)	Uzbird	England
Reginald W. James	Physicist	Jimmy	England
Robert S. Clark	Biologist	Bob	Scotland
James (Frank) Hurley	Photographer	The Prince	Australia
Thomas H. Orde Lees	Motor expert (storekeeper)	Colonel, Old Lady	England
George Marston	Artist	Putty	England
Harry McNeish	Carpenter	Chips, Chippy	Scotland
Charles Green	Cook	Doughballs	England
Walter How	Able seaman	Hownow	England
William Bakewell	Able seaman	Billy, Bakie	United States
Timothy McCarthy	Able seaman	Tim	Ireland
Thomas McLeod	Able seaman	Stornoway	Scotland
John Vincent	Able seaman	Bosun	England
Perce Blackborow	Steward	Blackie	Wales
Ernest Holness	Fireman*	Holie	England
William Stevenson	Fireman*	Steve	England

*Firemen on a ship take care of the engines.

FOR YOUNGER READERS:

Shipwreck at the Bottom of the World: The Extraordinary True Story of Shackleton and the Endurance, by Jennifer Armstrong. Crown, 1998.

FOR OLDER READERS:

Endurance: Shackleton's Incredible Voyage, by Alfred Lansing. Orion, 2000.

The Endurance: Shackleton's Legendary Antarctic Expedition, by Caroline Alexander. Knopf, 1998.

FOR THE TRULY ADDICTED:

Shackleton, by Roland Huntford. Carroll & Graf, 1985. Provides a fascinating and comprehensive (774 pages) history of polar exploration.

OTHER POLAR EXPLORATIONS:

The Worst Journey in the World, by Apsley Cherry-Garrard. Pimlico, 2004. A great book, telling the story of a young man's experience on Robert Scott's expedition to the South Pole.

Victoria McKernan started hitchhiking around the world at the age of eighteen and has had a lifelong interest in the sea. Since learning to scuba-dive on Australia's Great Barrier Reef, she has worked as a scuba instructor, dive master, underwater model, and support diver for Hydrolab, an underwater research habitat. She is also the author of four novels for adults.

Victoria McKernan lives in Washington, D.C., with a dog, two cats, and one boa constrictor.